CALLING FOR A FUNERAL

CALLING FOR A FUNERAL

CHRISTINE T. JORGENSEN

FIVE STAR

An imprint of Thomson Gale, a part of The Thomson Corporation

THOMSON

GALE

Detroit • New York • San Francisco • New Haven, Conn. • Waterville, Maine • London

THOMSON
™
GALE

LIBRARY OF CONGRESS CATALOGING-IN-PUBLICATION DATA

Jorgensen, Christine T.
   Calling for a funeral / Christine T. Jorgensen.—1st ed.
      p. cm.
   ISBN-13: 978-1-59414-535-3 (alk. paper)
   ISBN-10: 1-59414-535-0 (alk. paper)
   1. Single mothers—Fiction. 2. Supervisors—Crimes against—Fiction. 3. Telemarketing—Fiction. I. Title.
   PS3560.O765C35 2007
   813'.54—dc22
                                                        2006035933

First Edition. First Printing: March 2007.

Published in 2007 in conjunction with Tekno Books and Ed Gorman.

Printed in the United States of America on permanent paper
10 9 8 7 6 5 4 3 2 1

ACKNOWLEDGMENTS

This is a novel of crime fiction, and any resemblance to anyone living or dead is purely coincidental. The book, however, is based on information provided by many dedicated and knowledgeable people: Jamison Madson (www.caughtintheweb exotics.com), whose dedication and passion for creatures, especially arachnids, was invaluable; Vanessa Murdock, who patiently tutored me on computer matters; the Denver Police Department; the Butterfly Pavilion.

In addition, there were incredibly supportive and talented people who patiently read and critiqued the manuscript despite having important other matters to attend to: Jane Chelius, Kay Bergstrom, Carol Caverly, Dolores Johnson, Leslie O'Kane, Peggy Swager, and my husband, Jim, who read every draft from beginning to end without losing his sense of humor.

To Dana, Naya, and Eamon

CHAPTER 1

I sat in Helene Foster's little office, listening to the whisper of the air conditioning and the occasional sound of a paper turning as she paged through my report. I could have heard a pin drop. I did hear my stomach growl. And my heart thump with growing anxiety.

While Helene could be downright abrasive, she and I were old college roommates and only three months ago she had begged me to leave Chicago and come to Denver to work for her. This review must be a formality. Had to be, I told myself, and felt my pulse speed up. Passing my probationary period was important to me and not passing had dire implications for my grocery budget.

Barely ten months ago I acquired Mac, a nearly ten-year-old son, to care for. Motherhood, however abrupt and unplanned, had radically changed my life. The responsibility of rearing a child, of teaching him right from wrong—not a strong point in my family culture—and the sheer impact of loving him was breath-taking. To find that one young boy could mean so much to me left me aching to do right by him. On the practical side, the grocery bill alone staggered me.

Helene steepled her fingers, her fingernails perfect ovals of gleaming red. My utilitarian, square-cut nails needed filing; I curled them into my palms. Never a fast reader, Helene was taking ages to get through my report. Not lengthy, my report certainly was not fascinating and definitely not complicated. It was a simple compilation of sales, income, deposits, correlated with Helene's presence at the company in Denver. I figured she was curious about the effect she had on the company sales, possibly looking to justify requesting a salary boost.

Unfortunately, the data did not support the idea that she had any overall effect, but I buried that bit of information tactfully at the end. It was that last bit that had me a tad anxious. Helene, like a lot of us, wasn't keen on criticism.

I shifted in the chair, exhaling just loudly enough to prod her along. Finally she turned the last page. I sensed she was in distress, but she'd recently undergone a serious Botox treatment to her brow—so while her lips were distressed, her forehead was serene.

Then she made her hands into little fists and turned to stare out the window at the sky. Curious, and growing more uneasy, I followed her gaze. A tiny jet pierced the clear blue Denver sky, leaving a silvery contrail. An arrow into the heart of the universe?

Unable to tolerate her silence any longer I spoke up. "Helene, do you have any questions about the report? I believe I pulled together everything you asked about."

She was silent for another long minute, then dragged her gaze to meet mine and said calmly, "Francie, you're fired."

Surely, I heard wrong. "Fired?"

"Fired."

Fired. Job over. Well, damn!

Stunned, I watched as Helene slid the folder with my report into her bottom desk drawer and locked it, pocketing the key. When I could, I asked, "Why?"

"You're still on probation so I don't have to explain. I just made a terrible mistake."

What was she talking about? How could she fire me? She had begged me to come to Denver, now she was firing me?

She rose, opened her office door, and stood on the threshold where she could be seen and heard by the three other people in the office: her partner, Harris Bruckner; the company secretary, Lizzie Bruckner; and Sam Lawson, the only other employee besides me. It was a small company. Getting smaller fast.

In a melodramatic gesture, she cringed as if I were about to attack her. I was still sitting in the chair. It's darn near impossible to attack someone from a sitting position. So this was for show.

Still in the doorway, and just as she had done when she was the drama queen in our college theater group, Helene raised her voice, pitched it to the others in the office, and intoned, "You failed probation. Your work is incompetent."

What a farce. She hadn't been good at serious drama in college and now she was barely even comedic. If I hadn't been so angry, I might have laughed.

Mustering as much dignity as I could, I rose out of the chair. Still managing some control, although my thoughts came thick and fast, I said, measuring my words, "Every word of that report is true, every figure accurate—"

She interrupted, this time shouting, "You failed the simplest test!"

That project was no test. Those were people I worked with out there in the office and I resented the slur on my work. I glanced around the main office room.

In his early forties, Harris Bruckner stood across the room in his office door looking partner-ish, his thick, dark hair combed back, eyes narrowed and peering down his nose, with a guarded expression on his face, as though he wasn't really surprised.

Lizzie, his wife, stared open-mouthed, shocked, the telephone receiver forgotten in her hand.

Sam Lawson, nerdy but nice, sat at his desk, chewing on his lower lip just as Mac did when he was doing homework. Sam pretended to be working away on his latest software program,

11

yet he leaned our way to hear better.

Sam and Lizzie had been wonderful to me from the moment I came to work at Techlaw three months before. Every one of them had been to my house barely a week ago for a Fourth of July barbecue. What were they thinking?

My face flushed hot with sudden embarrassment.

A smooth male voice rolled out from safely behind Harris Bruckner's broad shoulders. "You need any help there, Helene?" It was Laurence Gifford, Techlaw's consulting attorney, stepped forward, looking casually elegant in his Armani, lean, muscular, and married, as I remembered. He had been closeted with Helene just before I went in and there was a hint of satisfaction in his expression. I had a sudden clear conviction that he'd had a hand in this.

At that moment I'd have given anything to come up with something really cutting and witty. Instead, I managed a calm voice laced with menace. "Damn you, Helene. Write me out of your life, if you *can*, 'cause you're out of mine."

The reference to writing was petty and mean because Helene was dyslexic and didn't want people to know, but I was hurt. Still, it sounded so lame that I added, "And if you ever, ever come near me again, I'll—kill you." Of course I regretted it as soon as I said it.

Helene paled. "I'll walk you out," she said and marched to my desk, positioning herself in front of my computer. As though I'd sit down and work another second in that company! She glared as best she could with her paralyzed forehead.

My humiliation was complete now. My firing and my fury had been witnessed by the entire company. The only person missing from this miserable vignette was the cleaning woman, Rosie, and her mop.

I glared back at Helene, yanked open my bottom desk drawer, snatched my purse, palmed the desk key, and marched out the door. Helene followed behind me and she really had to hustle, because she is barely five feet with short legs and I'm five nine with nice long ones.

I held my chin high and walked as fast as I could, just to make her work. She had hurt me deeply; humiliated me in front of people whose opinion I valued. In all the time I had known her, through all the troubles we shared in college, she had never shown that side of her. I could only think, I hadn't really known her at all. And now I didn't care to.

I sailed across the hot tarmac parking lot to my battered, aged Ford Galaxy, whose enormous trunk had trundled all my possessions out here from Chicago. Helene trotted in my wake. I had planned to buy a new—well newer—car with the next paycheck. Like so many things, that was now changed.

I had long given up locking the car—no one wanted to steal it—so I was already behind the wheel when Helene reached my side. The hot July breeze blew her fine blond hair across her face into her big, blue eyes, which looked a little bleak. "Francie, please believe me . . ." Her voice trailed off and she bit her lower lip with her very white little teeth.

There was no way I would accept an apology, or an explanation. This move had meant a chance to leave Chicago and start over, making a normal life for Mac and myself. I wanted to remind her of all that, but I knew I'd lose my composure, maybe even cry, so I simply said, "Too late, Helene. I don't want to hear it."

She glanced at the building where Harris, Lizzie, and Sam were at the window watching us, then looked back again at me. Her eyes clouded with an emotion I'd never seen in her before. Fear? Yeah, fear. Helene's botoxed forehead was smooth and untroubled, but her cheeks were pale, and her blue eyes huge in her face, almost tragic.

Well good. After what she had done, it was damned satisfying to see her upset.

She shivered, even in the noontime heat, and said, "It's for your own good—"

"Oh, don't start." I snarled and rolled up the window, as if my air conditioning still worked. I turned the ignition key, heard the satisfying roar of the engine, and screeched out of the parking lot.

Away from her. For good.

I had left jobs before, but always on my own terms. The job changes may have been a tad frequent, but they were usually for a better position, or better pay. But, then I'd been single. Now I was single and for the last year, the mother of a nearly ten-year-old son who consumed a considerable amount of daily bread.

At the corner I braked for the stop sign. It was then the full realization of my situation hit me. I was royally screwed. I had been fired before I was covered by unemployment insurance.

I sucked in a couple deep breaths and screamed, "Daaaaaamn!" It didn't help.

My foot firmly on the brake pedal, I wiped my eyes, blew my nose, combed my hair, and told myself it wasn't the first time I'd been screwed.

A few blocks farther on I told myself I almost always landed on my feet. Halfway home, I was vowing to reframe the whole horrible event and make it a celebration. To cheer myself up, I'd get the biggest three-layer carrot cake I could find, preferably with little frosting carrots dancing around the top. And if the sugar didn't get me high enough, I just might slurp down a glass of wine.

I was working hard on positive thinking.

And once I was actually thinking, I wished I had threatened Helene with my Uncle Louie, Louie the Knife as the papers called him. He'd have done it, he loved scaring people. That would have put enough fear in her to bust her Botox.

Mac and I lived in a semi-quiet south Denver neighborhood near the University of Denver. Semi-quiet because students rented a number of the houses on the block and they were gone for the summer. Ours was a miniscule, one-story frame house, no garage, on a narrow lot with a spreading cottonwood tree in the front. Perfect except that my kitchen window was directly opposite my neighbor Mrs. Folsom's kitchen window. Without a doubt she would note I was home early. She noted everything.

I parked in front of our house, took the cake inside, retrieved the morning paper from the trash, and started calling listings from the want-ads. Within an hour my head was pounding, but I had three interviews set for the next day. I was finishing my application résumé when Mac got home from day camp.

He dropped his backpack on the kitchen table and pushed his sweaty, dark blond curls back from his forehead. His face was rosy from the heat and his hands grubby. He dropped into a chair. "What's the cake for?"

"Wash your hands, you can have some."

He washed quickly, smeared the towel across his face, and watched me out of the corner of his eye to see if I'd notice and protest. I ignored it this time. Instead, I retrieved a couple of small plates and a knife to open the plastic box. The top was welded to the bottom. "Had a good day?"

"Yeah." He scratched the side of his nose, his gold-brown hair hovering over his forehead. "So how come the cake?"

"We're celebrating. I'm going to change jobs."

"I thought you liked your job. It pays good."

"Well. It paid well." I nodded, trying to smile. I took the butcher knife and tried to pry open the cake box.

Mac was watching with growing interest. "Need some help?"

"No, thanks." I gripped the knife firmly and rammed it into

15

the side of the box. "I got it. Everything is just fine."

I lifted the cake out. It was firm, heavy, and substantial. I set it down and sliced through it. The knife blade caught on the nuts. I pressed down hard. "I'm going to look around a bit. There are lots of job opportunities out there."

Mac's slab of cake balanced on the knife blade. My hand was trembling a bit. The cake tumbled to the counter. I picked it up and laid it on Mac's plate.

"You're saying this is a good thing?"

I pulled a big grin and put a fork on the plate and handed it to him. "Sure." I was pleased with myself. I was maintaining control.

A calculating expression crossed his young face. "If it's so good, can we get a dog? To celebrate? I need a companion."

This was probably his seventieth request for a dog. "You've got me for a companion."

His eyes narrowed. "I have to have you for a companion. I didn't get to choose you."

That stung. Control, I reminded myself. I was the adult and Mac was a child. "We just can't do a dog."

He stared at me until I felt uncomfortable. "You lost that job, huh?"

My hand trembled a bit more and a feeling of irritation bubbled in my chest. I cut a slice of cake for myself. It felt lovely slicing, pressing the knife through the firm layers of cake.

"True, but it's a good thing. I can get another."

"Do we have enough to eat?"

"Of course. There's not a thing to worry about." I cut another, smaller piece of cake, pressing harder on the knife, making a thin slice, in case we needed seconds. "I have a chance to try out some new skills."

It crumbled to the side. I sliced another. It felt good to cut it, to feel the knife catch on the nuts, then cut through with a jolt.

I sliced another. It felt great. I sliced another. Then I raised the knife and whacked the remaining cake into lots of little pieces. Kind of like a Japanese chef.

"Yeah?" Mac looked a bit shaken. "Is that a new way to fix cake?"

The irritation in my chest was gone. "Yes."

I scooped it into a large mixing bowl, took a spatula and pressed it flat, slapped it several times, and stood back. "English trifle."

I looked up. My neighbor, Mrs. Folsom, stood at her kitchen window, mouth agape. I was going to have to work some more on that control thing.

Two weeks later on a boiling hot Saturday morning at the end of July, we were in a one-hundred-year heat wave and I was in a cash crisis, still without a job, with my credit cards hanging heavy. Eating wasn't a habit we could break. We couldn't simply become breath-arians living on happy talk and vengeful thoughts. Mac was a growing boy. His mother had died when he was five and without his father I was *it*.

I had applied for jobs from secretary to stock broker to grocery clerk with no success. This oppressively hot and humid Saturday morning, I faced reality and admitted to myself there was probably only one option left. Depression clutched at my beating heart every time I thought about it. I fed my depression four slices of peanut butter toast and told myself, "I'm tough. I can do this."

As soon as Mac left for wrestling practice at the YMCA, I set off. I drove down snoozy streets humming with the sound of cicadas, each of whom seemed to rejoice in the one-hundred-and-two-degree heat. Even my old Ford Galaxy was depressed. Yesterday it had developed a tell-tale smell of imminent car-death. I suspected a discarded hard-boiled egg, not one of Mac's favorite foods. Or worse, a carburetor clog or a muffler meltdown, or whatever it was that could stink up a car.

The address I was looking for turned out to be on the fringe of downtown, treeless and roasting. The weary, one-story building might have once been a dry cleaners in a thriving working-class neighborhood, but now the broad windows were covered with brown-painted plywood and decorated with layers of graffiti. A dingy door bore the lettering "Level One Communications."

I parked in the broiling sun and got out, my teal-blue silk blouse sticking to my back. Flapping my arms, I tried to dry out and rid myself of car-stink. I went inside, the sulfurous odor of the car lingering in my nose. I hoped it wasn't following me into the interview.

No comforting hum of air conditioning came to my ears. The reception area was small and hot as Dante's Inferno. A large woman with limp hair and a heavy bead of perspiration on the dusky moustache of her upper lip looked up and said in a firm voice, "Francie Starzel?"

"Yes."

"I'm Ethel Green, supervisor. Please come this way." Ethel lumbered to her feet. "Sorry about the heat. The air conditioning went out this morning. It should be back on any minute."

I followed Ethel's sweat-stained back into a smaller, bleaker version of the first room. "We can talk in here," she said as she sat heavily at a small, bare table and motioned for me to sit in front of an open window that looked out onto an empty lot. A faint breeze stirred past me toward her. My potential boss's nose wrinkled daintily. Had the scent of *eau de car* come in with me?

I wished I'd aired out a bit longer. This might be the job from hell, but it would mean a paycheck, which I desperately needed.

She busied herself with papers, blinked rapidly, smiled thinly, and handed me a sheet of paper. "Please read this aloud."

I read one paragraph. She raised her hand to stop me. Peering at my résumé she said, "You write here that you last worked for Techlaw Inc. I haven't heard of it. Please describe."

"It's a small software company that develops customized software for law offices. I was an assistant to the sales manager, Helene Foster."

"I see." Her nose twitched. "Why did you leave?"

"A cutback." Actually a stab in the back, but I wanted to avoid that discussion.

She waited, so I added, "The company consists of two partners, Helene Foster and Harris Bruckner. Helene does all the sales, Harris develops and customizes the software with the assistance of a programmer, Sam Lawson." For the sake of simplicity I left out Lizzie, the wife *cum* receptionist. I tried hard to smile confidently. "Sam Lawson is a reference."

"So I see. Helene Foster was your immediate supervisor?"

Former boss, former friend, current backstabber, reason for my unemployment. I answered simply, "Yes."

"That's a very small company."

"The other jobs, like the accountant and lawyer, are contracted out. It keeps the overhead low."

She fanned herself with her plump hand. "You were paid quite well. Telemarketing will be quite a comedown."

Oh, to understate the obvious by about seventeen thousand percent. "The market is slow right now. I've worked telemarketing before, in Chicago. I noted it on the application." I hated it before too, but I kept that to myself.

"So I see now," she said and pulled a tissue from a box on the corner of her cluttered desk. Through the wad of tissue she asked, "Why do you want this job?"

I would do whatever it took to put food on the table for

Mac. I decided to throw it all to the winds. "I need to feed, clothe, and house my poor, fatherless ten-year-old."

She pondered.

I felt the job slipping away from me.

Finally she roused. "Can you start Monday?"

"Certainly."

Tissue crammed to her nose, she said, "You must do at least twenty hours of calls during the week, or more, and for the first two weeks you get a guaranteed ten dollars an hour. If your sales are good, you can get the higher of salary or commissions. Telemarketing is under pressure here. We've cut back more than fifty percent in the last year. I have to warn you, there's no job security in this field now."

The ten dollars an hour sold me. If I worked over, or got commissions, I could make it for a few weeks. "When will I be paid?"

She waved the tissue at me and stood. "Every two days if you work at least ten hours."

"What is my assignment?"

She sneezed. A huge, screaming loud sneeze. "Allergies," she gasped.

"I'm selling allergy medicines?"

"No. *I* have allergies. *You're* selling funeral services."

CHAPTER 2

The telemarketers, wearing headsets and peering at computer screens, sat at carrels in a large room. The air conditioning wound up and came back on as Ethel gave me a brief demonstration of the equipment. "The calls are computer generated, and switched to you only after someone has answered the call. On the computer screen you will see the name of the person responsible for the telephone bill and their address."

I nodded. "The size of this company is smaller, but otherwise, it's similar to my Chicago job."

Ethel smiled with only half her face. The result was disconcerting. She gave me materials to study. Leaflets on funeral possibilities, funeral insurance, funeral services, and funeral costs, all quite enlightening and very depressing. "Commissions come only on services actually contracted and paid for," she said.

That meant that my guaranteed two weeks of salary could run out long before I made enough commission to support us, but at least it was two weeks of cold cash. Hopefully by that time, I'd have another job offer.

I thanked her and started to leave. Suddenly one of the telemarketers raised her hands, stood, did a victory dance, and bowed to the applause of the other four workers. She'd made a sale. If they did all that for one sale, it wasn't very promising.

I made my way back to my sweltering car and fanned myself with the funeral pamphlets until I had the engine running and a breeze coming in the open window to clear the air. Telemarketing wasn't glamorous, and telemarketing funeral services would be a bare step above dog catching in Mac's eyes. How was I going to sell it as a good thing to him?

For that matter, how was I going to sell it to myself? I hated funerals. When Mac's dad died, he went in such a blaze of flame there were no remains, no casket necessary, and I had done my best to put it behind me as fast as possible. Maybe that had helped me decide to leave Chicago.

Mac was waiting for me at noon, outside the gym. Fortunately I had paid for his wrestling and his summer day camp in the flush old days before I was fired.

Mac took after his father, tall for a nearly ten-year-old, with gray eyes, thick and curly dark blond hair, and a sturdy build with brawny shoulders, so it was no surprise he was a heavyweight wrestler and quite good.

A bare year ago Dave had died, one week before we were to marry. I was left with a new dress and guardianship of Mac, his nine-year-old motherless son. I loved Mac dearly, but he had yet to call me Mom, and maybe after one too many losses, especially his father, he was afraid to count on me. In any case, he was careful to keep up his guard and I sometimes wondered if he tolerated me because I was all he had left.

I pulled up to the curb.

Mac tossed his gym bag in the back seat, climbed in, and arranged his feet in their size-ten gunboats on the floor. The tennies were new three weeks ago, which at the rate he was growing, meant I had maybe three weeks to go before he grew through the sides. The thought caused a fleeting sense of panic, but I calmed myself by gazing at his happy smile.

I reached to hug him but he pulled away. I ended up patting his shoulder and feeling frustrated and empty. If his father were still alive, I'd kill him.

"How'd wrestling go?"

"Coach says I've got a chance at winning in the next meet. And Sam—" He caught himself. "Mr. Lawson stopped by today to watch practice. He said hello."

Sam Lawson, computer nerd, had been really sweet and supportive since I'd been fired from Techlaw. He had taken Mac to baseball games a couple of times as well, but I was a little surprised to hear he'd come to wrestling practice. I steered the car away from the curb and entered the stream of traffic.

Mac's nose wrinkled. "It stinks bad in here."

"Someone must have stashed a hard-boiled egg."

"Don't look at me! It *really* stinks in here." He stuck his head out the window and sucked in several deep breaths, then asked, "Did you get a grocery store job?"

He had hopes of grazing while I worked. I shook my head and drove faster to circulate the air. "I'm on a will-call list there. I got something else to fill in."

"What?"

Stretching my face into a maxi-grin I said as brightly as I could, "Telemarketing. Funerals."

His face fell. "That's a sh—" He caught himself. "Shabby, *shabby* job."

"Think positive." I stretched my grin wider to convey enthusiasm and felt like a bobble-head. "I start Monday."

"But you hate telemarketers. And you hated doing it when you were one before. You said so."

"Hey! This is a good thing. It buys food, clothes, and house. And to celebrate I'll spring for a nice pet, say a goldfish."

He went very silent. A sure sign of disappointment.

"Or a Siamese fighting fish? They're cool. Five-ninety-five and they have personality. They even breathe air. How can you beat that?"

He rolled his eyes. "They're all wet. I want something furry I can pet."

I shook my head. "It has to be small, something that lives in an aquarium. Think about it."

We rolled to a stop in the Tropicana Pet Shop parking lot far away from other cars, leaving plenty of room in case we needed a tow truck. In spite of yearning for a furry friend, Mac perked up and headed inside.

He dutifully scrutinized the aquariums and the various fishes in them. I drifted toward the far end of the store to give him space to decide. He started talking to a tall young man with a thick ponytail, thin hips, and jeans that barely clung to his rump. I heard Mac exclaiming, "Oh, man, cool. Really cool."

Pleased, I rounded the corner and came face to face with a large, furry, plate-sized, eight-legged creature. Every hair on my body stood straight out. "Oh, my God in heaven!"

"Not that one, this one. What d'ya think?"

How did I miss seeing the word "Arachnids" over the section? "They're poisonous!"

The tall, thin fellow slouched closer. An earring and two studs glinted in the shell of one ear and his T-shirt said "Spider-Man." His employee's badge said "DUDE." He ran his tongue over an arrow-shaped stud in the middle of his lower lip and said in a voice that started out deep and ended up cracking, "Actually, they're great pets, like, probably the lowest maintenance pet you can find."

Be still my beating heart. "They have too many legs."

He shrugged. "They don't grow as big as iguanas. And, like, they're lots easier than a snake."

Now there was a selling point.

I looked desperately across the room to a dazed-looking woman badly in need of a good haircut gazing piteously back at me. "There's a customer over there waiting for you."

Dude glanced where I was pointing and made a snuffling, snorting noise that might have been a laugh. "That's a mirror, ma'am. That's you."

"Well, *someone* here must need you."

Mac stood up tall. "I do. How much is this tarantula?"

Jesus, Mary, and Joseph save me. I spoke up. "We're in the market for a *fish.*"

Dude ignored me. "These, like, range from fifteen ninety-nine, up to a hundred and fifty bucks, depends how common they are."

"They bite," I whined. "They're wild."

"There's docile ones and there's, like, aggressive ones." Dude was turning into a tall, thin devil. He pointed a knobby finger at the middle terrarium. "That one, his bite's a bee sting."

"People die of bee stings."

Mac's eyes lit up. "Tarantulas are so *cool.* No one else will have one of these. Which ones get tame? I want to have him crawl on my arm."

I started to hyperventilate.

Dude warmed to his subject. "Rose Hairs, Red Knees—probably Rose Hairs are your best bet. That one's a Rose Hair—she's usually fifteen ninety-nine, but today, on sale, she's nine ninety-nine." Dude pursed his lips. "But if you want her, I can make it eight bucks even. She's kind of old."

Mac was bobbing up and down with excitement. "What do they live in?"

"Oh, terrariums or little plastic cages. A little vermiculite on the bottom, hardly ever need to clean the cage."

"Hear that, Francie? And terrariums are just like aquariums, only without the water."

I pushed forward, determined. "Tarantulas eat people."

Dude made that snuffling sound again. "Crickets, actually. Three or four a week."

Oh, save me. "Mac, how about a mouse? Or a hamster, or any old rodent?"

He shook his head. "I've got money from my birthday. Lil sent it to me."

Lil, my mother, loving and generous, although eccentric. Mac took to her; why couldn't he take to me? "She wouldn't want you to spend it this way."

Mac looked me straight in the eye, his gaze steady and gray, mine sick and green. "Grandma Lil said to get something I really, really wanted. And I really, really want this." He added, "I'll keep her in my room."

My heart sank. "Mac—"

"You said my birthday money could be spent just as I wish. And this is my wish."

I couldn't find a suitable response so I asked, "How long do they live?" I prayed the answer would be one season, like Charlotte.

Dude, the devil with the studded lip, grinned. "Ten or fifteen years. Unless you breed them, then the female will cannibalize the males. Or unless you drop them. Then they'll bust a leg or abdomen and goo themselves to death."

"Goo?"

"They don't have blood. Best of all, they're hypoallergenic."

Oh, nice. A bloodless, fuzzy, plate-sized, cannabalizer that wouldn't make me sneeze or wheeze. "Just what every home needs," I said.

Mac handed over his birthday money. "She's *so* cool. The other kids will really be amazed."

Dude rang up the spider, a plastic cage, and half a dozen crickets. Then the devil said, "Yeah, they're sweet. Just stay *real* mellow with her. She doesn't like surprises."

"I'm going to name her Spike. What do you think, Francie?"

Whiskey, I need a drink. I said, "That's nice."

Mac trotted proudly out to the car. "Don't worry, Lil will be real happy. And if we have to move back to Chicago she'll be even happier. Grandma Lil wants us."

No, not that. Not in a million years. Give me a female arachnid named Spike any day. "Do you remember how I said I was coming to Denver for a better life?"

Mac climbed in the car, holding Spike in her plastic cage close to his face. "You said, you were following Bliss."

"Going back to Chicago would be giving up on my dream."

"Spike's my dream." He frowned. "What's yours?"

It was a surprisingly touching question. The answer that sprang to mind was that I wanted Mac to call me Mom, but it had to come naturally, not because I asked.

I said, "For us to be a family. A normal, law-abiding, honest, and happy family. And right now, that means a job that pays the bills."

I started the car and grinned with all my might. "And today I got a job that will pay some of the bills, so we're on our way. As Grandpa would say, 'The good times are just ahead.' "

Mac dragged his gray-eyed gaze away from Spike, looked at me flatly and said, "Grandpa's in jail."

Sunday morning dawned clear and, again, hot. By eleven o'clock it was sweltering and I was trying to ignore a worry in the back of my mind about the stink in my car by doing the Sunday crossword puzzle. In the margin of the paper I had listed ten words for hot and humid. I was stuck.

Sweat beaded my forehead and trickled down between my breasts in spite of a cool shower earlier. I laid the puzzle aside, trying hard to ignore Spike in her cage on the table. A cricket crawled over Spike's back.

I shuddered. "Something has to happen. We cannot sit all day sweating and watching Spike play with her food. I need to find what's stinking up the car and I want your help."

Mac frowned uncomfortably. "Uh, Sam . . . Mr. Lawson I

mean, asked me if we wanted to go to the ball game this afternoon. It's the Rockies and the Cubs. I can't miss the Cubs. Can't the car wait?"

"Sam is supposed to ask me first. Privately."

Mac's face was carefully blank. "I think he figured you'd say no."

Before I could reply, there was a knock on the front door. Through the screen I saw Sam on the front porch, his brown hair plastered flat to his head, his glasses halfway down his rounded nose. He wore cutoffs with a button-down, short-sleeved shirt only half tucked in, complete with ink stain on the pocket and mismatched socks. He was in his late thirties, bright and well-meaning, a whiz on the computer, but he dressed as though he hadn't a clue. And, in fact, I suspected he hadn't.

"Wait here a minute, Mac." I went to the door, stepped outside, and gave Sam a very stern glare.

He shuffled his feet awkwardly and shoved his glasses up on his nose. They slid down again immediately, emphasizing his lost-puppy look. "Uh, hi Francie. You ready?"

"You're supposed to ask me before you ask Mac."

"Sorry." He scratched his neck. "I thought it would be a treat for him. And for you. And me especially."

"Sam, I can't repay you. Helene still owes me for my last three weeks." I thought a minute. "Couldn't you push her to issue that check?"

"Sorry, no can do," he replied. Then looking shyly at me he added, "There's one way . . ."

Little alarm bells rang in my mind. When everyone from the company was here for the Fourth of July barbecue Sam had made it obvious he saw me as relationship potential. Much as I appreciated his attention, especially to Mac, I wasn't ready for serious dating. No quickening heart beat to make me want to deepen our friendship romantically. He was nice, more than helpful, but there was no zing. In fact, he was more like a second child, impossible to take seriously, or even stay mad at.

He must have seen it because he sobered. "You could come back to Techlaw. When you're there I don't feel like the odd man out."

Sam could sometimes be so socially dense it astounded me, but he looked so earnest I almost patted the top of his head. Instead I said, "You know that's impossible. Anyway, I have another job."

"Oh, yeah? What?"

Avoid that topic, I thought. "So, I can't go with you today. I need to get stuff in order to start Monday."

"I was hoping you would come. What do you have to do?"

"Clean the car, for one."

"You could do it later." He glanced at his watch. "Or we could work for a little while—"

"No, thanks. Just take Mac and you two have a good time, but after this, ask me first, Sam. Promise?"

He nodded and shoved his glasses up again. They slid back down, again.

I walked to the curb and watched them leave, then went to the Galaxy. I fitted the key into the trunk lock and turned it and lifted the trunk lid. I sucked air, my mouth cold and dry.

CHAPTER 3

Sweet Jesus. Maybe it was just my imagination. I closed my eyes, then opened them and lifted the trunk lid again.

Inside lay a body, fortunately facing away, bloated from deterioration. Blond hair, a black, crusted hole above the ear. A dainty black shoe. I didn't need to see any more. The odor was sickening, overwhelming. Gagging I pressed the trunk lid shut again. A woman. Very dead.

My heart went out to her.

Years ago in my episodic youth my family lived in Chicago's south side near a housing project. Irate drug dealers who thought they'd been shafted regularly handed out this kind of punishment—a bullet in the brain and a car-trunk coffin.

At the time, we had an old jalopy parked in the alley. I went out to go somewhere, I no longer remembered where, and found the trunk ajar. Stupidly, I lifted the lid. Back then, the body faced me, eyes open, burnt holes. I shrieked 'til Mom slapped my face.

Was this body the result of a drug deal gone bad? It was a pretty common result of not rendering unto the drug lord the drug lord's due in South Side Chicago, but Denver? Denver was upscale compared to South Side Chicago.

In slow stupid-time, questions stumbled through my mind, a kind of mental listing. I like lists. My pen and my paper, they comfort me. Too unsteady to write anything down, I mumbled to myself, "What am I going to do?"

How did she get in here? I always parked on the street. She must have been dumped in my trunk at night.

Why *my* trunk? There were twenty, thirty other cars on the street every night. Why mine? No answer for that one.

The stench from the body in the trunk wouldn't leave my nose and my knees weren't too steady. I sat down on the parking strip and dropped my head in my hands. I'm not good at death. It makes me queasy, sad, and a little stupid. And, very frightened.

What was I going to do? Call the police? I could hear Lil's voice in my mind. Lil didn't like police. She would say, "Dump it. They'll only blame you."

No, they won't, I told myself. *Let me think a minute.*

I closed my eyes, as though I could shut out that whole train of thought, then said aloud, "I'm going to do what's right."

My parents were good to me, loving and protective, and I loved them dearly in return, but as the social workers said, my parents lived in another value system. Dad's penchant for supplementing the family income with homemade money and rubber checks earned him the nickname Paperhanger. My brother, Andy, the indulged one of the two of us, could charm cash from a rutabaga. And Mom, distressed but ever indulgent, always put a positive spin to their behavior, almost as though she got some vicarious enjoyment from it.

"People enjoy giving Andrew money," she'd say, or "Dad believes in supporting us. Isn't that nice?"

As for me, I tried really hard to do right, but *right* wasn't in my family genes. So, in spite of thirty-four years of trying to extinguish criminal instincts, I still have to think things through in order to come to the lawful course of action.

Making a second mental list, I thought: *I will not flee the state. I will not dump the body elsewhere. I will not drive to the police station. I'll call them and have them meet me here.*

What would I say? I didn't know.

My lips were stiff and dry. I licked them. It didn't help. I staggered into the house, got my purse, ransacked it until I found the cell phone, and pressed in the numbers. What to say? Still no answer to that one.

My hands shook. I dropped the phone. I fished it up and put it to my ear. Surely when the cops answered, I'd have thought up something real smooth to say. Something tactful and classy.

"Emergency, how can I help you?"

"There's a dead body in my trunk."

When you call to complain that you heard a person screaming in the neighborhood it takes twenty, thirty minutes, but say you have a body in the trunk of your car, and they are quick. No twenty-minute wait. After an eternity of maybe three minutes, a police car pulled up in front.

I sat on the front steps of our house, aware of the neighbors peering out their windows. Especially Mrs. Folsom next door, who came out on her porch, scowled, and went back inside. No doubt her suspicion that we lowered the tone of the neighborhood was confirmed.

A stout officer whose navy uniform was stretched tight across his shoulders lumbered toward me. His eyes were deep set. His brass nametag said he was officer Bowden; his expression said I was dog meat.

He halted in front of me, one fleshy hand resting on a remarkably hefty gun that looked like a .357 Magnum, the other hand flexed as though it craved action. He could pound me into the ground with one thump. "Are you the one who phoned in?"

Unable to speak, I nodded, my eyes suddenly burning, I rose slowly, keeping my hands in view, and said in a choked voice, "I found it when I opened the trunk to . . . to clean out the car."

The officer raised his brow.

"It . . . the car had a bad stink."

"When did you notice the smell?"

"Yesterday. Morning. No, maybe a little on Friday, the day before yesterday."

His eyes narrowed to mere slits of suspicion.

"Actually the car never smelled too nice. It's old. I thought the smell was an old egg, a hardboiled egg. Maybe I smelled it . . ." I clapped my hand over my mouth to stop my babbling.

"Do you have the keys to the trunk?"

I handed them over. "The round key opens the trunk."

At the rear of the car he worked the key unsuccessfully, nearly lifting the car off its wheels when he tried to open the trunk. I tried to tell him how to open it, but he waved me away. I was afraid he'd break the key off in the lock, so I yelled anyway, "You have to press down on the lid."

He put a thick hand on the lid and pressed down. The trunk flew open. He stared for a seeming eternity, touched the body gently, then glanced over at me. "Is this what you found?"

"Yes."

"You know who this is?"

Why on earth would I know her? If I said I hadn't looked very closely, would he ask me to take a look? Probably. "No. Never seen her before."

Because my knees were wobbly, I stayed where I was, safely out of his reach. His size alone was frightening, but the naked suspicion on his face terrified me.

"Did you touch anything?"

"The trunk key, the trunk . . ." I stopped. Had I touched anything else? I didn't think so.

"Do you recognize the body?"

Why did he ask again? I shook my head. "No."

He gave me a long, skeptical scrutiny, during which I gave him a long, steady return-gaze. Then he pulled out his radio and pressed in a few buttons "Would you wait over there, please,

33

ma'am." He jerked his chin toward the squad car and talked softly into a cell phone.

I ignored his chin directions and went back to the porch steps, safely away from the squad car. I decided against going inside, for fear they would want to come inside to ask questions and then maybe poke around, and maybe—I didn't know what. Dad always said, "Never, ever let them inside." I think what scared me more than anything else was what I didn't know.

Another squad car pulled up and two more uniformed officers got out. After a brief conference, one strung yellow tape around the car and some of the street and yard, establishing the perimeter of the crime scene. From this point on, time moved exceedingly slowly. Neighbors stood around, stared brazenly at me, and whispered among themselves. Mrs. Folsom next door came out again, looked everything over, and went back inside, slamming her door. More police filled the street. I guess it was a slow crime afternoon in Denver.

About an hour later a very attractive male with rakish hair tumbling over his forehead sauntered up to the porch where I sat. Beneath his casual slacks and polo shirt were the muscles of a buff body and in his dark eyes lay the contained air of a person who memorized faces. He could have been a well-dressed reporter, or even a con-man on the prowl, but he was a cop. The ability to spot a cop is a genetic predisposition in my family.

No doubt attempting to disarm me with his good looks and a casual air, he smiled and stuck out a strong, square hand. "Hi."

I didn't shake hands. Mine were too cold and I didn't want him to warm them up. I settled for a simple "Hello."

He retracted his hand and introduced himself. "I'm Detective Dominic Wolfe and I need to ask you a few questions."

Twice he took my statement of what happened, then a third time, questioning each event as though he thought I'd change the story. It took the luster off his attractiveness.

A photographer with flash camera and video recorder, print men, the whole forensic unit as far as I could see, all came and took endless pains to record everything about the car. At some point in my fourth telling of the finding of the body, I noticed an odd-looking white station wagon pull up outside the ring of crime tape. Two thin men in black suits unfolded themselves from the front seat and leaned against the side of the vehicle. One lit a cigarette and shook out the match in an arc, blowing twin streams of smoke out of his nostrils into the baking mid-afternoon air. He glanced my way, then looked up, watching the smoke of his cigarette curl upward. I realized, with a slight shock, that they were morgue attendants.

A television crew with lights arrived along with a reporter I thought I recognized from the nightly news. Her red hair, varnished into place, never moved in the light breeze. She wore earrings, a stylish jacket, and beneath all that style, she wore torn cutoffs where they'd never show. I moved away from the cameras.

Detective Wolfe followed. "If your car was locked, how did the victim get in your car?"

He already had my answer to this, so why was he going over it again? Still, I answered him. "It's not hard to break into the front. Jimmy the front door window and pull the trunk lever."

"When did you notice the odor?"

"Yesterday, maybe the night before."

"And you didn't look then?"

I had had too much on my mind, like how was I going to make the house payment, how far would my meager savings go? "I figured my son had left a lunch somewhere under a seat."

Suspicion tightened his lips as he made a lengthy note. "Who would want to kill her?"

"I don't know."

"No idea?"

"I don't know who she is. I never saw her before in my life. I have no idea why she's there. I've said that over and over."

"When did you last open the trunk of your car?"

I shook my head. "I don't know, a couple weeks ago, I guess. When I shopped for the July fourth barbecue."

"That's almost three weeks ago. Kind of a long time, wouldn't you say? Where do you put your groceries?"

"The trunk sticks sometimes," I said. "It's cleaner and easier to get them out from the back seat."

"Have you seen anyone suspicious in the neighborhood?"

"The woman next door, Mrs. Folsom, is very suspicious. She peeks in my kitchen window all the time. Very suspicious."

He scowled. "This is nothing to joke about. A woman has just been found murdered in the trunk of your car."

"Of course you're right. It isn't a joking matter, but I have answered your questions the best I can."

The detective made note of where I worked and I asked him his name again. Detective Dominic Wolfe. He looked hard at me. He had nice eyes, the kind that looked like they were made to smile, but now they were cold and flat.

I looked back just as steadily. Straight in the eyes with no shifting, like Dad taught us. A tow truck edged up the street. "Are you planning to take my car?"

"It's evidence, ma'am."

"When will I get it back?"

He rubbed his jaw, looking very satisfied. "Hard to say, ma'am."

"How long will you need to keep it?"

"Hard to say, ma'am. Maybe a week, or two, or so."

"How am I supposed to get to work, without a car. Dang, getting around without a car is tough and takes forever."

He ignored my question and turned fully toward me. "This

has all the earmarks of a drug deal gone bad."

"I didn't kill her. I just found her."

He jammed his notebook into his breast pocket. "How do you explain all this?"

"I *don't*. I don't know what, how, or why this happened." But the old creeping feeling that I'd somehow done something wrong, something terrible, that had brought down doom, was crawling around in my chest. I dropped my gaze so he wouldn't see it in my eyes.

He nodded and started to walk away, then turned back. "By the way, do you own a gun?"

"No." The lie was out of my mouth before I could think. A chill went over my skin. A very small, hammerless .38, lay hidden on the slat in the box springs of my bed. Gift from my loving brother Andrew. No one knew about it. Now, what to do? Retract my words? I'd look guilty as hell. And it would get no better when he discovered the thing was unregistered. Stricken, I turned away so he wouldn't see the guilt in my eyes.

He stood still, frowning and thinking, his arms hanging loose from his powerful shoulders.

A young officer came to his side. "Sir? We think we've got a possible ID. Found a wallet."

Detective Wolfe roused, his dark eyes sharp. He stepped away, moving down the steps toward the Galaxy.

The officer's words floated back to me on a light, late afternoon breeze. "The name in the wallet is Helene Foster."

CHAPTER 4

Not a word came from my lips. I couldn't speak or even think beyond trying to absorb the fact that the poor woman in the trunk of my car was Helene.

Detective Wolfe and the uniformed officer stopped on the parking strip, their heads close together, talking softly.

Shivers started at the crown of my head and washed down, raising goose bumps along my spine. The vision of the back of Helene's head, the small deadly hole above her ear where the bullet had entered—I closed my eyes, tight, trying to block the memory and think my way out of this nightmare. Rewrite this scenario, like I did my bad dreams. Why had I not looked more closely? Why hadn't I seen it was her? If I had, what would I have done differently?

Could they be wrong? Maybe it was only Helene's wallet and the body of someone else. Someone else with fine blond hair and petite black shoes. Such as she always wore. Why in God's name hadn't I recognized her?

Through a veil of disbelief I saw the morgue attendant drop his cigarette butt on the ground, crush it out, and wheel the gurney to the rear of my car. I buried my head in my hands. When next I looked, they were wheeling the gurney with the zippered black plastic body bag to the nondescript white wagon.

A tear slipped down my cheek. Poor Helene. I had been so angry with her, but that would have faded in time. We went all through college together, roomed together three of those years, and survived several huge arguments because she would ask for truth and I would tell her. We had kept in touch over the years, though not as frequently after she married Stewart Foster. We would have gotten over this last episode, just as we had all the other ones.

And what of Stewart, Helene's husband? Where was he? What was he doing? Was he making a nice Sunday dinner for them, as I had been doing when the police knocked on my door with their long faces and guarded expressions to tell me Mac's father was dead?

I imagined Stewart, tall and lean in a homey apron while he tossed a salad, his blond hair falling in his eyes. I had been shredding chicken meat when the officers tore apart my life and Mac's.

Finally the tow truck loaded up my Galaxy and left. The reporters left. The cops straggled to their cars. The neighbors retreated to their homes to peer from the front windows or catch the newscast on their televisions.

I closed my eyes and saw Helene again, almost like a silent movie. Helene, petite, worried, in the bar of the hotel in Chicago, begging me to move to Denver. Helene showing me around the office my first day. Helene reading the report I'd written, her fine blond hair swinging into her face, her lips thin, looking worried. Helene saying, "I've made a terrible mistake. You're fired. Go. Now."

Standing before me angry, frightened. Walking me out to the parking lot, looking up from her five-foot-two to my five-foot-eight, her blue eyes miserable, troubled. And I'd thought, good, feel bad. Feel terrible.

She gave me dreams, then dashed them. She caused me pain, and cost me a fortune. But, worst of all, she humiliated me. She accused me of being incompetent right there in the office in front of all of them, Harris, Lizzie, and Sam, and even Laurence Gifford.

That was the last time I saw her.

Now? I felt awful. Empty. Sick. But not angry, not at her. What had gone so wrong? Why was she in the trunk of my car? And what would happen when they realized I did know her?

Would they believe that I had assumed it was a drug-related death, and so didn't look to see if it was anyone I knew? Helene, with her rigid moral standards, was the last person I'd connect to a drug-related crime. Would they buy that I hadn't wanted to look at her because it was too almighty horrifying to see someone dead, much less shot and decaying? Scenes such as that burn themselves into the memory bank and rise at night in nightmares that linger for months, years, like that time in Chicago.

I realized with a chill that any digging Detective Wolfe did in Chicago into my background was unlikely to help my cause. There was dear old Dad and Uncle Roy and even Andrew, my brother, who never did learn right from wrong. Or right from left for that matter. Mine was a family whose primary coping mechanism was crime. The motto on my family escutcheon would be "Expedience First." Charming, lovable, but criminal.

Once the police tumbled to that, I was afraid they wouldn't look under any rocks to find who really killed Helene. They'd settle for me. The operative word here was "afraid." I was afraid.

The psychiatric sorts maintain that talking about things eases the burden, but admitting fear even to myself made it worse. My adrenal glands immediately went to work again. I had to do something if I were going to avoid being dog meat for Wolfe. Had to have a plan, but what? To make it worse, I had no spare money for a lawyer. Helene still owed me my last paycheck.

Oh, save me! I'd left a threatening message on her machine. As soon as Detective Wolfe heard the message he would know that I knew her and that I'd threatened her. I was in trouble. Big trouble.

Luckily, Mac and Sam stopped for a burger after the game so the police had left before they got home. No one should be exposed to such violence, but I especially wanted to protect Mac. He'd had enough trauma in his short lifetime; he didn't need to add this. I sanitized the details and told them briefly what had happened so they wouldn't be blindsided by the news in the media.

I was so glad I did. Mac's young face looked stricken and Sam bit his lower lip and shook his head until I thought his glasses would slide right off the end of his nose. He rubbed his face for the nth time and asked, "How could her body get into the trunk of your car?"

I sighed. "I park on the street."

Sam frowned. "Don't you lock your car?"

"I think I did. I usually do, but it's no trick to jimmy it. I've done it dozens of times, whenever I lock myself out."

"I've never seen it."

He probably hadn't. He wasn't an observant man. If he were, his socks would match. "Well, everyone else in the world has. My neighbors have, Mrs. Folsom next door who sees me as her private entertainment center has, certainly the people in the Techlaw parking lot have."

Mac said, "It's real easy to get into the Galaxy. Even my friend Barry can do it. Then you only have to pull the trunk lever." He got up and went to the kitchen where I could hear him open the refrigerator. Grazing.

Sam finally left and I poured myself an eight-ounce glass of Bon Vie wine, cheap and nasty, to ward off my demons.

Mac sat at the little card table we used in the kitchen. Eyeball to eyeball with Spike, Mac munched the last of a dill pickle. I

41

wondered if he would be traumatized by all this and decided a little questioning was in order. "How are you doing?"

He looked up. "I'm still a little hungry."

I put together a cheese sandwich and tried again, from a different angle. "Was it a good game?"

"The Cubs won, of course. And Sam, Mr. Lawson, had a cool camcorder, so he got all kinds of pictures of me there and talking, and he even got one of Sosa hitting a homer. It was great."

"That's wonderful. How are you feeling? About Mrs. Foster?"

He shrugged and bit into the sandwich. "It doesn't seem very real. I just wonder why she was in our car."

Was it a positive sign of incipient affection that he saw it as *our* car?

"I don't know why she was in our car," I said. Of course I wondered if it was to frame me, but I didn't tell Mac. It would only worry him. "I think because it's easy to open."

Mac swilled down a third glass of milk and looked thoughtfully at me. "Do you s'pose she fired anyone else? Maybe they killed her."

"I'm the only one she fired."

"Too bad." He chewed while I drained my wine and poured another.

Mac finished the last of the fig bars and said, "We could take off. Alaska. They've got lots of woods and bears and wolves and fish. It'd be perfect. I've got my survival book. We could live off the land."

"It's a thought." I envisioned us living off the land. Mac was nearly all muscle and definitely all appetite. Anywhere we settled would be deforested and barren of any life form in three months. "I think it takes more nerve to stay here and fight it out."

"What if we don't win?"

"But we will." With an air of bravado, I tossed off the last of my second glass of wine. "Now, it's ten-thirty, past time for you to go to bed." I poured a third glass of wine. It tasted better now that my tongue was numb. Everything was better, almost.

He frowned. "But really, if we don't win, then can we go to Alaska?"

Alaska was sounding better, too. "Sure." Thinking it was far better for Mac to fall asleep remembering his wonderful afternoon at the ball game, I said. "Now, tell me about the game today."

"Sam is amazing. He knows all about computers and comics and baseball." Mac was off, talking happily about Sam almost catching a pop-up foul at the game, having a comic book collection, writing comic books, then about the hot dog, the ice cream, the soda, the popcorn, and the chips which Mac had consumed. "And Sam can toss four popcorns in the air and catch all of them in his mouth at one time!"

Talent to live by.

Mac went to bed satisfied and maybe twenty minutes later I turned off the living room lights, pulled the window shades, flicked on a light in the bathroom, and checked on him. He was on his back, snoring heavily. His survival book covered his face.

Setting his book aside, I tucked him in and kissed his sleep-flushed cheek. For the millionth time I wondered if I would be able to rear this child. If loving him counted, he'd be in clover, but if wisdom were needed, he'd be cheated. What had his father been thinking to leave me as Mac's guardian? I pulled down his window shade and tiptoed back through the house to the front window in the dark.

The phone rang its special long-distance ring. I remembered I hadn't made my Sunday call to Lil. I called weekly in the belief that she'd feel sufficiently connected to us that she would stay comfortably in Chicago. All I needed now was Lil swoop-

43

ing in to muddy the waters.

Forcing cheer into my voice, I said, "Hi, Mom. What's up?"

Mom's voice poured into my ears from the cell phone. "I guess this means you're not in jail."

Ah, the family refrain.

"Of course I'm not in jail."

"I don't hear from you, I figure there's trouble."

"We just had a big day and I forgot to call. How're things there?"

Lil sighed heavily. "I told you it was a mistake to leave Chicago. You just throw your clothes and Mac in the car and come right back home, where you belong." She clipped her last three words so I'd know she really meant it.

The four glasses of wine made my tongue stiff. "We're fine here, Mom."

"I don't believe it. Helene is trouble. I told you before you left that she'd be the devil to work for."

It's better to screen what's said to Lil. Unfortunately, four glasses of wine ripped my good sense. "Helene's dead, Mom. Someone killed her."

"Oh, my God. You don't call, I know there's trouble, but I don't expect to hear murder. What kind of a city are you in?"

"It's a good city. A terrible thing happened."

Mom made one short, soothing, crooning sound, then moved straight to problem solving, which for her is much more comfortable than dealing with emotions. "You have to think this through. There's no connection to you."

There was another long silence from Lil. She was thinking and it made me nervous. She's smart, but she jumps to conclusions sometimes. I heard her breathing, then she plunged ahead. "I'll bet she got someone else to do a report, then fired them, and they killed her. What was that report anyway?"

It seemed a lot safer to talk about the report. "It was crazy. I don't know why she had me do it. She asked me to compare and contrast her daily schedule, the sales reports, the office repairs, and I don't know what all. She said it was important. Then, the day she fired me, she said it was a test and I failed."

"Is there a lawyer in that company? You find a lawyer, you find trouble—"

"Mom!"

"Or maybe you were too much competition. Maybe you were threatening to Helene."

"Helene was the one killed. If I were competition, I'd have been killed."

"Do you still have that gun? You may need it."

She scared me. "Stop, Mom, you're getting too far out there." I said it to reassure myself, but I still peeked out the front window. My house was mid-block on a dark, quiet street and the only movement outside was the sway of the tree branches in the summer night. I peered up and down the street.

At either end of the block a street light shed bright cones of light on the pavement, but none of it extended to my little house, huddled between two larger ones. On either side of the street, cars stood nose to tail like so many black beetles, in a line interrupted only by narrow driveways. No shadows moved, no cigarettes glowed in any of them.

"It's okay, Mom. All quiet here." Then just as I started to let the curtain fall back in place, a car slowly rounded the corner, tires crunching on the pavement, headlights casting beams down the street. A dark-colored, two-door with a spoiler, a semi-sporty car of the sort seniors drive when they feel young but need the comfort of a sedan, crept along.

The car passed my house and moved on, without pausing, but it left a familiar tension I thought I had left behind in Chicago—the kind of tension no amount of wine, good or not, would erase. Was the driver really looking for a parking space?

Or was someone watching me?

I let out breath I hadn't realized I'd been holding and eased back onto the couch. "Mom? Still there?"

"And where would I go? Did I say goodbye?"

Before I could answer, Lil spoke again, her tone placating. "Don't get mad, just think about it. Do you want me to come out and drive you back here?"

A streak of acute panic struck somewhere in my midriff. A lone car in the street was nothing compared to the mere idea of Lil descending on us. "No! I'm staying here. My job starts tomorrow. And you need to stay *there*, for Dad and Andy."

I heard grave disappointment in her voice when she said, "If you change your mind, I can always come."

It occurred to me that Mom had survived all these years by simply moving on from all things unpleasant, without regrets, by dwelling only on her love for us.

The tip of my nose stung like it always does when I'm near tears. "Thanks, Mom. I love you, too."

Lil sniffled. "Change jobs as soon as possible. Telemarketing causes tumors."

CHAPTER 5

Tumors were the least of my worries. I hung up after telling her what Mac ate for supper, what the weather was like, and all those trivial little details that somehow made up the threads that tied our lives together.

I double-checked the locks on the front and back doors and the window stop-locks, then sat in the darkened living room, hyper-alert to every little sound, watching out the window, unable to think of sleep. The chirp of the crickets and drone of the cicadas drifted in through the window screen. Mrs. Folsom's swamp cooler kicked on.

To accept help from Lil or my loving brother, Andy, was to entangle myself forever in their love and their lifestyle. I couldn't do it, to myself or to Mac. When I was a kid we'd moved nearly every year, accounting for the sixteen schools I'd attended in twelve years. Other families might have a motto like "Stand Fast." Mine had the motto "Move Fast."

My heart started thumping heavily; breathing was tough. I wanted to pack my bags, grab Mac, and run. Far and fast. It might be in the genes, the need to move on whenever it gets tough. Then, I had hated it, but right now it sure sounded attractive.

Of course, the next best thing was chocolate, so I went straight to the fridge, took out the can of chocolate syrup, and drank it.

If there was one thing I wanted to give Mac and myself, it

was a break from my family, especially right now. Since Mac didn't have our genes, he had a chance at a normal life, but fleeing would set an example I might never be able to turn around.

Had I any cash, I could hire a lawyer, but a lawyer would simply bill me, then hire an investigator who would check out my story at my expense, with no guarantee of finding out who really killed Helene.

Then, still sitting in the dark, I riffled through my memories to talk myself out of running away. I got a pencil and my little notepad to make a list. It was nearly impossible to see in the dark but it felt comforting somehow. I love lists. They always help. I wrote down:

Run:

Mexico

Canada

Brazil

A fellow I knew from my last high school disappeared for eight years before he was found. Supposing I could do as well, that would get Mac to seventeen, his senior year in high school. Not a good age to have your mother arrested for murder. How would I apply for scholarships for him? Occupation: murder suspect? Income, zilch?

Life as a fugitive meant living on the run. How would I do that with a kid who has to eat regularly? By the time I lived that long as a fugitive I'd be crazed. I'd heard you could telemarket from jail. Could you do it from a mental institution?

Three things were clear through the wine and chocolate haze. One, it couldn't get much worse. Two, I was set up. And three, no one was going to rescue me.

I was on my own.

Dad always said, "If you want it done right, do it yourself."

Of course, he was talking about theft, but surely the principle could apply.

I woke the next morning, the pencil grooving my cheek, the pad of paper wrinkled under my chin, with a mammoth headache and a decision—well, really more of a vision: Me, as a detective.

I would start with three basic things. I found comfort in threes. The first was to avoid the police as long as possible. The second was to say as little as possible. And third, for the kind of information I would have to get, I needed some kind of traction, leverage, inside information, grit, whatever. An "in" person.

Lizzie Bruckner was Techlaw's secretary/receptionist and telephone wizard. She was a lively, impish, dark-haired font of information with an inside track.

She answered on the third ring, all perky questions and gushing sympathy over the trauma of finding Helene. She would be glad to meet me for lunch. We settled on Betty's Corner, a tiny little lunch restaurant near Techlaw's offices.

I dressed carefully in fresh jeans, my favorite ones, with large, shouting-red lips embroidered on the butt. I topped them off with a silk blouse and a squirt of Carolina Herrera perfume that I had bought in the flush days before I was fired. Now all I had to do was sell a few funeral services at the Level One telemarketing empire.

Minutes after Mac left for school the doorbell rang. I tiptoed to the door and peeped through the fisheye. The little hairs on the back of my neck rose.

Detective Wolfe, wearing navy slacks and a light blue shirt, lounged against the porch railing, his back to me. If he were here to arrest me, I thought, he'd have brought a witness.

He turned and leaned toward the fisheye, his face distorted into a long, long oval with dark hair, bug eyes, and a very long nose. He even looked a little like a wolf.

I waited, barely breathing, until he took out a slip of paper, made a quick note on it, and left it jammed in the door.

He walked across and a little down the street to a black two-door car with a spoiler on the tail, too flashy to be used for surveillance. Most official police cars in Denver are white, and usually marked. This one looked a lot like the dark car that had come slowly down the street last night. He got in and drove away.

I waited five more minutes, then left by the back door to avoid the note. A note I hadn't read was a note I could ignore. No car started up, no one followed me. My heart only raced for the first block; it had settled to near normal rate by the time I reached the bus stop.

The bus went west to the industrial area of south Platte Valley, characterized by dust, heat, and urban renewal in the larval stage. The Level One Communications company's nondescript building sported florid fresh graffiti.

I entered, noticing with thankfulness that the air conditioning was fixed, and saw for the first time the motto: "Happy Voices, Selling Calls."

Only three of the dozen phone carrels in the large open room were occupied. Morning hours are the worst for sales.

I clocked in, found my folder with the printed paragraphs of information to read to those who would listen, and took a carrel. Ethel had explained that I received a one-dollar commission for a referral for further information, a two-dollar commission for an appointment with the funeral salesman, and a one percent commission on any money actually paid. The bigger the funeral, the better the commission.

Three hang-ups and one cursing-out later, someone talked to me. Her name was Mazie Glowitz, and by her voice I judged her to be an elderly woman whose mild lisp was caused by ill-fitting dentures. I gave her my name. "I'm calling to tell you

about this great opportunity to plan for the death of your life—
you don't want to go disorganized."

"Dearie, if I go it'll be from chronic constipation. Enemas are
the only way to go. Like Mae West, a colonic a day keeps death
away." She chortled.

Oh, dear. Should I hang up? Did nut cases count as contacts?
"May I send you information about our select service? Planning
ahead saves you money."

"*Proof*, Dearie, that's what's important. Do I care about
money? Where I'm going, money won't be an issue."

I was getting confused trying to follow her thinking. "Your
family will—"

"Proof is colonics. Good old warm coffee, full of caffeine.
Now if you can prove—"

I couldn't hang up fast enough. I stood up, pitched out the
tail-end of my cup of coffee, and took a quick spin around the
room to settle my stomach.

My next call I spent thirty minutes talking services and
mortuary sympathy until my head was spinning, only to discover
that the funeral being planned was a cat's funeral.

The murmur of little telemarketer voices diminished, replaced
by the pungent aroma of tuna fish and potato chips. Noontime.
I rubbed my eyes, stretched, picked up my purse, and left. Not
a single dollar earned.

I remembered loud and clear why I'd hated this job before.
And back then I'd been lucky enough to sell dog food. People
buy dog food.

CHAPTER 6

North Capitol Hill was largely built up at the turn of the century and still marked by shaded streets and large two- and three-story brick homes on small lots set close enough to ensure that no conversation would go unheard any time the windows were open.

Previously decaying and subdivided, many of the houses had been converted into yuppie professional offices, the back yards made into parking spaces. A few blocks north, several hospitals sprawled in glassy splendor. I guess the lawyers figured their clients could stagger north to medical care and bottled oxygen after they were presented with their bills.

Alone on a triangular bit of land in the midst of a convergence of streets, Betty's Corner did a humming business in chicken burritos, fish tacos, and shrimp enchiladas. Probably the most famous item on the menu was the green chili ice cream sundae, but the *best* item was Betty's baked chili rellenos—large dark-green poblano peppers stuffed with Monterey jack cheese and baked with chopped tomatoes and just a hint of cilantro. I smelled them as soon as the bus let me off on the corner and merely followed my nose to Betty's.

Inside, the smell of chili and the sibilant murmur of Spanish filled the tiny café. Ah, comfort. A place that smelled like heaven. My plan was simple: eat chilies, grill Lizzie, and get my paycheck reissued. Mustn't forget the cash.

Three little tables along the far wall were filled with people, a counter with a cash register stood to my left, and on the wall was a blackboard menu. Lizzie stood in front of the menu, her superb figure outlined by a simple blue dress. I sucked in my belly automatically. It's hard to feel elegant in jeans with red lips on the rump.

Lizzie was a fine-boned woman with a poof of brown hair and eyebrows arched in permanent, wide-eyed surprise, a life-sized doll whose age hadn't risen over twenty-eight in the last seven years. Her face, made for smiles and laughter, was tense; her lips were pursed and her eyes reddened, as though she had been crying. Something obviously had changed from earlier this morning when I talked to her.

I touched her shoulder to let her know I was there. She started and stepped back from me as though I carried the plague. I wished I'd cleared my throat or something. It doesn't help to scare a person to death just before you ask them to talk about their murdered boss.

I thanked her for meeting me and suggested we order so she wouldn't be late when she returned to the office. She twitched in a kind of smile and ordered a fish taco, which sounded ghastly. I ordered chili rellenos. The waitress at the counter wrote quickly. "Drinks?"

Lizzie answered, "Coffee for me. You, too?"

Not after Mazie on the phone this morning, telling me about her caffeine colonics. "Ice water."

We took our drinks to a tiny corner table and sat to wait for our meals. Lizzie stirred her coffee endlessly. "I'm just a bit on edge," she said.

When she started to stir again I put a hand out to stop her. She jerked back as if I were a rattlesnake, and I said, "Hey, what's going on?"

Lizzie blinked very slowly, then faster as tears gathered in her eyes. "The police came this morning."

"And?"

Her gaze darted nervously away. I braced for a white lie, but she looked back straight into my eyes, almost daring me to doubt her. "They were real interested in the fact that you were fired. I got the idea they think you killed her."

Judging from the expression in her eyes, that was exactly what she thought, too. I spoke slowly so she wouldn't miss a word. "Oh, Lizzie, I am so sorry. It must have taken all your nerve just to come meet me this noon."

Tears gathered in her eyes and threatened to spill over onto her cheeks. "I didn't tell anyone I was coming, especially not Harris." She looked nervously away. "He's . . . he's a little negative, if you know what I mean."

She was married to the guy, so that was probably as critical as she could get, but Harris was more than a little negative. Being a borderline genius is no excuse for being chronically worried, abstracted, and impatient. For Lizzie's sake I murmured, "Stressed."

She burst out, "We're all stressed! He's . . . unreasonable."

The last thing I wanted was to be caught in a tirade about her marital troubles. I had enough problems of my own and I needed to get on with solving them.

"Look, Lizzie." I emphasized her name to drag her gaze to mine, to make sure she was listening to me. "I was stunned when Helene fired me, because she had promised me a job with a great salary and I loved working at Techlaw, but I *did not* kill her."

Lizzie was silent, staring at the tabletop, tracing an endless pattern on it with her finger. Finally she said, "You left her a message threatening to kill her if she didn't send you your last paycheck."

Ouch. There was that. Helene still owed me for my last three weeks and I'd left that nasty, furious message on her phone, unfortunately at work as well as at home. "But haven't you ever said something like that when you were pissed? 'Do it again and I'll kill you?' or 'I could've strangled her?' It was just an expression."

Lizzie swiped at her eyes.

I continued. "I was angry then, but I didn't kill her. Helene was a friend. I thought, I still think, that she cared about me and I don't know why she fired me. I didn't make any mistakes on the report I did for her. Not one."

Lizzie blew her nose gently and dabbed at her eyes. Her mascara ran in smutty marks from her eyes to her cheeks, much like the sad clown faces in the circus that used to scare me as a child. I couldn't tell if she'd believed me, but she looked less frightened.

I leaned forward just a little. "Lizzie, when did you see Helene last?"

She blinked rapidly. "Thursday. I saw her Thursday and then Friday morning she left me a phone message saying she wouldn't be in."

"Who did she see Thursday?"

Lizzie shrugged. "I don't know. Laurence Gifford, in the morning I think, but I didn't have her schedule. You know what she was like lately. She didn't tell anyone what she was doing."

Laurence Gifford was the company consulting attorney and auditor. True, Techlaw Inc. couldn't have been making oodles of cash, not with the economy as it was, but if I'd merely been a layoff, why would Helene have fired me in the way she did, humiliating me in front of everyone. Wouldn't she have simply said I was being laid off? Helene could be cold, but she wasn't rotten. There had to be more to it. "What was Helene working on? Was it connected to Gifford?"

Lizzie spoke carefully, as though she was thinking back, but I wondered if she was making it up. "Something at night, I think," she said, "after we all went home. Helene never told me."

"Did she use the files I had? For my report?"

"I don't know about any files you had. Or a report."

Her gaze was tight on the tabletop, her little hand tensed. I thought she lied.

"Did you tell the police about that?" As soon as I said it, I knew I'd made a mistake.

She flinched and her voice sounded defensive and evasive. "I was upset. I don't remember exactly what I said."

I hurried to reassure her, to try to smooth over the breach. "It's all right. You have to answer their questions. I'm not worried about that."

The waitress slid our food down on the tabletop. The fish tacos smelled fantastic. Food helps. It quiets the fires of unrest and irritation in my breast. I hoped it would help Lizzie.

As soon as she had consumed nearly a half of her second taco I started in again. "Let's go back a bit. What did Helene say to you about hiring me?"

"Nothing."

"I mean, last fall maybe? Not recently."

The tension in her shoulders seemed to ease. The past was clearly a safer subject than the present. Maybe it was for most people.

She chewed slowly, swallowed, and said, "I think last October or maybe November, she started to stay late. She'd get that icy, distant look in her eyes that just stopped me in my tracks. Arctic cold, you know? Almost accusing. I felt like she stopped trusting me or something, because she stopped talking to me much. Just clammed up."

Secrets do that. They make people go silent. So as long ago as October or November Helene had something she didn't want to tell Lizzie. And since Lizzie was married to Harris, presumably Helene didn't want to tell Harris either. "What do you think it was?"

Lizzie shook her head, but she blinked nervously. "I don't know."

"What happened?"

"She was gone a lot, distracted when she was in the office, and then in January she went to Chicago and hired you."

Helene's offer of the perfect job in Denver had been a godsend. I needed to get out of Chicago. Being so eager to start fresh, I had jumped too soon, asked too few questions. Lizzie was chewing slowly. I asked, "Had Helene advertised the position?"

Lizzie didn't meet my gaze. "Not a word. She just marched into Harris's office one afternoon and before the door banged shut I heard her say, 'We've got to have more help and I know the person.' They argued. I heard the blurred voices rise and fall, kind of angry, you know?"

"Harris didn't tell you about it later?"

She looked at me as though I was too, too naïve. "No. Helene flew to Chicago, came back, and said she had hired you."

"And you have no idea why?"

She shook her head, her lips pressed together as though she knew, but was determined not to say.

"That must have been unnerving for you."

"Oh, no," she said, "not for me."

Of course, she was married to one of the bosses.

Lizzie finally looked me in the eye. "Laurence Gifford was really put out. And although he was really pleased later, I think Sam was surprised."

"Did he say so?"

"You know how he is. Doesn't ever really come out and say anything, just grunts and snorts, but he lets you know."

I nodded. Sam Lawton had sub-vocal animal sounds down to a fine art. And he'd been generous in teaching them to Mac.

"When you packed up my desk, what did you do with the files in the bottom drawer?"

Her high, rounded eyebrows climbed a tad higher. "The drawer was empty."

"Nothing at all?" A tiny frown grew on her forehead and I hastened to add, "There were a few odds and ends I forgot to pick up when I left."

She shook her head in little movements. "Nothing but a bit of foil from a Hershey's Kiss candy." She looked thoughtful for a long moment, then said, "Notes from your report?"

I shrugged. "Like I said, just scratch papers."

Except they weren't. They were the notes I'd kept after I finished the project for Helene. Was Lizzie lying? I couldn't tell. "Did Helene have you clean it out right away?"

"That afternoon."

"Did anyone else go through the desk?"

"No."

"I locked the drawer the day I left the office. And I still have the key." I waited for her to react.

Her small white teeth caught her lower lip as my words sank in. "I used to have your desk. I still have a key to it." Lizzie picked up her purse. "I thought you knew. I'm sorry, but I need to get back to the office."

I almost forgot to ask about my paycheck. "Did Helene order my terminal paycheck?"

She shook her head. "Not that I know. You'll have to go to Harris."

Ouch. "Lizzie, just one more question. Did you ever have reason to think Helene might have used drugs?"

She didn't answer for a long time, then she said softly, "I, I don't . . ." She hesitated, then looked me straight in the eye. "Yes. I saw her in the bathroom once, tossing back some pills."

"Medication?"

"Maybe, but she had mood swings. And she seemed so edgy. Stu mentioned . . ."

Helene never called her husband "Stu." Lizzie noticed my surprise and bit back whatever she was going to say next.

"Stu mentioned what, Lizzie?"

"Forget I said that. And don't ask him about it."

"But surely—"

"Why are you asking all these questions?" She glanced around then leaned toward me. "You aren't trying to investigate this, are you?"

The intensity of her expression made me hesitate. Why would she care? "Just trying to understand."

"Well, you better be careful." She stood, clutching her purse to her chest.

"What do you mean?"

Lizzie's face was pinched, making her look suddenly older. She leaned toward me. Keeping her voice low but urgent, she said, "First, Julia. Now Helene is dead."

"Julia?" Startled, I asked, "Who's Julia?"

"Julia Orbach. She had your job before you."

I felt a cold draft on my arms. "I thought Helene was doing it all."

"She was. Harris wanted to save money, so they didn't replace Julia after she was gone."

"Where did Julia go?" I asked, expecting to hear she got married and moved to the 'burbs, or southern California, or had a kid.

"She died in a car accident in the mountains. About this time last year."

Why hadn't anyone mentioned her? Was it a conspiracy of silence? My mouth went dry. The seconds stretched out long and cold. I finally said, "Are you saying Julia's death wasn't an accident?"

Lizzie stepped back and glanced around. "I'm not saying another word. You've got Mac to think of."

Techlaw Inc. was a very small company with a disturbingly high death rate. I stared at Lizzie's retreating back, one thought cycling in my mind. *What if Julia's death wasn't an accident?*

If by any chance Julia Orbach's accident wasn't an accident, then forty percent of Techlaw had been murdered. Very bad odds.

CHAPTER 7

Outside, the breeze lifted my hair off my neck and cooled my face. The sun seemed to have dimmed a bit. I found myself checking more carefully to see if anyone followed me. Even Lizzie had been frazzled, and she either lied or forgot things she should have remembered, like my report. Something big was going on with her. Was she protecting someone, or herself?

Harris was worried and it was rubbing off on their marriage. The undertones of marital discord had been present in little references to Harris's dedication to work and her self-pitying comments. And as I thought of it, I remembered other incidents in the past when Lizzie had made an offhand comment about Harris that in this light now sounded like a plea for attention.

Marriages, even troubled ones, were miracles of trust and communication. In the course of a marriage, people talk to their spouses. I remembered my parents, who certainly talked. They had masses to hide and still talked to each other, and not just because spouses couldn't be forced to testify against each other. Then I wondered, what had Helene talked about to Stewart? And what were Stewart's funeral plans? How was he handling this terrible tragedy?

I came to a retaining wall and sat down on it. I flashed back to the day I learned Mac's father was dead: the stultifying air in the room, the wind that howled around the corner of the apartment building that night, the emptiness of the bed, so vast I couldn't sleep. How was Helene's husband sleeping?

Stewart had both the pain and the relief of funereal duties to complete—the arrangements, the visitation, the ordering of the house, all the things that help to make death real, immutable, and, at last, final so that you can move on. None of that had been available to me.

Mac's father, Dave McGraw, said he was going for doughnuts early one Sunday morning, but ended up somewhere else, caught in an all-consuming fire. It was devastating. There had been nothing left of him, except his nearly nine-year-old boy, who had never really wanted my intrusion in their life. A horrible shock for me, but especially for Mac.

I had thought it couldn't get any worse, and then it did. I learned Dave hadn't been going for doughnuts. He was in a meth lab that blew up, going for dough, not doughnuts. The one thing I had thought was wonderful in my life had been a lie.

Lizzie was right. I had to think of Mac. He was paramount in my life. He *was* my life. His happiness was why I moved to Colorado, his safety was why I worried in the small hours of the night, his future was why I had to make sure I didn't get stuck with a murder rap. Bad enough Mac's father was dead; he sure didn't deserve to have me in the joint, or worse. Colorado still had the death penalty.

The breeze caught a thin plastic grocery bag from a doorway across the street and lifted it high, then bounced it along the pavement until it rolled into the street. A truck went by, crushing it beneath its wheels. Not unlike my lover and Helene, both taken so quickly and violently.

I shook myself. I could sit here and be pitiful, or I could do something constructive.

I took out my little notepad and jotted:
Helene killed:
What about noise?

Duct tape silencer?
Stuffed in trunk: takes muscle
Petite but heavy when limp
Drugs
Problems: Blood
Witnesses who saw?
Julia Orbach
On the next page I added:
My car?
Who did she see Thursday?
Why didn't she come to work Friday?
These I would focus on. I shoved the little notepad into my purse, which I laid across my lap.

Helene's current life, who she liked, who she socialized with, and how she and hubby were getting along, could all be unknowns. Even Stewart, her husband, was a relatively large question mark. She'd met and married him after she moved to Colorado, so I didn't know him well.

In spite of the heat, I shivered, discovered the notepad had fallen to the ground, picked it up, and shoved it in my pocket.

I rang Helene's home on my cell phone. The housekeeper answered and said there was a home visitation tomorrow night. Services would be the following afternoon at the McLaren Funeral Home. I rang off. It seemed so soon, so rushed. Did Stewart want to get it over with quickly? Or was it so painful for him that he only wanted everything done? Still, visitation was a good place to start gathering answers. Someone had to know something.

I set off for the bus stop.

About mid-block, before the mouth of an alley, a dark car with a spoiler pulled up, the privacy-glass window sliding down. "Hey, there, stop!"

I recognized the voice. Detective Wolfe. My heart rate

skyrocketed. What did he want?

He climbed out of his car, adjusted a lightweight tan jacket, and came toward me in long, athletic strides. He stopped a scant four feet away, his hands loose at his sides. "Let's just talk a minute, cool down a little."

Was he going to ask about the message I'd left for Helene on her telephone answering machine, the one where I said I'd kill her if she didn't pay me?

My heart rate lowered a bit, still thumping though, from GAAC, generalized-anxiety-associated-with-cops, another one of those Starzel family syndromes. I had tried to rid myself of it by being a law-abiding, honest, truthful, and upright citizen as much as possible. It didn't work. Maybe it was another genetic thing.

Or maybe he didn't know about the message yet. My heart rate dropped from the 200s down closer to normal.

"You looked like you were going to run."

What could I say? That I knew he wore his jacket to cover a shoulder holster? That he was a cop and my family viewed cops the same way ranchers viewed wolves? As the enemy?

I licked my lips. "In the neighborhoods where I grew up there were two kinds of people—the quick and the dead."

A flicker of amusement showed in his eyes, then he said, "We need to talk."

He took another step toward me. "You said you didn't recognize the body in your trunk, but she was your boss. So explain."

I backed up. "She was unrecognizable. You saw her, she was swollen, bloated . . ." I started to feel ill and stopped for a breath. "I didn't know who it was until . . ." I caught myself, then told the truth. "Until you were leaving and I overheard an officer tell you her name."

There was an angry flicker deep in his dark eyes. "Why didn't you say something then?"

"I was too stunned and you were in your car leaving before I could even think."

Wolfe looked as though he was weighing what I'd said for truth value, then rubbed his chin and said, "I've got something for you." He reached inside his jacket.

I sucked in a breath. Going for handcuffs? His gun?

Pulling out a slip of paper, he took a quick step forward, grabbed my hand, and slapped the paper in it. "Your appointment. Tomorrow morning," he said and walked back to his car.

"I can't make it. Work."

"Work is no excuse." He stopped just before climbing into the car. "We have a lot to cover. Take the morning off. And in the meantime, think about telling the truth when you come."

I yelled after him, "I told you the truth."

He smiled slowly. "Not all of it."

Actually, I'd been telling the truth, at some risk in fact. And I was even more irritated because this was no accidental meeting. He must have followed me, which meant along with everything else she told him, Lizzie must have told him we were meeting for lunch. Lizzie had very loose lips.

I watched him drive away and told myself I'd learned two things. One, I needed to be careful about being followed, and two, I could not trust Lizzie.

Everything seemed to be closing in on me. If I intended to remain a free woman and a loving mother, I had lots to do. Justice was out there and I was going to find it, starting with Laurence Gifford, Techlaw's consulting attorney. Fortunately, his offices weren't far.

As I was doing my report for Helene, I had noted that Laurence Gifford had appointments with Helene, and he usually had them prior to conferences with both Harris and Helene. At the time, I hadn't thought it important; now I wondered if there was more to it.

The only times I'd ever seen the man was from a distance as he whisked into the office. And the infamous day of my firing. I didn't remember much except that he was sort-of tall and sort-of good looking and sort-of well dressed in a suit sort-of way. All totaled, he was a "sort-of" kind of guy in a good suit, which is the same as saying I didn't remember him at all.

Four blocks later I found his law offices occupying a peaked-roof Victorian home which had gingerbread woodwork quaintly picked out in three contrasting colors. It was so Hansel and Gretel I almost expected to be greeted by a wicked witch.

The bell rang solidly, the door buzzed, and I pushed it open. The foyer was small, with heavy oak woodwork and a floor done in small green and white hexagonal ceramic tiles. A small infrared alarm device was planted unobtrusively on the wall at knee level. Dad taught us early to notice such things.

A grandmotherly secretary with a pile of marvelous white hair sat behind an antique oak desk. She smiled and asked if I had an appointment.

Reminding myself I was a compassionate, truthful person who wouldn't lie to a woman who probably baked snickerdoodle cookies every morning before work, I said, "No, but I really need to see him."

Her jaw firmed. She looked less grandmotherly, more stern. "I'm afraid he has a very tight schedule. Maybe I can answer your questions? Or make an appointment for a consultation?"

At an astronomical fee, no doubt. I didn't want to mention Helene's name because that would undoubtedly earn a refusal all day, so I said, "I'm part of Techlaw and just need to ask him a quick question. It won't take long."

Her facial expression hardened. "I don't understand."

She was *really* wearing thin. "You don't need to understand."

The grandmotherly surface cracked open. She was hardened

steel underneath. "Yes, I do."

That did it. She was a professional gatekeeper but my feet hurt from walking, and I was feeling mulish, determined to see him. I gazed back at her and very deliberately patted my belly in a woman-to-woman message. "It's *very* personal. He *needs* to see me."

Now she looked as though she'd discovered a cockroach in her Raisin Bran. "If you wish to see Mr. Gifford, you will need to make an appointment and the fee is $350 an hour."

"And even higher if I make a stink?"

"Correct."

I stretched my lips into a menacing smile. "If he plans to remain a free and unfettered man, he'll see me in less time than it takes to zip up, if you get my drift."

The expression in her eyes turned glacial. She was angry, but not shocked. Was he some kind of Lothario with a string of women on the side, or was she simply very controlled?

I thought she'd pick up the phone and call back to him, but instead she rose and marched into his office.

Now that was a mistake. One should never leave one's desk when there is an angry Starzel in the room.

The daily appointment calendar lay open on her desk. I leaned over and read his schedule. He had seen Harris Bruckner at one o'clock until half an hour ago. I flipped a page back to the previous week's layout. Thursday at two p.m. he had seen Helene Foster, the afternoon before the night she was killed. Friday a dark line ran through appointments. He had cancelled Friday. Why?

Hearing rapid footsteps, I flipped back the page and pretended to be gazing at a pair of Western prints, one a sun-baked cow's skull in a bed of bluebells.

I don't think she was fooled for a minute. There was a look of chagrin on her face as though she had just realized her mistake in leaving her desk. Her eyes were slits of suspicion. "He'll see you, but only for a few minutes."

"Thank you," I said and sailed down the hall to what had at one time been a lovely, wood-paneled dining room and now was an office with glass-paned French doors. If I hadn't been so annoyed, I probably would have admired the extensive renovation.

Lawrence Gifford sat behind an antique carved desk beside a bay with three windows looking out onto a narrow strip of grass and a large, old maple tree. Tasteful Western prints hung from a plate rail. I knocked lightly and entered.

He was tall and well-muscled, which showed when he stood and offered his hand in a dry, firm handshake. He had sharp cold eyes with fine crow's feet at the corners and hooded eyelids that gave him the appearance of a lizard watching his potential dinner. Me. From the brief quirk of his eyebrow I knew he recognized me, no doubt from Helene's fire-Francie scene at Techlaw. I took a seat.

He sat and leaned back, his elbows on the chair arms, hands folded over his flat abdomen. The top of his head came to just below an array of diplomas: college, law school, the Colorado bar association, even a CPA certificate. It was a very effective way to impress his clientele. I made a mental note to dust off my own diplomas: high school, college, and one award for citizenship from junior high school. I could frame them up for the next time I had a real job.

Patronizing and patient, but just barely, he said, "My secretary said you had a personal matter? I have to warn you that my practice is strictly in corporate law. I don't do divorces, private investigations—"

"Or paternity suits?"

He stared briefly, then laughed, although the expression in his eyes was wary. "From what Jeannie said, I figured you were a piece of work."

I wasn't sure how to begin. "You worked with Helene Foster. In fact, you met with her just before I did, two weeks ago."

"The day she fired you."

I was going to ignore that, then decided to use it instead. "Yes, and that's what I need to talk about. The firing process was not properly followed and I'm considering a lawsuit against Techlaw. You will be named, of course."

"You have no grounds."

"If you can convince me that your dealings with Helene that morning did not involve me, I will leave you out of the suit."

The corner of his mouth twitched in what might have been a suppressed smirk. "That was a nice try, but you know I can't divulge information about a client."

"In a sense, I'm your client, as well."

He twirled the broad gold wedding band on his ring finger. "I don't think being fired from the company qualifies you as a client. Why don't you tell me why you are really here?"

In an odd, tic-like mannerism, he glanced quickly to the right, out the side windows, then back to me. The turn of his face, the corner of his jaw, the habit of suddenly glancing to the right was an odd, distinctive mannerism. And one I had seen before. Where?

"I see from your licenses on the wall that you're a certified public accountant. I know that in addition to being legal counselor for Techlaw, you're also the auditor."

He shrugged. "I have consulted with Techlaw, which you already know because you worked there. And I've been their auditor. There has never, I repeat, never been any irregularity."

I wasn't getting anywhere. What would happen if I angered him? Would he blurt out something? "That's a flat-out lie," I said, "and you know it."

"I know no such thing."

"That's why you told Helene to fire me, isn't it? Because my

69

report made it clear that your audits were faulty. And for some reason, Helene went along with you. Why was that? Did you threaten her? Have something on her?"

Only his eyes moved under their hooded lids.

I looked at him hard, trying to see behind his very controlled façade. "Did she tell you Thursday that she was going to expose you?" His face flushed. "Did you convince her to meet with you Thursday night and lose your temper?"

He rose and loomed over his desk toward me. "That's enough! Time is up!"

"She was petite but she had a sharp tongue. Did she infuriate you then?"

"Don't say another word."

I really should have shut up, but I didn't. "I'm going to find her killer, if I have to die trying."

"At the rate you're going, you may indeed."

CHAPTER 8

Laurence Gifford was as cool as lizard skin on a mountain morning, cool enough to make me shudder inside. I left. Fast.

Outside I walked, checking around and behind myself. My report had told Helene something, perhaps had pointed to a crooked audit by Gifford, and Helene had fired me publicly, thinking it would protect me. I had just undone that and exposed myself to a man with the nerve and intelligence to kill and get away with it.

If all that wasn't bad enough, I'd lied, menaced, and been ready to cheat, steal, and attack just to set myself up like a ten-pin ready to be felled. I walked faster, my sore feet no longer important.

It would have been no trick at all for this fit, well-muscled man to dump her body in the trunk of my car. I wasn't even sure I locked the thing. He could find out where I lived from personnel records. And he'd seen me fired in a dramatic scene where I'd told Helene she'd be sorry in front of the whole staff. It all fit very neatly, but it would be tough to prove. And now I was a moving target. Literally.

When I reached my house, there was no dark car with a spoiler parked on the street, waiting, a wolf stalking its prey. I was the tiniest bit disappointed, and in that moment, I thought I finally understood why Little Red Riding Hood talked to the wolf. They aren't entirely unattractive.

There was, however, a white, nondescript four-door Ford

that had the earmark of a cop car—extra antenna and a large spotlight on the driver's side—parked down a house. I didn't know whether that was a good thing or not.

I decided to avoid my front door and trailed down the alley behind our house, slipped in the back gate, and entered through the back door. Mac came in barely five minutes later, looking happy and relaxed.

That was what I wanted to preserve above all else. His safety and happiness. I wish I'd remembered that when I was in Gifford's office. I pasted on a smile and asked, "How was camp? You're a little late."

"I stopped at Barry's house on the way."

Barry, his best friend, lives a bit more than a block away. "Did you tell him about Spike?"

"Yeah. He's coming over to see her tomorrow. *His* mom lets *him* keep a snake."

The happiness I want to preserve in Mac does not extend to reptiles. "Are you hungry?"

"No, *she* has cookies, too. Oatmeal. She baked them." Mac dropped into a chair. "I could use some pickles though."

"I'm usually good for a pickle or two." I pulled a jar of dills out of the cupboard, opened it, and handed it over.

"Hey, Francie," he said around a large mouthful of partially chewed dill pickle. "There's a weirdo sitting out front in a white car. Think we should call the police?" He pulled a note out of his pocket. "And I found this on the porch."

It was the appointment slip Wolfe had left on the porch this morning. "Oh, thanks," I said and stuffed it in the pocket of my jeans.

"What about the guy in the car?"

"I think he's just hiding out from his wife. She probably doesn't let him smoke in the house."

"Oh. Some people are weird, you know?"

"Absolutely." And unpredictable. I had to remember that. Dangerously unpredictable.

As Dad always said, "Why make it easy for them?"

The next morning the bus was late, by maybe four and a half minutes. I decided it was a crucial four and a half, taking way too much time out of my work day, so I skipped the appointment with Detective Handsome and went straight to work. I got to Level One a little early, clocked in, and surveyed my work area.

The sun shone through the dirty window panes, sending bars of warm light on the dusty old oak flooring of the room. Years ago it must have been a nice building. It looked pretty good right now. Better by far than the police station.

I selected a carrel next to a window where, if my calls were slow, I could watch the crows on the rooftop across the street. I logged in and waited for the first call. It was 9:05 a.m. As soon as I got the cue I started my pitch.

A loud hoot came over the phone line. "Hah! Selling funerals, huh? I've a question for you, miss. How much do you make doing this job?"

Ten dollars an hour, but of course I wasn't going to tell him. I ignored his question and intoned the memorized paragraph. "One of the newest product lines is the art casket. You can choose a scene or a motif and have it imprinted on the side of your casket for an original design, unique to you that will express your most passionate feelings, even after death."

"I asked how much do you make doing this lousy job?"

That was it for the written text. "Very little because people do not enjoy looking ahead into reality and planning for it."

"Do you plan for it?"

I couldn't answer just then. Detective Wolfe, a slight flush on his cheeks, wearing a blue oxford cloth shirt and light jacket to cover the standard shoulder-holster-with-.38, was at my side. His face, I decided, was essentially a nice face, maybe even a great-looking face if you like them rugged, square-jawed, and almost handsome. Aside from memorizing exactly how good he looked, I paid him no attention.

The irate voice of my callee boomed out of the earphones. "Miss? You there? You should get out of that business. It ain't good for you to be calling up people and talking about death."

"You're right, sir. Maybe I can simply mail out some information—"

"No. Don't want nothing, except for you to get off this phone."

"Thank you, sir." I hung up.

Wolfe had a sliver of a scar on his right temple and a small pulse just below it. His hands rested on his hips, waiting, I guess, for me to say something. I accepted another call. "Good morning, my name is—"

He reached over and disconnected the line. "You missed your appointment."

"I told you I couldn't make it."

"You can make it now. I talked to your supervisor."

"You're going to get me fired."

He glanced pointedly around the room as if to say: *This? You'll miss this?* Then he looked back at me. "Might be a favor for everyone. Come now." He was not amused.

I followed him outside to his car, where I halted, arms at my sides. His car was parked in a loading zone, obviously ready to whisk me to headquarters. If I got in I was tacitly agreeing to a questioning. I couldn't do that. Dad's voice was practically screaming in the back of my mind, "Don't ever agree to questioning without a lawyer." I had no lawyer.

"I refuse to go downtown, Detective."

He leaned against the side of the car, folded his arms across his chest, and looked at me. I was a little relieved his arms were crossed. People usually don't grab you from that position.

It was an uncomfortable few seconds while he scanned my face and I wondered what he was thinking. He was good at keeping his expression hidden. He was probably good at poker, too. For a while neither one of us spoke, in a kind of contest to see who would ask the first question. Then he spoke up. "Let's talk about finding the victim in your car. You found her when?"

"I've already been through this. You know exactly when I found her. You wrote it all down. I'm not willing to go through it again."

"Most people cooperate with police in the interest of finding the guilty person."

That was because most people are not only innocent, but they're unacquainted with police. I, on the other hand, have had much indoctrination from my family. "I have cooperated. I've told you everything I know. I'm not willing to repeat it endlessly merely because you don't have any new questions to ask or to satisfy some obsessive-compulsive tendency you have."

Mildly annoyed he said, "We can do this easy or we can do it hard."

"There is nothing to do. Do you have a warrant for my arrest?"

"No," he said and waved a notepad in a plastic baggie at me. "I have this."

My notepad! I grabbed for it, but he snatched it away from my fingers. My forehead dampened with a fine, nervous sweat. "Where'd you get that?"

"You dropped it yesterday. It makes some interesting reading. Looks to me like you need to explain it. It says here, 'Kill Helene Foster.' "

I corrected him. "It says 'Helene killed.' It's a simple list. It's my way of thinking things out."

"Sort of like a diary?"

"I don't keep . . ."

A memory flashed, drowning out whatever he said next. Helene had kept a diary, volumes of diaries, really journals. But the police must have searched Helene's home. Surely they'd found her journals. Could they have missed them? Or was this a trap?

Wolfe straightened. "I don't understand your game, but the district attorney is going to have a lot of questions for you when he sees this." He waved the list again, then pocketed it.

A flood of adrenaline rushed through my veins. "Do you have anything else you want to ask me?"

"I ran your name through the computer and came up with some very interesting information. You have some bad connections in Chicago. And there was mention of drug involvement."

"Not me."

"Oh, a frame is it? They all say that."

"They, who?"

"They, the criminals, the species, the druggies, the dealers. They."

I'd never been had up for drugs in any way. I couldn't swear I'd never ever tried them, but I'd never used. Nor was it in my records. He was just trying to get me to respond, and anything I said or did would only make the situation worse. I could hear Dad's voice in my mind. "Don't say a dad-gummed thing, Francie. They'll just twist it."

I straightened. "Am I under arrest?"

Pause. "No." Implication: *not yet.*

"Then I have nothing further to say."

His jaw set and his eyes were intense and angry. "You are going to have to talk to us one of these days and the longer you put it off, the worse it will be for you."

CHAPTER 9

I stalked back inside the building and took my seat at the phones. I was so strung out my gut quivered, but I knew what I had to do next. I had to find Helene's journal. I was sure she still kept one. She would have written down all her thoughts and suspicions, why she fired me, why she humiliated me, and even what had happened to Julia Orbach. And I had the perfect entrance to her house. The visitation.

It was hard to concentrate on selling funeral service contracts. Helene's journals were all I could think about. She was slightly dyslexic. The diaries were part of her exercises to overcome it. She hadn't viewed them as necessarily private in college, and had read them to me at times, proud of her life, at least in the good old days when we were young and trusting.

Even though Helene was found in the trunk of my car, the police would have searched her house. Spouses are always viewed with suspicion in a murder. Unless she had taken to hiding the journals, the cops should have found them. Still, there had been no mention of journals or a diary in the papers, so maybe, *maybe*, she had hidden them. And if she had, who would be best at finding them? A burglar or his apprentice, that's who. It had been ages, literally over twenty-five years, since Andy had taught me to skin through a place at the age of eight, but like riding a bike, some things stick with you. My palms itched.

Time dragged until two o'clock, when I hung up my headset and left. Because Mac was due home early, I went straight there, waltzing up the front porch steps, figuring anybody who surveilled would be rewarded and perhaps think I was too obvious to be guilty.

Mac arrived shortly after I did, his friend Barry in tow. Barry was on the small, thin side of ten years old, with a thatch of dark hair that fell into his eyes, a nose that needed constant attention, and two enormous front teeth that for years would be out of proportion until the rest of his face caught up. He was suitably impressed with Spike.

"Way cool. You s'pose Spike and Gilda would get along?"

Gilda, he told me, was his pet garter snake.

"Why yes," was on the tip of my tongue, but Mac headed me off with a firm, " 'Course not. Spike would kill her."

Barry left, mildly disgruntled.

Spike was obviously not only to raise Mac's cachet with his buddies, she was to bolster Mac's sagging self-confidence. Better a spider than a gun, I thought, and wished for the hundredth time that I weren't so new to this mothering thing.

After supper—macaroni and cheese—I looked speculatively at Mac, who instantly understood I had something in mind. He's had to go with me a zillion places because there was no one, or no one suitable, to care for him while I went alone.

His face wrinkled in dismay. "I don't want to go."

"You don't know what I'm thinking of."

"It doesn't matter, I don't want to go."

"This is a reception, Mac, at Helene's house. It won't take too long. I want to talk to some of Helene's friends, and Stewart, her husband."

"You can go to the funeral when I'm in school."

"I'll go, but a funeral is different. People act differently at them and a lot of people can't go because they have to work." *And the funeral won't be in Helene's home, so I can't scan for journals,* I thought.

"I don't want to talk to old folks. Can't I just stay home?"

"I really need you, Mac. You can be a help to me." That was true, but he scowled.

"It's a nighttime bus ride," I added. Mac loves riding buses. His scowl lightened.

I hit him with the clincher. "If there are refreshments, you can have all you want." He caved.

I took a page from the burglary bible; the first rule was to blend in. I dressed in a plain black skirt, a simple white silk blouse, and low-heeled shoes. I could almost pass as a waitress or the office clerical staff. The second rule was to be forgettable, so I tucked a pair of wire-rimmed reading glasses into a pocket. Glasses make me forgettable, in fact invisible.

As an extra precaution, I decided to take along my little Baby Browning. It would fit in my purse.

I reached under my bed, inside the box springs where I kept it. The slat was empty. I felt along the lining material. Nothing. It was gone. It took ten minutes to quiet my nerves.

The bus let us off four blocks from Helene's home, and since there were no sidewalks because no one in that neighborhood walked farther than their garage, we trudged along the edge of the street while I kept an eye out for lurking evil-doers.

Helene and Stewart lived in a lovely big-tree area of Denver called Crestmoor, east of Colorado Boulevard, where there were large manicured lawns and a genteel patina of manners and money—a nice place to live. At seven-thirty the hum of traffic diminished, the air softened and cooled, and the first hint of twilight began to settle over the neighborhood as the sun sank to the mountaintops.

A half a block from Helene and Stewart's large gracious home, cars lined the curbs and lights streamed from the windows. The huge front door stood open, air conditioning the entire neighborhood. From that distance the grillwork of the security door looked uncomfortably like a prison cell door. I hoped it wasn't an omen.

I pulled out the glasses and put them on, acting carefully indifferent as I noticed the semi-sporty black car with a spoiler on the trunk parked across the street. If Detective Dominic Wolf wanted to sit in the heat and take note of the callers, so be it. I riffled my fingers in his direction, so he'd know I knew he was there.

Inside, the foyer divided the living room from a formal dining room where a lavish buffet was laid out. Mac sighed with contentment.

Directly in front of us, stairs led up. I considered darting straight up so I could whip through Helene's upstairs while there was still a houseful of callers. Then I noticed several floral arrangements on the fourth stair, clearly to discourage people from ascending, and a caterer in black skirt and white blouse watching me.

Of course I could ignore her and step over the flowers and go up anyway, but I decided to head first for Helene's little home office off the living room.

"Stick with me, sweetie. We'll be in and out," I said and edged into the large, narrow living room, crowded with people, many of whom held dainty glass plates filled with a variety of finger food. At least with this many people, I might be able to move about without bumping into people I knew.

Mac tugged on my elbow and looked at me with rounded, begging eyes and mouthed the word, *food.*

I answered, "Hold on a bit, sweetie."

"He can go with me," said a familiar masculine voice. Sam Lawson stood behind us, his glasses riding at half-mast, his face lined with strain in spite of his smile. He looked at me closely. "I didn't know you wore glasses."

An entire crowd in a room and I immediately run into another Techlaw employee. "I was trying to be inconspicuous, Sam."

He pushed his glasses up and tugged at his tie, his elbows awkward in a sports jacket. "Oh, I was trying to be dressy." He flapped the jacket lightly and said, "Weddings and funerals only. Now if I could just find a wedding." He laughed in a burst of awkward noise.

I looked at the room, long, baronial, filled with probably close to twenty-five people. At the far end of the room, standing in front of a massive marble fireplace so pristine it could never have held a fire, stood Stewart Foster.

Stewart had the lean, long-boned look of a man who, in a former life, was a champion greyhound. The last time I'd seen him was at my house on July fourth. He'd been lightning quick and laughing then, with a dry wit and warm brown eyes. Tonight, though, his narrow head and long face made him seem taller than his six-feet-two, especially with his hair combed back to reveal a deep widow's peak. Although he was only in his late thirties, he seemed to move stiffly, as if Helene's death weighed on him, swelling his joints like an aging, arthritic racing hound.

I felt a deep twinge of pity for him. All those people to talk to, all those painful condolences to accept. I had met Stewart when I moved to Colorado and didn't know him well, but he had always seemed a nice warm foil to Helene's cool beauty.

Mac tugged at my elbow. "Food, please?"

Sam said, "I'd be glad to take Mac to the refreshments while you speak to Stewart. I'll bet Mac would rather eat than trail you through that mob."

It would be a hundred times better if Mac were not at my side. "Stay right in that room," I told him. "Do *not* go wandering around."

Sam said, "I'll keep an eye on him," and followed Mac.

A waiter came by, offering mini shrimp cocktails. I took one and drifted toward Helene's office, easing between people chatting in small groups. I was nearly at the door to the home office when a small, rounded woman with strong shoulders stepped forward, blocking my way.

"Miss Starzel? I never knew you wore glasses." Rosie. She cleaned our offices every night. Her round, prematurely lined face was lit with a warm smile and surrounded by thick, black curls.

I smiled back, even though she blocked the way to Helene's office.

"Hey, I was sorry to hear you got fired." She raised a little hors d'oeurves plate, piled with food. No carefully polished long nails—her hands were thick, reddened, her nails cut square across. She clutched a cheese puff. "There's enough cholesterol on that table to stop a herd of bison. It's set up for carnivores, you know." She took a dainty bite of the cheese puff and watched me closely.

I was caught off guard a bit and grinned. "Trans-fats heaven."

"Helene wouldn't have had this kind of coronary killer-food on the table. I know. I used to clean here for her, before I got on with the Kwick Kleaners. She was a vegetarian. Not like that husband, Stewart. Now there's a carnivore."

Rosie moved close to my elbow, practically speaking into my ear. "You were in school with her, weren't you? You knew her for what, sixteen, seventeen years?"

"How'd you know?"

"You figure she wouldn't talk to me 'cause I push a broom?" Rosie's voice sounded defensive.

"I thought no such thing. I was just surprised you knew."

A slightly shuttered look in her eyes as she sized me up. "I know a lot, I'll tell you." As if to emphasize it, she bit sharply into another cheese puff, chewed, and swallowed. "I loved her, you know? She was real good to me. She could be an out-and-out bitch, but she was smart, real smart. And loyal to those she liked." Rosie shook her head. "She was real upset about firing you."

"Did she talk to you about it?"

"Nope. I could just tell. She was worried about something, but she wouldn't talk about it."

"We were friends in college, even shared diaries. Did you see her write in a diary or a journal?"

Rosie's head tilted as though she were working something out. She looked at me almost sideways, a little like Spike, I decided. It was disconcerting.

Rosie took her time answering, and when she finally replied, her voice was thick. "She did, but she didn't share them."

Before I realized what I was saying, I blurted out, "Do you know where she kept them?"

Rosie considered her answer, then said, "Used to be in her home office. I thought you'd know."

"We grew apart some after college, after she married . . ." I felt myself start to choke up and took a sip of wine. Recomposed, I asked, "Did you ever see Helene taking medicine?"

"She never used drugs and whoever killed her murdered her out of sheer meanness." Rosie bit into another cheese puff.

I kept my expression as neutral as possible. "Did you know an employee named Julia? She had the job I was hired for."

Rosie's mouth drew up as though the cheese puff had suddenly soured. "Helene said you would help her. She wouldn't have brought you out here if she planned to fire you."

She frowned around the room. I couldn't tell whether she was looking for someone or simply stalling for time. Finally she glared at me and said quietly, "You gotta be real careful. This room is full of carnivores. If anyone invites you for dinner, you'd better make sure you're not the entree."

"What?"

"Don't trust *anyone*." She turned away and shouldered her way toward the dining room.

I was tempted to go after her and ask who she suspected, but I could see her later and my time here was limited. I needed to stick with finding those journals.

I squeezed past a small clutch of suited persons murmuring in low voices about their weekend plans, and was nearly at the door to Helene's office when I found myself face-to-face with one very good-looking woman, Georgia Jenson, Stewart's secretary.

In the blush of her late twenties, she had the same cool blond beauty that Helene had had, only where Helene had been petite, Georgia was tall. She even had Helene's rather cynical, blue-eyed look of calculation. Georgia frowned very becomingly, the way I wished I could frown, and said, "Excuse me, no one's allowed in the library."

So, now Helene's home office was called a library. "I was just hoping for a quiet place . . . feeling a bit dizzy." I wasn't entirely lying. The smell of the shrimp cocktail was unappetizing and the blood-red sauce definitely so.

Georgia looked closer at me. "I didn't know you wore glasses, Francie. And I'm really surprised to see you here."

My hackles rose. "Why is that?"

I waited for her to confess that she figured I was Helene's killer. Instead her cheeks pinked up and her lips thinned out. Score one for me. I shook my head in what I hoped would be a disarming gesture. "How is Stewart bearing up?"

She hesitated, then replied, "Amazingly well, everything considered. So difficult, you know, not *quite* knowing who killed her." Score one for sweet Georgia.

We had traded barbs, so I figured it was time to get down to basic information. "You've been with Stewart for years?"

"About a year. I took the job a year ago when Lizzie and I sort of traded jobs and she went to work for Helene and Harris. At Techlaw."

"Why did Lizzie leave? Is Stewart hard to work for?"

Georgia shook her head. "Stewart's great, *very* considerate." Her eyes were almost misty and some of her hostility seemed to drop away.

Hero worship? Was she a little bit in love with him? He wasn't my type, but good-looking if you like them greyhound lean and handsome. I preferred men a little sweaty, musky with an edge, but then my taste in men had left me single, with a nine-year-old boy to rear. "Lizzie must have had mixed feelings. Would you want to work for your husband and his partner? What if things didn't go right?"

Georgia shrugged an elegant shoulder. "She said it was to save Techlaw money, but I think Harris pressured her to do it. He always worries about money."

I leaned closer to her. "You said you worked for Harris before Stewart."

She reddened. "Very briefly."

I waited for her to explain, but she simply stood there, sipping her wine to fill the gap in conversation. I capitulated and said, "Helene could be a bit exacting."

Georgia's eyebrows lifted like little wings taking off. "Oh, a bit! I just didn't quite fit in . . . with Helene."

"You must have known a woman at Techlaw named Julia Orbach."

Distinctly uncomfortable, she quickly said, "I didn't really know her."

"Do you remember anything about the accident?"

Georgia brushed a lock of her hair back from her cheeks. "Nothing really. She was so young . . . excuse me, I need to say a word to . . ." and she eased away, practically evaporating into the crowd.

Yet again I started to enter Helene's office, hoping my glasses would keep me sort of invisible.

"Francie, I see you're wearing glasses," a voice boomed.

Stewart materialized at my elbow. So much for glasses being a disguise. For a moment I felt irritated, as though I were being purposely kept out of Helene's office. Then I saw the deep, vertical lines creasing his cheeks and remembered how difficult these times must be for him. Juggling the shrimp cocktail, I said, "Stewart, I'm so sorry."

To my surprise, he grasped my one free hand in his two cold ones. "Thank you for coming. I know it's difficult for you, too. It must have been . . . awful. How are you?"

"It's not easy."

"I saw you talking to Rosie."

I started to withdraw my hand from his. "I understand she worked here at the house for you and Helene before she worked at the office."

He clung to my hand like a lifeline. "She's the strangest woman on the planet. Hope she didn't upset you. Helene said she's on medication. Can't see that it helps."

"She was quite devoted to Helene. As I was."

He finally let go and rubbed his jaw. "Helene was so happy when you came in April. She said it would solve a problem." He passed a hand over his eyes. "I should have asked her about it. I should have tried harder to help out, but you know how she was. She didn't talk about the business, or much of anything else lately . . ." He let his voice drop off.

I tried to smile but it was hard and my face felt stretched out in a grimace. I looked for a place to put down the shrimp cocktail. "Stewart, I know you have a lot of people to see tonight, but did you know a woman named Julia who worked at

Techlaw maybe a year ago?"

"Julia?" He shook his head. "She left a long time ago."

"A year ago. And she died."

His gaze darted pointedly around the room, universal body language for *There must be someone, anybody else I could talk to.* The mere mention of Julia Orbach had first Rosie, then Georgia, and now Stewart oozing out of range as fast as possible. He squeezed my arm, just a tad firmly, and said, "Now don't be a stranger," and escaped to another person.

The person Stewart moved on to was Lizzie Bruckner. She looked far more upset tonight than she had been earlier at lunchtime. Her eyes were huge with dark grief smudges beneath them in her ashen face. Stewart gripped her hand as he had mine, then folded her into his arms in a soft hug, patting her back and murmuring something into her ear.

I was finally stepping into the library when a young business type squeezed by and thrust a plate with shrimp shells and a full cup of cocktail sauce at me. "Thank you, ma'am," he said.

So the dull outfit and glasses worked on people who didn't know me. I looked around for a place to ditch the plates.

Stewart and Lizzie were just steps from me. Stewart's hand was on Lizzie's arm and she was pulling back from him, her cheeks pinker. Unaware that I was behind her, she took a sudden step back. To avoid a collision I jumped back and lifted up the shrimp dishes so I wouldn't dump bright red all over her.

A shot rang out.

The room was stunned into momentary silence. Lizzie gasped. Her hand flew to her breast.

A second shot sounded. Louder because of the silence. This time I felt air move beside my head and heard a smack behind me. A bullet.

Lizzie sagged against me, crumpling. I dropped the plates and tried to grab her. She slipped through my fingers to the floor. Bright red oozed in her hair and across her face and smeared down her front.

"Lizzie!" Harris's voice called out. "Oh, my God, my wife's been shot."

Then I heard a hysterical woman shriek, "Mac! Where are you! Mac!"

It was me.

And there was no answer.

CHAPTER 10

In seeming slow motion my gaze fell on a single calm, cold face staring at me. Laurence Gifford. His cool, hooded gaze caught on mine, leaving me strangely more frightened than the gunshots had, maybe because it felt so personally menacing, especially after our little hostile exchange that afternoon.

I tried to move forward to see if he indeed held a gun, but Lizzie lay right before me on the floor, sticky red on her head and the side of her face. The sight of her with blood spattered all over was horrific. People surged, some trying to see, others trying to flee.

As the living room burst into pandemonium, Gifford disappeared among the crowd like a snake in grass. Was it simple aversion to me or to blood? Or something more? Could he have fired the shot? If Lizzie hadn't stepped back into me I'd have been exactly where she was when she went down. Was the bullet aimed at Lizzie? Or at me?

I shouted again. "Mac!" Where was he?

I tried to move to the dining room to look for him, but the crowd crushed toward us. I shoved in return. "Get back, give her air! Go back!" I held out my arms to keep the crowd from stepping on Lizzie and shouted yet again, "Mac! Sam!"

Finally I heard an answering, "Yo!" from Sam. At least Mac was with Sam. I relaxed and turned to Lizzie, still unconscious on the floor. The crowd was pressing in. I realized that if I knelt beside her, I was likely to get stepped on. In fact, if they moved any closer she was going to be trampled.

"Get back," I yelled again, and pushed on the person next to me. "Get these people back, so I can help her. Call the police, too."

As soon as the crowd inched away, I knelt beside Lizzie. The distinct scent of horseradish and catsup filled my nose. Now, I saw that the "blood" on her blouse looked definitely unbloodlike. I peeked under her blouse. No torn, bleeding flesh or blackened hole. Only healthy skin. It was shrimp cocktail sauce on her head and down her blouse, not blood. I reached for her wrist to check her pulse. It was fast and strong.

I shouted into a crowd of legs. "She's all right. She only fainted."

No one listened.

The bulky figure of Harris, her husband, dropped to his knees beside me. He grabbed her hand. "Oh, Lizzie. Don't die."

"She's all right. She fainted."

"She's bleeding."

"It's cocktail sauce. Smell it?"

Disbelieving, he bellowed again, "She's shot."

"Harris," I said and grabbed his chin, pulling his gaze to mine. "Look at me. She's not dead. She fainted. Fan her face."

"Then why—" He looked at me. "You're bleeding, too."

I stared into his eyes. "Harris, get a grip. It's shrimp cocktail sauce. Look at her."

Thank God her eyelids fluttered. He never would have believed me. He crooned over her. "Lizzie? Are you all right?"

"Keep them from stepping on her," I ordered. "She needs air and I need some napkins to get this stuff off her."

I rose to my feet. I had to find Mac and Sam.

"Mac! Sam!"

"Yo, here!" Sam shoved his way up to my side and peered at my shirt and raised his hands. "My God, there's blood on you!"

"Cocktail sauce." There was no Mac. I grabbed his jacket lapels. "Where's Mac?"

He dodged back, pulling his jacket out of my hands. "One minute he was at the table, snacking, and the next thing I know, he disappeared."

"I trusted you!" Barely containing myself, I strong-armed my way through to the foyer, then into the dining room, Sam at my heels, tugging at my elbow.

"Jesus, there's a hole dripping water in the foyer ceiling," he said.

"Screw the ceiling. Where's Mac?" Surely Mac was here somewhere. I scanned the room from right to left. He wasn't there. "Mac!"

"Maybe he's in the kitchen. He really liked the shrimp."

"It's not funny!"

"Really, try the kitchen. I'm sure he went in there."

I walked straight through the swinging door into a large, incredibly well-appointed kitchen. Two caterers huddled in a corner.

"Have you seen a young boy?"

One of the caterers looked up, face pale. She pointed with her elbow to a nearly hidden back staircase and mumbled, "One came through here earlier. I think he went up the stairs."

At the foot of the stairs, I hesitated briefly, shouting, "Mac! Are you here?"

What if he were lying shot, bleeding his little life away? What if—I raced up the stairs. Halfway, the staircase turned and angled up the rest of the way. I shouted again from the landing. "Mac!"

"Francie?" His voice sounded wobbly and scared.

"Mac!" I bolted up the last of the stairs. "Where are you?"

"Here." A door halfway down the hallway creaked open and Mac's pale face peered out. "Here."

I rushed down the hallway, flung wide the door, and gathered him into my arms. "Are you hurt?"

"No." His arms went gingerly around me, awkward and tentative. I was so glad he was all right he could have kicked me in the shins and I'd have been glad. As it was, he was giving me a hug, a feeble one, but still a hug. Warm and wonderful. My first from him.

"I didn't mean to do it."

I loosened my grip. "Do what?"

"It just went off."

My feet were cold—shock, I guessed. "What do you mean, 'it went off'? *You* shot?"

He nodded, tiny almost invisible little movements, his eyes huge and frightened in his pale face.

"*You* shot? Twice?"

He nodded, chin trembling.

So Gifford hadn't been trying to kill Lizzie or me. But what about the bullet I'd felt go by? Had it come from up here? "Tell me what happened."

"I had to go to the bathroom. There wasn't any toilet paper, so I looked in the cupboard. I found this neat-looking gun. I thought it was a toy. And when I clicked it, it went off. And now there's all this water."

I looked down. No wonder my feet were cold. Water was bubbling up from the flooring, oozing out the door of the bathroom, soaking the carpeting.

Footsteps pounded up the stairs. A rough hand on my shoulder pushed me aside. Detective Dominic Wolfe stepped inside. "What happened here?"

Mac pointed toward the bathroom floor. In half an inch of water, next to a sodden towel, lay a remarkably small, hammerless little Baby Browning. The kind of gun a person carries for self-defense. The kind you can discharge right out of a pocket or a purse because it has no hammer to get tangled in the cloth. Ten ounces of up-close and personal protection. Deadly enough. I knew. I had one just like it. *Had* had one.

I steered Mac across the hall and returned, jammed my hands in my pockets, and leaned over Wolfe's shoulder. That gun looked real familiar. A fine mist of nervous sweat formed on my forehead. I could not pull my gaze away from the gun.

Wolfe squatted, scrutinized it, then rose. "Wait there," he ordered and pointed me to a doorway across and down the hall. He pulled a cell phone from his pocket, pressed in a number, and put it to his ear.

I said, "Better have Stewart turn off the water."

He waved me away.

I tried to hear what he said, but his words were carefully muffled and the noise from downstairs overlay his conversation. I peeked into the door behind me.

It opened into an extra bedroom, used for storage. A God-given opportunity. I hadn't gotten into Helene's office, the so-called library downstairs, but I could at least try this room. "Mac, stay here at the door and if anyone comes, yell out to me that you want to leave."

"Let's go, please," Mac whined. "I don't feel so good."

"Mighty soon," I said and entered, leaving the door scarcely ajar. I figured I had at least three or four minutes.

The room was cool from air conditioning, but smelled of dust and a hint of something sweet, like rose water. Clothing, both men's and women's, lay atop the double bed as though awaiting someone to take them to the Goodwill.

I glanced in the closet where a Stairmaster and a treadmill stood folded up against the wall. That seems to be where most of them end up. Dust lay on the top of them. So much for fitness. At the far end of the room, shelves of books. I went straight for them.

Floor to ceiling in a tall, narrow bookcase, the books they really read were shelved and at least two shelves full had the blank spines and dull dark red color that Helene liked to use for her journals. I pulled the last one and opened it. Helene's awkward, heavily slanted hand filled the pages. I flipped to the last page, searching for a date. I found one. Two years ago.

I replaced it, careful to put it back exactly where it had been. There were dust lines to assist. Where were her recent journals? The police must have been here and taken them. Or someone else who knew she kept journals.

The shelf below held a stack of worn paperbacks, but there were two clean strips. Two large books had recently been there and now were gone. The recent diaries. Gone now.

I glanced around the room. A desk stood in front of the window, top covered with a fine dust. My hand was on the desk drawer pull when I heard Mac whine, "I wanna go home now."

Time was up.

I raced to the door, eased out, and joined Mac. The bathroom door was closed. The carpeting in front of the bathroom squished under the feet of Wolfe and Stewart advancing toward us. Stewart's face was grim. Wolfe was talking. "I've called a car."

I tried for a comradely grin, but failed. "Did you get the water turned off?"

They stared blankly at me.

"In the basement," I prompted. "Turn off the water?" I looked at Wolfe. "Stewart needs help. The bullet must have sheared a water pipe in the bathroom floor."

Stewart finally seemed to grasp what I was saying. He ran for the back stairs.

Wolfe looked at me. "I don't want one word out of you." Then he scowled at Mac. "Tell me exactly what happened here."

Mac stammered through the same story he'd told me, his

eyes round and solemn, his chin trembling. Wolfe made Mac explain again where he'd found the Browning, then detail the shooting. Finally Wolfe said, "You two go downstairs. *Now.* Do not leave."

Downstairs, the crowd had thinned considerably. Water dripped lightly in the foyer, the ceiling damp and bulging slightly. Two officers appeared at the front door. I pointed them upstairs. They trooped up, stepping around the flower arrangements on the fourth step.

Minutes later Stewart appeared, his cheeks slightly pink. He looked definitely rattled and ran upstairs to Wolfe. They both came back down and disappeared into the kitchen. I winced. Stewart was clearly having water problems.

From where Mac and I sat, the hole in the ceiling was not too visible. Miraculously, it still seemed to drip only a little water, but a nasty damp look had grown and there was a faint wet streak on the beautiful oriental-design wall paper with the metallic background. Helene would not have been amused. If the water got much worse it would leave a dreadful stain.

A large hand fell on my shoulder. "Francie."

I looked up and saw Harris Bruckner. A streak of shrimp sauce smeared his cheek, another streak stained his broad shirt front. He glanced quickly around the room, his gaze falling on Mac, slouched in his chair, engrossed in gazing up at the foyer ceiling.

Harris's voice faltered, awkward and uncomfortable. "I'm waiting for Lizzie to clean up a little." He hesitated, ran his hand through his thick hair, then added in a rush, "Thank you for helping Lizzie back there, and me. I kinda lost my head when I thought she was shot."

"I'm glad she's okay."

"Thanks. And I'm sorry about the way things turned out. At Techlaw, I mean."

"So am I."

"Have you found another job?"

I nodded. "By the way, I've never received the check for my July hours."

"It'll be issued this week."

"Lizzie said Helene talked to you about hiring me before she came to Chicago."

He frowned even more deeply, if that was possible, and shrugged his thick shoulders. "Helene didn't tell me she had someone in mind who would have to *move* here. I wouldn't have okayed that. It's too risky. And in this case, you now know why."

"I'm not sure I do."

"We could hire someone here cheaper and if it didn't work out, they wouldn't have uprooted their family."

"Did you think it wouldn't work out?"

"Nothing personal, I simply didn't think we needed to hire someone. It was an expense we didn't need to handle. But Helene insisted. She had more reasons written down than—"

Lizzie appeared from the powder room, still pale, her hair wet and plastered to her head. She barely glanced at me. "Now there's no water at all."

Harris took her elbow. "Stewart probably turned it off."

"Well, did he have to turn the whole house off, for God's sake?"

"Let's go, Lizzie. You can clean up at home."

"I want to say goodbye to poor Stewart." Her voice rose with an edge to it.

"We're going, now. If you'll excuse us . . ." He pushed Lizzie toward the door.

A large drop of water landed on my head. I looked up. The ceiling had developed a definite, nasty wet look. It was going to be very ugly by tomorrow. I turned to find Sam standing behind me.

He laughed awkwardly and pushed his glasses up on his nose. They immediately slid back down his nose. "Glad to see Mac's all right." He glanced down the room toward Stewart, now talking to Harris. Before I could comment, Sam continued. "You know he and Helene weren't getting along."

"Yeah, Harris just told me he disagreed with Helene about hiring me."

Sam looked at me, a puzzled expression clouding his dark eyes. "I was talking about *Stewart*. He and Helene were . . . talking the big split. Helene thought he had an outside—"

"Hey, Francie," Mac interrupted, "do you think that's a plaster ceiling?"

"Why do you ask?"

He scratched his head. "Well, Dad and I had one in our old house and when I let the tub run over, or left the shower curtain outside, it got wet."

"This is probably modern wallboard."

Mac shook his head. "Yeah, but Dad said old-fashioned plaster ceilings were big trouble when they got wet. First they get wet." He swung his feet in gleeful anticipation. "Then they get a bulge—"

"Relax, Stewart turned off the water," I said. "Besides, there's hardly any water coming out of the hole." Then I noticed several drops of water drip from the light fixture in the middle of the foyer. That wasn't a good sign.

Mac stood up and moved closer to the foyer, gazing intently at the ceiling. He pointed. "Yup, it's got a bulge."

He was right, it was growing. Mac had a nose for disasters.

Wolfe had told us to wait, but it was getting late. I signaled Mac and we started for the door.

As my hand gripped the doorknob I saw Stewart moving

stiffly through to the remaining visitors. Had he heard Sam's comment? I glanced up to the ceiling, now swelling more noticeably. I called out, "Stewart!"

He turned slowly and said through clenched teeth, "What?"

I pointed to the ceiling and the chandelier. "I think there's a problem here. Maybe you want to get a tarp."

He looked up, frowned, and muttered, "Stay there, I'll get something." He hurried toward the kitchen.

"Come on, Mac."

Mac resisted. "But I want to watch."

I pulled him toward the front door. Sam followed. "I thought the detective told you to stay."

"Yeah, well, he knows where to find me."

The water drops were becoming a thin stream, but the chandelier wasn't the problem. It would be anchored in the ceiling beams. It was the rest of the ceiling. It now had a definite bulge. And growing.

"There are some things we don't need to be present for. Come, *now.*" I pulled Mac to the door and shoved him out. Sam loped after him, looking curious. I started after them, then saw Stewart returning with a mixing bowl. "Uh, I think you're going to need something bigger."

He ignored me and placed the bowl under the stream, adjusting it carefully.

"Stewart! The whole ceiling is going to—" The word *drop* died on my lips. I eased back out the door, as I watched in mute fascination. The center of the ceiling groaned and cracked. Stewart looked up and raised his hands overhead, as though he might halt the impending disaster.

A cascade of filthy water poured onto his upturned face. Then the center of the ceiling broke away and fell in a gush of water and sodden plaster. Two large, ragged pieces of soaked plaster ceiling dropped to the floor, one where I had been standing. Several smaller chunks followed.

Stewart, dripping water and plaster bits, shook his fists at the now-bare laths above and yelled, "Nooooo!"

Behind him, like a thick, wild-haired wrestler, Harris shook water from his head and wiped plaster dust from his face. Lizzie, her blouse wet and clinging to her every curve and chilled nipples, shrieked, "What happened?"

The once-elegant foyer was a sodden wreck.

Stewart seemed frozen in place, water dripping onto his hair, soaking his suit, emphasizing his long, lean body. Globs of wet plaster smudged his face while his arms dangled helplessly at his sides. His jaw somewhat slack, he turned slowly to glare at me.

Mac breathed, "Awesome, man."

Behind me, Sam murmured, "Bummer."

I closed the security door gently.

CHAPTER 11

The look in Stewart's eyes made me uncomfortable, as though he blamed me for everything. I tried to melt into the darkness outside and bumped into Sam instead.

Sam, with awe in his voice, looked admiringly at me and said, "I can't believe you did all that in one simple evening. A masterpiece of chaos. God almighty, marriage and kids looks better by the minute." He clapped Mac on the shoulder. "Way to go, Mac."

"This is not funny, Sam."

Through the security door I saw Wolfe come downstairs, stop on the third from the bottom step, and take in the scene. He glared into the living room. I put a hand on Mac's shoulder and we eased off the porch, heading for the sidewalk.

The door opened and Detective Wolfe stepped out. "Hold it! Ms. Starzel, I told you to wait."

"We're still here. Keeping out of the way."

"You are *not* to leave."

Sam's shoulders straightened, his expression hardening. I could practically feel his testosterone rise. "Is this official?" he asked.

Wolfe answered pleasantly, "You have a problem with this, Mr. Lawson?"

Sam drew in a deep breath and seemed to puff up.

It was nice to have someone be worried for me, but I needed to stand up for myself. I put a restraining hand on Sam's arm.

"It's okay, Sam. I can handle this. Please."

Sam glanced back and forth between Detective Wolfe and me, then said, "I'll catch you later." He walked toward his car parked a couple houses down the street, which in this neighborhood meant nearly a block away.

"What do you want, Detective?"

"I want to talk to you. To both of you. Sit there for a minute. I'll give you a ride home."

"We're taking the bus, thank you."

"You just missed it. The next one won't be by for almost an hour."

I checked my watch. He was right. We had missed the bus and it only ran every hour. "Don't you need to stay here?"

"For a few minutes. Stay there. Do not move. Please accept my offer. There are no strings attached."

When anyone says that, it means there *are* strings attached, but it was late and I was very tired. Mac tugged on my sleeve. "Yeah, it'll be cool to ride in a real cop car. That'll really impress the kids."

Real cool. But at least it would indicate to Mac that I trusted cops, even though I didn't much. "All right." Mac and I sat on the lawn and waited. Mac tried to find shooting stars. I tried to find my wits.

In about twenty minutes Wolfe finished up. Mac was nearly asleep, his head in my lap. Wolfe helped get him up and walking.

"Tell you what," Wolfe said to me. "You can choose the seat you ride in. It's not a squad car, you know."

"Presumably, that means I can open the door from the inside?"

He grinned. It was a nice grin, and looked genuine. Maybe he had a redeeming sense of humor. He led the way to his car across the street and opened the back passenger door.

I tried the handle to see if it would in fact open from the inside. It would. Mac got in. I started to get in next to him, but Wolfe put a strong, square hand on my forearm and I smelled the scent of his shaving lotion, warm and a little sharp. I thought of a cat's paw, claws sheathed.

"Why don't you sit up front? I won't bite."

"I thought all wolves bit" fell out before I could stop it and for a hot five seconds I liked the whole thought of it. Then I mentally shook myself, but I sat up front.

He drove carefully, turning at the corner, the street lamp illuminating the car. A flash of gold on his finger, a wedding ring on his left hand, gleamed dully in the light. Oh, darn.

I was a little surprised at myself. I hadn't thought of cops in terms of family before, but it made him safer, less available and less lone-wolf-like. The silence spun out.

I finally asked, "Do you have any news about my car being released?"

"It won't be for some time yet. You might as well rent one. Your insurance might cover the cost." He turned south, toward my house. "I've got a question for you." He paused, I guess to see if I would protest. When I didn't he continued, "Why did you leave Chicago?"

Most regular families don't talk about sex and money; mine didn't talk about sex, money, jobs, past history, or much of anything except the most superficial of things—weather, clothes, more weather. In my case, any discussion of leaving Chicago would reopen wounds for Mac around his dad's death. In addition, one of the side effects of a "counterculture family"—as social workers had called mine—was a reluctance to divulge information. "I came out here for the job."

"Nothing is ever quite that simple."

"It is with me."

Mac piped up from the back seat. "She was following some

guy named Bliss. I think he dumped her."

We rode in silence until Wolfe pulled up in front of our house and said, "Wait a minute, after Mac is out." To Mac he said, "I may need to talk to you again, Mac. What you did tonight was very dangerous. You could have killed or injured someone."

"I'm really sorry. I didn't mean to do it, it just went off. Am I going to go to jail?" His voice quavered at the last word.

"I'm not sure what will come of this."

Mac climbed out of the car.

"I'll be there in a sec," I said to Mac and watched as he walked to the front porch.

I had my hand on the door handle, pressing down so that I could spring from the car at any time. "Mac is a good kid. There's no need to bully him."

"Listen to me very carefully," Wolfe said. "You're walking a very fine line. And the way you've behaved has only reinforced that. In addition, you don't seem to understand the seriousness of your son's behavior. He could be in huge trouble."

I had a much better understanding than Wolfe knew, but I wasn't going to admit it. "I suppose I'm at the top of your suspect list, and that's your excuse for the stakeout of my house," I said. "An older white four-door Ford with a searchlight on the driver's side?"

His expression was very still. "We don't have the manpower for a stakeout at your place."

That was scary. I tried to cover up my reaction with sarcasm. "Well! What a relief! Here I thought you guys had murder one pinned on me." It didn't work. A chill broke out on my neck. If the cops weren't out front watching me, who was? I started to get out of the car.

He rested his forearm over the rim of the steering wheel, turning further toward me. "This is not a game. A woman has been murdered. You seem to be convinced that I'm your biggest problem, but believe me, if you're innocent, your biggest problem is the killer."

He shook his head then continued, his voice low and intimate. "Look, I know you don't have anyone to lean on. In this case, the last thing you should do is trust any of your friends, because if you aren't the murderer, one of them is."

I wanted to run inside, lock the doors and hide, but I made myself calm down and think it through. The one friend in this town I thought I could trust had fired me and then turned up dead in my car. I really didn't trust anyone.

His face was dark and unreadable in the shadows. When he spoke again his voice was quiet, almost resigned. "You know, if you go poking around in this, you'll get hurt."

"And if I don't, the D.A. will lay it all at my feet."

"Feels like a no-win situation, doesn't it?" He sighed. "Your only chance is to talk to me. In spite of what you think, I am not simply building a case against you."

I didn't believe him, but at least I figured he wasn't the killer and I could use someone to talk to. I only had to remember he was a cop. He wasn't really in my corner.

He stirred, and keeping his voice quiet he asked, "What were you looking for in the Foster house?"

Of course, I knew it was part of the "good guy" role, but I couldn't figure out how it would hurt to tell him and maybe it would help.

"Helene always kept journals. She started it young, as an exercise to help her compensate for her dyslexia. I was hoping I could find her most recent ones. Her current one would detail what she was thinking when she fired me, but I was also hoping to get the one that covered the time period when Julia Orbach worked for Techlaw and when she died. No one will talk about it, and that seems to me to be significant."

"How do you know she still kept a journal at all?"

"Rosie, who worked for her, and later for the cleaning service at Techlaw, said she saw Helene writing in a journal. I didn't get a chance tonight to look in the master bedroom or anywhere else she might have hidden the most current one, but I found a shelf of old ones in the house. The latest two are missing. Your men searched the house already. Either you took them, or someone else did."

He looked aside, his expression stony. "Why didn't you mention those this morning?"

"You *didn't* find them, did you?" His silence confirmed it. So, if they hadn't found the journals, someone else had. "I wonder why Stewart would have hidden or disposed of them?" And then I remembered the warmth of the hug he'd given Lizzie.

"What else did you ferret out tonight?"

"Lizzie Bruckner used to work for Stewart but switched jobs with Georgia Jenson about a year ago. Not long after, Julia Orbach died. Georgia is quite laudatory about Stewart, finds him very considerate. And finally, Stewart likes to read men's action adventure stories."

"You know that because . . . ?"

"Just a guess." I started to get out, then stopped. "Techlaw has a consulting lawyer, Laurence Gifford. He's also their auditor and Helene met with him right before she fired me."

"You're not just a little biased here?"

"I don't like the guy. Nevertheless, you might look at the money trail. I wrote a report for Helene which she read and locked up in her desk at Techlaw when she fired me. I think it was part of the reason she fired me."

"Where is it now?"

"She put it in her bottom file drawer that morning. It was in a thin file, had my name on the front."

"No report from you was found. What was it?"

"At the time, it was seemingly inconsequential—her activity log for the past year and the coming three months, the sales and receipts for the last year, and inventory. The inventory I had done last. Everything had matched up. Beautifully. It was a compilation of records they already had, easily available."

"So why would anyone bother stealing it?"

"To frame me."

"You knew all about her journals—you could have taken them."

"Am I so interesting that you can't look beyond me?"

His cheeks seemed to darken. Did he flush, or was it my imagination? I smiled, suddenly amused. "You're attracted to me, aren't you? That's why you continue to focus on me. How bloody ironic, you'll convict me because you like me. Or rather because you're attracted, but you don't like me. God, what a twist!" That time his cheeks definitely flushed.

Inside my house, my amusement faded as Wolfe drove away. I was in a jam. I seemed to be everyone's bull's eye. My primary hope was that so long as the killer who had framed me thought it was working and the cops suspected me, I would be safe for a while.

What did this mean for Mac, though? How could I protect him? Mac was so easy to love, but hard to protect. Bright, strong in so many ways, he was older than his years, having had to grow up early. I tended to treat him as far more mature and capable than he could possibly be at his age. This mothering business was so new and I had so much to learn. I only hoped I learned it in time.

Wolfe had said the cops weren't doing a stakeout. True? I had thought so, but maybe he really didn't know. Or perhaps he lied.

Why had I trusted him? Wasn't making the suspect feel comfortable all part of being a good cop? Getting them to confide. And I had done just that. He was truly good at the "good guy" role. It made me angry because I felt like I'd been duped, like a simple, stupid criminal.

I realized Mac was looking at me, his face intense. "What's the matter?"

I tried to smooth out my face. "Nothing, why?"

"You look kind of sad."

Sad? I looked sad? I wasn't sad, I was worried and angry. Furious, in fact. At Wolfe for being a cop, for saying my report wasn't there, for being someone who made me want to trust him, for being—married? Impossible. "Too much going on, I guess, Mac."

"We're in big trouble and it's my fault."

At that very moment he looked such a young child, but he had to understand how close to real disaster he had come tonight. "Mac, what you did was serious and could have been a complete disaster. It's bad enough to ruin Stewart's ceiling, but that bullet went right by a lot of people. Think how awful you'd had felt if someone was hurt, or killed."

"I really didn't mean to do it."

"I know, but that's the trouble with guns. If you don't know what you're doing . . ."

He chewed on his lip for a few minutes, then said, "Do we have to pay for the ceiling?"

"Maybe. I need to offer at least."

"I'll give up my allowance."

I nodded. "That will help."

"It's a real big worry isn't it?"

"I'll work it out."

"Chocolate ice cream helps."

"Would it help you?"

"Especially if it had chocolate sauce on it."

"Chocolate sauce is gone."

"Oh. How 'bout Oreos?"

"Gone."

"Then what do we have?"

"Cocoa powder."

"Homemade chocolate sauce?" He must have seen my expression because he added hastily, "I know how to make it in the microwave. Grandma Lil showed me before we moved. She wants us to come back to Chicago."

"And you want to go?"

He looked hard at the floor. "I kind of miss her and Uncle Andy."

"I miss them too, sweetie." Like a toothache, or a migraine, or a fire at sea. I gave him a hug. He stiffened, but held still for it. "But it's important for us to make our own life."

He stirred up cocoa, sugar, and a lump of butter, shoved the bowl into the microwave, and licked the spoon while it cooked. "When I'm with Grandma Lil I want to be away, and when I'm here I want to be there."

"It's called ambivalence."

"It makes me want to eat."

It made me want to run, but at least for the moment, I was determined to stay and fight. But it's one thing to decide to stay and fight; it's another to sleep through the night when you feel someone watching.

After sitting in the dark and looking at the street, I was up three times in the wee hours, checking to see if there was any suspicious activity or lack thereof. The only thing I noticed was Mrs. Folsom in her kitchen window, staring at me. I couldn't decide whether it was a good thing or not. If I had a sexy night life, it would have been irritating to the nth, but given that my night life was lit only by fears, it was almost reassuring. Almost.

CHAPTER 12

Wednesday morning dawned warm and bright, with a sky so clear it took my breath away. How much safer and positive things seemed in the strong morning sunshine. I made coffee and found my nighttime willies ridiculous, even though there was a lurking sense of danger at the back of the messy closet that was my mind.

Anticipating Helene's funeral that afternoon, I dressed in a simple, black sheath dress and black sandals, uncomfortable, not made for walking, but sexy. For the pleasure, I wore leopard-print panties, bra, and slip underneath. No one would see them, of course, but it lifted my spirits simply knowing that underneath my drab outside there was an exciting inside. Sort of symbolic.

The real me wasn't a frightened, single, sudden-mother working a temporary job with no future, calling people who hated to be called about a service they daily prayed they wouldn't need. The real me wouldn't be on a collision course with disaster, chasing shadows and glancing over her shoulder every ten minutes.

Right now, the real me was a thirty-four-year-old woman who still looked thirty, could look sexy, was usually sensible, or at least practical, with a tendency to get into trouble and a habit of picking inappropriate lovers, men who looked good and turned out to have a criminal twist hidden inside. The latest one of whom had given me his darling son before he was murdered. The real me was hip-deep in trouble, but by God, I told myself,

I wasn't beat yet. My version of a locker-room morale raiser.

Because I planned to leave Level One in time for Helene's funeral, Mac and I left home early, and in spite of his protests I walked him to within sight of his day camp. "Don't talk to strangers."

He looked at me, rolling his eyes. "Don't treat me like a baby. You're getting a little weird, Francie."

Maybe, but I wanted us to stay alive. I waited until I saw him enter the building.

The bus was warm, crowded, and full of exhaust fumes. Unable to shake the shadow of fear, I scrutinized the passengers and glanced out the back of the bus to see if it was being followed. Of course it was; it was rush hour. If I had a car, I told myself, I would at least be in charge of my own destiny, however miserable it was. My car insurance, though, the cheapest going, did not provide for a rental. By the time I got to work my nerves were taut.

That morning Level One's main room was still surprisingly empty at eight o'clock. The desks were largely unoccupied, the phones silent. Sun streaked in through the narrow windows, spreading a mellow, gold light that made the room almost pleasant. I wondered if there was something about Wednesday mornings that I didn't know, like maybe they were terrible times for sales, so everyone stayed home.

The carrel I'd used yesterday was empty. I slipped into it, stowed my purse, and put on my headphones. My job with Helene had been wonderful, interesting, and well paying. Now I was selling funerals over the phone. Would it be better selling something like, say, specialty pet food? Or magazines? Or insurance? At the rate I was going, would I ever find out? I almost wept.

My seventh call was a voice that sounded older than God and shouted, "Yeah?"

"How are you doing, sir?" I asked, trying to keep my voice light.

"If I was doing well I wouldn't be at home right now talking to you."

"I'm sorry to hear you're not well."

"Who said I'm not well? I'm fine. I'm great." His voice wobbled. It sounded as though he was sipping something. "I couldn't be any better."

"I'm glad to hear it. It's important to plan ahead, though, for the days when you're not so well. When you need the services of the hereafter."

"Here after what? What's after me?"

"Nobody, I meant—"

"Nobody better be after me. I got a shotgun and I'll plaster their brass with shot."

"I was trying to tell you about the Everlasting Homes services, sir."

"I got a home. I don't need another."

"Funeral services, sir, for when you, er, one dies."

"What one? Who died?"

"No one died."

"You're lying to me. Girly, people lie all the time. Just 'cause I'm stuck here in this place don't mean you can lie to me, too. You just wait 'til you're in a hard spot and they tell you they're gonna get you hearing aids and take care of you. You'll find out what lies are. Hah! No one lied, my foot! Can't trust a soul. Now I gotta go get my car—"

This madman had a car? That did it. I didn't care how bad it would drain the savings account, I was getting a car. I looked up. Ethel Green, my supervisor was standing beside me, her hands planted on her hips. "I'll drop some information in the mail for you, sir."

"Don't send me nothing. The dog chewed my glasses and I

111

can't see a thing. Nice talkin' to you. Call again sometime when you feel better."

"Good day, sir."

Ethel waited for me to pull down my headphones, then handed me several pamphlets. "Francie, here is some new material that may help. Everlasting has a new line they'd like you to push."

I looked at the folders in my hand, colorful pictures of caskets, one with a woodland scene on the side. A second had a flight of doves. Artful. This was sure to help.

Ethel cleared her throat. "You're not making any sales. Not a single one so far. You must do better."

"Funerals are a hard sell."

"Well, they can't be that hard. Everyone's going to need one sooner or later. And it's a bad idea to use your own name. I'm surprised you didn't know that. You said you worked at this before."

I was selling pet food then, super-easy by comparison.

She continued. "You need to make up a decent, earnest name—something that makes people want to say 'yes.'"

I stared at her; she was serious. "Thank you for the help."

What was I saying? I was becoming a groveling idiot. Telemarketing didn't cause tumors, it caused brain drain.

"I'm afraid I have to say you're not working out very well at this."

I was failing at telemarketing? Tell me it wasn't true. How humiliating! It was worse than failing ballet because I couldn't tell left from right and leaped onto the only boy in the class with disastrous results. You know how few boys take ballet? One fewer after I landed on him.

I pulled on my headphones. Another call came through. Clearing my throat, I spread out the pamphlets so I could use phrases from them and launched in.

"Hello, this is Susie M. Sellall calling and I'd like to talk to you about planning for your life. We all face an unpleasant truth—someday we're going to die. What I'd like to do is help you to plan for that glorious event so that it's the best show you ever put on and one you can be proud of every day you're up in heaven."

There was a long silence, then a timid voice said, "Really?"

"Did you know you can order your own eternal . . . eternal resting place, your comfort zone, now, and install in it all the comforts you've ever wanted? And if you do it now, today, you'll get the privilege of selecting a scene to go on the side of your . . . heavenly eternal resting . . . coach. Think of it as a celestial limousine with a mural on the side, immortalizing you. The Bright Light model." I sucked in a huge breath. "Think of it as a graceful fainting couch, like the Victorians used and looked so wonderful on, but better because it will have a beautiful scene on the side."

"A scene?"

"Yes, a kind of icon to your eternal web page."

"Eternal web page?"

"Everlasting Homes is sure to make your departure the one of your dreams."

"Are we talking about a cruise?"

"Sort of. I like to think of it as the cruise of your future . . . life."

"Is this a prize?"

I whacked myself on the forehead. "No. I'm talking about funeral services that will be remembered by one and all for the rest of time."

Long silence. Then she said, "I'd get to put a picture on my eternal couch?"

"You can choose from a selection of beautiful scenes. It's the latest fashion in funerals. A sylvan scene on your casket or any of several choices, doves, a sunrise, or for the dedicated sports fan, the logo and colors of your favorite football team, or for the racier model, NASCAR racing scenes."

Silence, then, "My family would choose the race scenes. They're always trying to rush me into the grave."

Was Stewart rushing Helene into the grave? Had Helene made prearrangements? I shuddered.

The timid little voice droned on. "I worry I'll still be alive. Will the funeral home check for that?"

"They only bury dead people. Hate burying live ones." What was I saying? "If you make your own arrangements, you'll have *control* over these things."

"How much is it?"

"If you make a deposit of ninety-nine dollars today on your credit card, this scene will be yours at no additional cost. Then a representative of the Everlasting Homes will call you to arrange the details which will set the final cost."

"Can I have my cat in my scene?"

"Those are details you work out with the Everlasting Homes. All you have to do is put down this small deposit through a credit card payment so I can authorize the free-scene special."

"I think I'd like that."

For God's sake. I'd made a sale, or what they considered a sale. Hallelujah! I got Ethel Green on line to verify it and take down all her details. My first. I stood and did a dance. Two other telemarketers cheered.

Not so bad. If I kept that up, maybe I'd get promoted to tombstones. If I could do *that*, maybe I could get out of the trouble I was in *before* Detective Wolfe put my sweet assets in jail.

It was heady success and I was hot for a car, the very first one that didn't cost over two hundred and fifty dollars. I figured it was crucial to get wheels if I was going to snoop, because standing at bus stops took a lot of time. Besides, it made me far too vulnerable.

I left Level One at twelve-thirty, promising myself I'd work extra hours the next day, and took the number 15 bus, known as the Colfax mobile mental health station because there was always at least one florid schizophrenic on board. I rode it straight east, until I came to a suitably shabby used-car dealer, Reliable Auto Sales. The sign hung by one corner. The salesman, wearing an eye-blinding yellow and gray plaid jacket, helped me pick out a rambling hunk of rust that had once been a metallic green queen and now was a bilious variegated khaki, as if it wore filthy camouflage. The wheels went in slightly different directions and the brakes squealed to let me know they were there but next to stripped. So long as I drove with the windows open I probably wouldn't be asphyxiated.

I was signing the papers when my cell phone rang. It was Sam, offering me a ride to Helene's service. "Hey, thanks Sam, but I just bought some transportation. It's cheap and it's mine. You don't know how confining it is to be without."

"Yeah, well, I didn't like the idea of you standing on the street corners." He paused. I pictured him pushing his glasses up on his nose. "Well, see you later." He sounded disappointed.

The salesman gave me a can of power-steering fluid as well as a can of brake fluid as a bonus.

At the funeral chapel parking lot I parked in two spaces because the car turned in what the salesman had described euphemistically as "an elegant wide arc." I made a mental note to add power-steering fluid after Helene's funeral.

I was a bit early for the service. The usher handed me a program and, at my request, seated me in the back row, close to the door. At the front of the chapel stood a magnificent mahogany casket, closed, with a large spray of delicate yellow roses next to a portrait of Helene, taken at college graduation on the steps of our dormitory.

She had always been adventurous, open, friendly, and full of life. I had been quiet, brought up to keep family secrets in the closet, and slow to make friends. Helene gradually brought me out of my shell. We had shared so many things then.

Hot tears burned my eyes. She had been so lovely, and a good friend in college.

In Denver I had hoped to regain that same level of intimacy, but after a brief, wonderful start, Helene had became increasingly irritable and distant, until, by the day she fired me, she had seemed almost frightened.

Goodbyes, though, were important to me as a way of bringing issues to a close, and I hoped this service would do that to the extent possible. I also wanted to see what reactions the others were having. I wasn't sure what specifically I hoped to gain, but some hint of relationships, or emotions, or—I couldn't put a finger on it, so as the little chapel gradually filled up with somberly attired people wearing long faces and fashionable dresses, I watched everyone come in. How they walked, to whom they talked, where they sat, hoping something would stand out.

Moments before the service started, Detective Wolfe sat down next to me. I moved over. He followed, leaning over to whisper, "They ran out of programs, would you share?"

I thrust mine at him.

He took it and nodded. "Nice car you got."

"My good one was taken, stolen, by your henchmen."

"You have two weeks to pass the safety inspection."

"You need one of the services I'm selling." I thought I saw the glimmer of a smile in the corner of his eye.

Organ music swelled; we all stood. Stewart entered, his cheeks lined and pale, his step almost hesitant. Barely thirty-eight, that afternoon he could have passed for sixty-eight. He walked down the center aisle alone to the front, where he took a seat. There were no other family members. Helene was an only child and her parents had died while we were in college. I knew nothing of Stewart's family, but he sat alone in the pew, looking forlorn. Harris and Lizzie Bruckner sat in the pew behind him. Lizzie patted him on the shoulder when she and Harris sat down.

The funeral was dismal, impersonal, and blessedly short. Helene's life, her accomplishments, her vivid drive and personality were all wrapped in solemn, dirge-laden words that came nowhere close to describing the woman I had known.

It was a very wet scene for me. I went through a dozen tissues, blotting tears, a lot for Helene, and even more for the revived memory of Mac's father's funeral, also small, tragically impersonal, and crushing.

When the organ music signaled it was over, we all stood again while Stewart followed the casket out. I saw Rosie scuttle toward the door and tried to get her attention without success. I hoped to ask her about Helene's journals, but she was out and gone before I could catch up with her.

Once outside, I waited for Harris Bruckner to ask him about my report. Surely Helene would have discussed it with him. I spotted his bulky shoulders and Lizzie's tall, slender frame coming out the chapel door. I apologized to Lizzie for the interruption. She smiled through reddened eyes and said she'd meet him at the car. I decided she was genuinely sad and shaken at Helene's death.

"Harris, I won't keep you, but I want to ask if Helene mentioned my report to you and perhaps gave you a copy?"

He frowned and shook his head. "What report?"

I drew in a breath. "Helene assigned me a project which I completed. She read it and locked it in her desk drawer. Yet when I asked the police about it, they said there was no report in her desk. I figure you probably knew about it, or at least went

117

through her desk."

He tossed his head. "I don't know what you're talking about. I have to go. Lizzie is upset and waiting."

"But you are sure? She locked it in her desk drawer."

"Trust me. I checked the drawer myself." He spun on his heel and strode quickly to his car, where Lizzie was talking to Georgia Jenson, Stewart's secretary. I sidled up feeling a bit like a "preying" mantis. "Lizzie, could I get a quick word with you?"

Her eyes, behind the netting of her little black hat, narrowed into icy blue slits. "Please, leave me alone."

I was shocked by her change of attitude. "But you said—"

"I don't have to talk to you."

Stewart came up in time to hear her. "Francie, for God's sake. Haven't you done enough?" He grabbed Lizzie's elbow and steered her into the crowd of people, many of whom were staring at me.

Detective Wolfe's voice came from behind me. "You're about as popular as a ghoul at a garden party."

"Oh, go away."

He placidly watched the crowd disperse. "Remember what I said last night, Francie?"

"I should stand idly by and let you and your team of hotshots nail me to the wall? I don't think so. Your men missed the journals altogether and you haven't even made a decent search for that report."

"There's no evidence it existed, much less that it pertains to anything. Everyone at the office says you were fired because you failed probation."

"I didn't fail a thing. I was simply fired. I did a good job and I was honest. I don't know how that report fits into anything, but the fact that it's missing tells me it's important."

I glanced around to see where people were. Sam waved and gestured as though he was offering to come and interrupt. I shook my head. It was nice of him, but it would only complicate matters.

Wolfe caught the exchange. "He keeps a good eye on you."

"He's been helpful." The sun streaked Wolfe's hair and slanted into his eyes. For a moment I felt I could see inside him and was struck again with the thought that in other circumstances he would be nice to get to know. In these circumstances, though, it was like getting acquainted with a scorpion. You could never tell when you'd be stung. "It's nice to have at least one person in my corner," I said, and added mentally, *even if he is an overgrown boy.*

"You can't afford to trust anyone, Francie." Wolfe held my gaze with his and I felt an uncomfortable flutter in my stomach. "You'll hear about it on the news tonight. Helene was killed Thursday night."

"*Thursday* night? But she called in the next morning and talked to Lizzie."

"Actually, it was a message for Lizzie, which Lizzie found Friday morning."

"Didn't Stewart notice Helene was missing?"

"He left town Thursday afternoon for a convention in Albuquerque."

"That's only four hundred miles away, and on an interstate. He could have driven back, killed her, and returned. For that matter, so could Sam. He was in Aspen. That's only one hundred and eighty miles away."

Wolfe was looking at me the way I look at Mac when I ask him if he ate the last of the ice cream, and then wait for him to 'fess up. I straightened. Nothing looks more like guilt than slumping. "I was home Thursday night; you can ask Mac."

"What time did he go to sleep?"

"Nine."

Wolfe shook his head. "You could have slipped out after he

went to sleep. You're not off the hook."

"Except for Helene's body in my trunk, you don't have anything that ties me to her murder, not really."

"You mean, if we also ignore the fact that she fired you, owed you money, and you left a threat on her answering machine?"

"Circumstantial. And you don't even know for sure where she was killed."

He glanced at the dwindling crowd of mourners, then looked back at me, the expression in his eyes unreadable. "She was shot in her own driveway. I believe you're familiar with it. The consensus is that we have plenty. We meet with the district attorney in two days."

CHAPTER 13

Why had Wolfe even told me that? A warning? Or a setup to frighten me into some incriminating action? I swallowed a large lump in my throat. Two days wasn't much time, not nearly enough. Two days put me at Friday. I *had* to find those journals, or at the very least, my report.

I marched to my car, wearing indignation like it was proof positive of my innocence, but this was serious. I had no proof of anything. The only thing I'd ever had was my report and it had been in Helene's hands the day I left the company. It had to be important if someone took it or destroyed it.

I fired up the Rust, as I now thought of my cheap heap, and left in a cloud of exhaust, much like an octopus leaves in a cloud of ink. The brakes were a tad squashy but I didn't want the whole parking lot full of Helene's mourners and Detective Wolfe to observe my refilling of the brake fluid. Some things are simply too humiliating.

I drove a few blocks, turned into a side street, waited to see if anyone turned in after me. When no one did, I got out and raised the hood. The Rust may have been cheap to purchase, but the fluid consumption alone was going to be a sizeable maintenance item. One more thing to worry about.

As I topped up the brake fluid, I realized I had completely overlooked the possibility that Helene could have left her journals in her car. It was practically a traveling office. In fact, she could have left my report there as well. Given my background, and depending on the type of car, I might be able to jimmy it in a flash.

Right now Stewart would be at the graveside for Helene's interment and there was almost an hour before I needed to pick up Mac from wrestling practice. Plenty of time.

At Helene's home, I parked around the corner on the far side of a magnificent blue spruce that really needed to be trimmed, because it offered too much cover and invited burglars.

From the good old days when Helene and I were friendly, I knew there was a hidden garage door button. I found it, pressed it, and waited while the door raised, then I entered, closed the door, and moved through the mixed scent of dirt, oil, and polished car to her Mercedes. Of course it was locked. A little red blinking light on the door verified it.

Blinking red light . . . alarm . . . oh, crap! I turned and glanced quickly at the walls of the garage. Dammit! I slapped my forehead. Attached to the garage wall by the door was a silent house alarm which would sound at the police station. I probably had about three minutes before I was dead meat.

Not enough time to get inside her car. And the jimmy bar I used to get into my old car was *in* my old car at the police car pound. And even if a coat hanger would work, which it probably wouldn't on Helene's car, I didn't have one.

Two minutes left.

I smudged my fingerprint on the garage door button on the way out, ran to the Rust, coaxed her into starting, and was turning the corner when the cops pulled up to Helene's. Resisting the urge to race away, I turned very carefully and got as far as the mid-block alley before I whipped into the alley, mashed the gas pedal, sped through to the other end and emerged, turning east. No one followed.

How dumb could I be? What in the world had I been thinking?

If I were going to break the law, I would have to get a lot better at it, or as old Dad would say, I'd be jailed for stupidity and have earned every day of it. Maybe I wasn't terminally stupid, only prone to low blood sugar. Which would probably be a tough defense in a courtroom.

I drove straight to the South Colorado Boulevard Dairy Queen and ordered a hot fudge sundae. As I sat in a booth spooning it into my mouth my world looked pretty glum. I had to find a way to put in more hours at Level One soon to feed Mac and pay bills, but if I didn't figure out who killed Helene pretty quick, the only telephone I'd be using would be in the Colorado Women's Penitentiary.

Once chocolate hit my blood stream I grew more optimistic. My mountain of troubles seemed to shrink a bit. Or I just had a better perspective. I had to get better at this sleuthing business. Right now I was my own worst enemy. Worse than Wolfe.

I dragged out a pad and began to make a list. *Motives for killing:*

Money—one of the most common motives, but Stewart would be her beneficiary and he had a lot of money and she had all hers tied up in Techlaw. Techlaw, that is Harris, might want her dead to save her salary. Especially if there was partner insurance, and there probably was. I wrote *Harris* after *Money*.

Power—I didn't know how this one could fit, unless again, it was Harris who simply wanted the whole burrito for himself.

Love, or its opposite—very possible. Sam said Helene and Stewart were on the outs.

Jealousy—possible, but likely?

Greed—covered under money.

Rage—Helene could be a bitch, but murder from rage seemed an impulse crime and it took planning to frame me.

Revenge—the one the police believed in.

To cover up another crime—this one could fit with my report.

My report, or something in it, could be the key.

I underlined *love* and *jealousy*, and double-underlined the cover-up motive. They seemed the most logical. This time, I very carefully put the pad inside my purse.

There was one last place to look for my report and Helene's journals: Techlaw. And the sooner the better. As long as there was a chance the report still existed on my hard drive, I had to get inside the office, preferably when no one else was around.

I dug out a tissue from my purse to clean the chocolate off my fingers and discovered a chunk of chewing gum wadded in the folds. And stuck to the gum was a bright brass key. My office key that I had never turned in, that Helene had neglected to ask for.

I pried the key loose and pocketed it carefully. This would simplify things enormously. With this key I could get into the Techlaw offices to look for my report. First, all I had to do was weasel a way inside the building and past the guard.

Oh, Lord in heaven above. It was practically a directive from the gods. Go forth and be sleuthful.

That evening Mac pronounced the Rust ugly but comfortable. Unfortunately, we also discovered that the front passenger door didn't open from the inside. I reminded him it had cost only two hundred and fifty dollars and he worked hard to find something nice to say about it. He finally came up with the fact that the exhaust poured out the back as though the car were a rocket blasting off. "Way cool," he said.

It occurred to me that that same exhaust would prevent it from passing the safety inspection. I hoped I could get my car back in time.

After dinner I called my neighbor, not the window-peering Mrs. Folsom but the neighbor on the other side, who nicely agreed to sit for Mac while I went out. Once they were both settled I slipped into my black jeans and a dark T-shirt and took my pack containing a carefully chosen recovery software program, two fresh chunks of Mac's bubble gum, and a set of lock picks—a Christmas gift one year from my darling brother Andy.

The lock picks were for Helene's desk on the off chance her journal was there. The software was to recover my report from my computer hard drive. Whoever took the folder would most likely have erased the report on the computer, but maybe it could be recovered—a long shot, because everyone at Techlaw was a computer expert.

At a little before ten I pulled up in the parking lot and noticed the lights were on in our office. I had a moment of panic, then remembered the lights stayed on until Rosie finished cleaning.

I pulled to the back of the parking lot and parked in the shadows. The Rust's afterburner died an ugly death. I waited for the air to clear before attempting to open the car door. The Rust was a dubious beast, but at least it ran.

In stark contrast to the front parking area with its bright lighting and carefully landscaped beds of grass, evergreens, and shade trees, the back parking lot was a broad tarmac lot dimly lit from the spotlights on the ledges of the building's roof. Because I had parked toward the rear of the lot next to the trash bins, the Rust barely stood out. For all practical purposes it was hidden.

The cleaning crew for the building came on between ten and eleven. Soon they arrived. There were supposed to be five in the crew. I was looking for Rosie's characteristic heavy, rolling gait, caused by bad knees and swollen ankles. I broke out Mac's bubble gum, warmed it in the palm of my hand, and waited. My plan hinged on Rosie coming to work tonight.

Four people arrived at 10:15. No Rosie.

I got out of the car and hailed the last of the four cleaners as she neared the door. The others went inside, leaving her standing in the open door. I knew she'd hold it, because only the crew captain had a key.

She turned, peering toward me, her round face and blunt features emphasized under the back door spotlight into patches of light and dark. Her broad body cast a heavy pool of shadow around her feet.

I trotted up, panting. "Where's Rosie? I was waiting to talk to her."

The woman pursed her lips, her eyes hidden in the shadow of her brow. "Didn't show."

I moved in close, figuring she would automatically back up to preserve her personal space, and caught the acrid scent of old cigarette smoke and bacon grease from her clothing. She stepped back, possibly a little frightened, her hand gripping the safety bar on the door. I stuck one of the unwrapped, warmed pieces of bubble gum to my palm then grasped the edge of the door at the latch, pressing the gum in hard and tight as I spoke. "Do you think Rosie is sick?"

"She's had trouble since we switched to nights." The woman's expression was solemn, even furtive with the odd overhead shadows. I probably looked as scary to her, maybe more.

Leaning heavily against the edge of the door I pressed the gum deep into the latch, hoping it would hold.

She inched back, pulling on the door. "I don't know 'bout Rosie. All I know is it means we work extra if she don't come. I gotta go now."

I put a foot out to block the door. "I owe Rosie some money," I said, talking loud and fast to distract her while I leaned to the jamb side and shoved the other chunk of gum into the retainer in the latch plate. "I kinda wanted to pay it off tonight. Tell Rosie I was here, okay?"

She nodded and put her considerable weight into pulling on

the door. I stepped back, released the door, and it shut. I started slowly back toward the Rust in case she checked. The gum had to hold for a few minutes, long enough for her to get up the stairs so she wouldn't see me open the door.

Sure enough. I was only a few feet away when the door opened and she poked her head out. She scanned the lot then slammed the door. I couldn't tell if the latch had gone home or not. I kept on walking in case she checked again. The door stayed closed.

I gave it four minutes or so, then scurried back to the door and stood flattened against the building. Heat still radiated from the wall of the building, although the sun had been down for over an hour.

Two very long minutes later I tried the door. The knob turned easily. I pulled slowly. And slowly it came open, spilling out a gust of cement-scented air as if the building were exhaling. I stepped inside and pulled the gum from the latch and the retainer, pocketed it, and moved as naturally as possible along to the stair landing, where I would be out of sight of a security camera and could listen to locate the cleaning crew. My ears rang in the silence, exactly as they had when years ago, as a child, I'd stood watch for Andy before I was old enough to know I shouldn't. Every whisper of the building sounded as if it were a living thing that could either protect or betray me at any minute.

A vacuum cleaner whined on the first floor. I stole up the stairs past the first-floor door to the second floor and listened there at the door. Silence.

It was twenty-nine minutes past ten now. I had about thirty minutes to work, *if* the cleaning crew did their areas first and filled in Rosie's assignment afterward.

I cracked the door and peeked into the bright fluorescent-lit hallway. No whine of vacuum cleaners, no sign of cleaning staff.

At the far end of the hall I saw through the glass wall to Lizzie's empty reception desk, behind it the half wall into Techlaw's open-plan office room. The lights were on and it appeared no one was home.

I stepped out and walked quickly to the office door. The key slipped into the keyhole easily in spite of a few flecks of sticky gum. The lock turned and I entered in one almost-swift motion, the hair on my head raised in sheer fear. Because of the glass wall I could be seen from the hallway. My palms were slick with sweat.

I crouched behind Lizzie's desk for a bit of cover in case a cleaning person came down the hall. I couldn't see over the half wall dividing the reception area from the office area where my desk stood along with Sam Lawson's, but my heart needed time to settle down anyway. There was no sound except the quiet whir of the air conditioning which kept the air moving much too slowly through the building.

I had come for my report but so long as I was here, I decided to have a quick poke through Lizzie's desk. Maybe something there would explain Lizzie's evasiveness.

Although it was locked, her desk had a surprisingly simple lock. Thanks to Andy's careful lessons, I had it open in minutes. I justified the break-in to myself by saying I wasn't stealing anything, only looking.

The top drawer held a wide selection of designer teas arranged in alphabetical order. Great.

The second drawer was tidily arranged into stacks of 3 × 5 and 5 × 8 cards and colored pens, in the order of the rainbow. I could only guess about her kitchen; maybe the knives were arranged in order of sharpness? Or length? Or lethality? Big money that the soups were alphabetical. Also big money that she wouldn't kill unless it was by something very sure and very clean. An overdose of sleeping pills most likely. Did the fact that she was obsessively tidy indicate she'd never be responsible for a messy murder?

I sobered up thinking about the possibility that Helene had been dosed with a sedative before being killed. Could I get that information by brazening my way into the medical examiner's office? Did I *want* to go there?

In the deep bottom drawer in a manila file I had hoped might contain my report, I found a fascinating little printout, a bank summary of Lizzie and Harris's saving account. It showed steady, large withdrawals until very recently, when the account was down to two thousand dollars. In all, three hundred and forty thousand dollars had been drained from that account in the last sixteen months. That was a lot of cash. A lifetime of savings, I'd bet.

Where was it all going?

Was one of them feathering a nest for the future? Was Lizzie checking up on Harris's activities, or was she keeping track of her own transactions? Was this evidence of blackmail? In any case, it explained some of the marital tension I'd sensed. I replaced it carefully where I'd found it, beneath the fingernail polish tray.

I rose, then ducked around the half wall where I could stand hidden from the front glass behind a row of file drawers with a large split-leaf philodendron on top. Harris and Helene each had an office with solid wood doors to the side; otherwise the room was an open expanse of desks. A glance at my desk and my heart sank. My desktop was clean, the computer gone. A quick check of the drawers showed them to be empty, wiped clean. The Snickers bar I'd been saving in the bottom drawer was gone. Even the cookie crumbs were wiped clean, no doubt by Lizzie, the neat freak.

I heard a drawer shut and a chair creak.

Someone was in Harris's office. A chair pushed back.

I looked for a place to hide. Nothing was really big enough. Heavy footsteps; the floor vibrated lightly.

I dropped to the floor and squeezed into the kneehole of my desk. Scant cover. I wished I hadn't had that hot fudge sundae this afternoon. I think it was sticking out of the kneehole.

It was nearly eleven o'clock at night; who could possibly be here? I squeezed harder into the kneehole, my legs folded so that my chin rested on them. I could hardly breathe. I crammed my head in as far as possible so I couldn't see out and instantly understood the comfort ostriches have when they bury their heads in the sand.

My desk stood sideways to Harris's office. If the person so much as looked to the side they'd see me curled up there. I pulled the wastebasket around in front. Not much help. It felt like every Snickers bar I ever ate, and they were considerable in number, stuck out in plain sight.

His office door opened. My mouth went desert dry.

Heavy footsteps. I twisted painfully to see out and recognized the shoes. Worn black wing-tips. Harris Bruckner.

CHAPTER 14

What was he doing here? I couldn't take my eyes off him.

He hesitated.

Oh, my God, could he feel me looking? Did terror have weight? He'd never impressed me as sensitive, but . . .

He stood there, frowning and rubbing his neck. He looked up, stretching, twisting his head back and forth. Were his eyes closed?

Blood pounded in my ears. I held my breath in case he could hear me breathing and closed my eyes to nearly shut, so that I was looking through the veil of my eyelashes. Irrational, but maybe it would cut the weight of my horrified stare and he wouldn't feel it.

Then he exhaled heavily and started toward the front. He was a heavy walker. The floor trembled as he lumbered to the lobby, then out the door. I didn't see where he went, but he was in shirtsleeves and had left his office door open. Big money, he went to the can.

It was nighttime. Two to one I had only minutes, unless he had prostate trouble—then I had more, but not much.

My knees were cramped and aching. I scrambled out and scuttled into Harris's office. No obsessive tidiness there. I couldn't see his laptop. Given the mess, it must have been buried there. For that matter, a body could have been buried there. Papers overflowed his desk onto the floor as though they had fallen like autumn leaves. Lengthy printouts of accounts.

A very cursory read indicated money coming and going, mostly going—for the last year at least. In fact, the last month's balance was negative, very negative. A very different story from the one I'd seen in December's figures, the last month for which I'd done the figures for Helene. How could that be? What had changed?

There wasn't enough time for me to figure it out. His desk was such a mess he probably wouldn't miss a sheet or two. I quickly folded one of the printouts and shoved it into the top of my underwear. Harris might search pockets, but I didn't think he'd do underwear. I made a mental list. *Harris: Motive: Money.* Was there a company insurance policy on Helene? Had Harris already filed for it?

I scuttled to Helene's door. Through the glass panel next to the door I saw my computer on the floor next to her desk, probably wiped clean, like her office. The desktop was clear, except for her slim-line monitor.

A large desk calendar lay open. It was not the little worn one I'd seen her whip out of her briefcase whenever she needed to consult a phone number, date, or appointment. Had it been put there for appearance's sake by the killer? Who had taken her working calendar?

I tried the doorknob. Locked.

If only I could get in there. Harris wouldn't see me unless he came all the way in.

My hands were shaking. Nerves. It had been too long since I'd been at this lock business. I tried with my little tool. Slipped. Missed. Tried again. Failed.

Down the hall a door shut.

I grabbed a plastic card, my miserable $300-limit card, and shoved it roughly in the jamb. It worked. I slipped inside, closed and leaned against the door. Panting. Knees still sore and shaking.

It had taken maybe a minute to get through that lock. He'd be coming in the office front door now. I could barely hear the sound of it shutting.

I tried to swallow and moisten my throat. No spit. The floor shook. He was at his door. He stopped. A heavy step. He stood right on the other side of the door. Did he sense me? Could he hear my heart thudding? Yeah. Probably. God knows I could.

Oh, no. I forgot to lock the door when I sprang it with my card. I turned to reach for the doorknob lock. Too late. It turned.

Harris knew it should be locked. His voice boomed out, "Who's there?"

Crap!

The door of the office burst open.

The thrust of the door slammed me back into the wall with a thud that shook the room.

He roared, furious, "What the hell!"

Terror set in. Adrenaline hit my bloodstream. I shrieked louder, "What are *you* doing here?"

He was stunned. It gave me a precious second.

I screamed again. "Who do you think you are? You could have killed me!"

His face flushed the nasty, dull color of outrage. "What the—"

"Why are you here?"

"I own this place! What are you—"

"You're lucky I'm not half dead!"

"You're lucky I don't have a loaded gun in my hand!"

"There's a cleaning crew up here. Touch me and I'll SCREAM!"

His brow was a single angry line across his face, hiding his eyes, no doubt a blazing fiery red. "You're already screaming."

"Kill me and you're in so much trouble . . ."

He glared.

I glared back.

His fists bunched at his sides. He looked as though he was getting ready to throttle me. "This is *my* office. What are *you* doing here?"

"It's Helene's office and I'm here to get the information off my computer that you're hiding!"

He took a step toward me. "You've got no right."

I was actually getting angry myself. It helped. "Yes, I have. It's my report, my creation. I've got rights!"

"No, you don't. I own it. This is my business."

Not safe to lower my attack level yet. "Maybe it's your computer, but it has *my* report."

"How did you get in here?"

I took a dangerous step toward him. "I walked in. Not one thing here is locked worth a tinker's damn!" I figured the nearly archaic expression would calm his seething fury.

It seemed to be working. I took another itsy-bitsy step toward him, keeping one foot back so I could spin away if he reached toward me. "If you're so worried about security, you ought to get some decent locks, and then use them!"

The muscles at the side of his face sprang in and out as his jaw worked, clenching and unclenching. "You are the most brazen, unethical, snooping, lying—"

"Hold it! I'm not sitting around letting some vicious killer get away with murder. What are you doing, anyway? So far as I can see, you're whining over money while your poor partner is moldering in her grave."

He was gasping for breath. "I don't believe—"

"I don't believe the report, either. Someone's lying about the income around here and it isn't me!"

His jaw dropped. "What?"

"I saw those sheets in there. Something's wrong. If you don't straighten it out, it's going to look like you've been siphoning out the income the whole time."

"You've been reading my papers."

"And I'm telling you, I'm leaving if you don't calm down."

He stared at me. "This is ludicrous!"

"That's better." I shook my shoulders as though something had been decided and stretched my mouth into something I hoped approximated a pleasant look without smiling, which *would* have been ludicrous. "Now, if you're ready to talk, maybe we can learn something important here."

To be safe, I moved to the other side of the desk, quickly opening desk drawers. They were all empty. "We'd better hurry. The cleaning crew is right down the hall."

He didn't seem to catch the inanity of that. I hurried on. "Now, help me get this up where we can work on it." I pointed to my computer. "This could hold the answers."

Of course, if it did and he was the killer, I was in for some huge problems. I didn't want to think about it then. It would have left me gagging from delayed reaction nerves. Not a position of strength.

"What do you—"

"Don't talk." I interrupted him yet again to keep him off balance. Apparently, he wasn't used to it. "Lift my tower up here where we can get at it."

He picked it up with alarming ease, which told me he had significant muscular strength and I'd be a mere matchstick in his grip. He set it on the desktop. "What do you really want, Francie?"

I'm really not a very good liar. I told the truth. "I came to find a copy of the last report I gave Helene. I figure it might be on the hard drive."

"Why didn't you call if you were so interested? Why come here at, what? At nearly eleven at night?"

"I don't sleep well. I just happened to drive by and saw lights. I know you work late. What's so hard to believe about that?"

"The guard wouldn't have let you in."

"I walked in behind the cleaning crew."

He rolled his eyes. "Even supposing that's the truth, what is all this about a report for Helene? If it were so important, she would have mentioned it to me."

"Only if she trusted you."

He stiffened. "What are you implying?"

"I'm not implying anything. I merely answered your question. If the report is still in the machine, I'll print it out and you can have a copy. What do you have to lose?"

He was silent.

"Did you have the tower brought in here?"

He looked at me, puzzled and blinking.

I repeated, "Did you or Helene ask for it to be brought in here?"

"I believe Helene did. I saw her at your desk working at the computer, then the next I knew it was in here."

I swallowed and said to Harris, "There may not be anything left on the hard drive."

Powerful heavy lines creased his forehead in between his eyebrows. He stared at the desk as if he thought it would offer up some suggestion, or maybe he was simply searching for another reason to refuse me. "There may have been nothing on it to begin with."

"Then, as I said, what do you have to lose?"

He shrugged.

I opened the programs. Excel and Word were the two I'd used. There was nothing there. I went to the Recycle Bin; nothing there either. I went to Find, riffled through the files available. Nothing I had done remained. I installed the CD with the recovery program I was familiar with. Nothing. The report was definitely gone.

Emptiness spread through my belly, leaving a vast black hole, sucking up all my life, light, and energy. Betrayed. Had Helene erased it all to protect me? Or was there more to it? Or could she have put it on a CD before erasing it? "Looks like there's nothing there."

Harris snorted. "Thought so."

If Helene had fired me to protect me, she might also have erased my report so the killer wouldn't read my data. Or had Helene discovered it was already erased? If that were the case, then the killer already knew about the report and had a copy of it. And that made me a very big target.

He loomed over me, easily twice my size, in his forties and very muscular and fit, although heavy. I eased out of the chair and put it between us. "Were there any CDs that she left for you?"

"This has gone far enough."

His quiet menace was far worse than his shouting. And now that my terror and anger were gone I didn't have the strength of panic.

I made for the door, talking as I went. "I think Helene was worrying about improprieties in the company. She knew something was wrong and she was determined to find out what it was."

He laughed, a sharp, nasty sound that made me want to get far away from him. "You were being used by Helene, like everyone else. She used people. Get over it. And get out."

"You put up a good show, Harris, but nobody works this late this often if the company is healthy." I reached the door. "Partner insurance. I'll bet you're counting on partner insurance to pull Techlaw out of the red."

"You're trying to shift blame from yourself to anyone else you can find. Get out of here."

I felt my lips twitch from sheer nervousness. It had the effect of enraging him further.

His face mottled. "Get out!" He smashed his fist down on the desktop, then stepped toward me. I held my ground in a brief act of defiance and bravado, then I got sensible and backed out, keeping my eyes on him the whole time.

He raised a fist at me. "Don't contact anyone in this company again. If you do, you'll pay for it."

When I was safely close to the door, I asked, "What about Julia Orbach? Do you ever wonder about that accident?"

The red color in his cheeks paled. "How dare you!" He started toward me.

I sidled to the door. "What about my check?"

His expression said I'd sunk my chance for reimbursement.

CHAPTER 15

The door to the offices swung closed with a final little snick and I stood in the empty hallway, bathed in the cold glow of indirect fluorescent light. The paycheck was money, but the report was my chance to figure out what was going on around here and maybe catch Helene's killer. I couldn't even begin to describe the pit in my gut over the loss of it. I had Harris's printout, but beyond that, nothing. I was sick.

What had made me think I could figure this out? What inborn arrogance made me think I was a detective at all? Then I remembered. It wasn't that I could do it, it was that no one else would. They'd just yell "Hallelujah, we've got our fall guy" and point their fingers at me.

It took me at least two minutes of despair, leaning against the wall with my forehead in my hand, to pull myself together. Delayed nerves. It's handy to have good reactive responses in an emergency, but it sure plays havoc afterwards.

As soon as I could hear over the sound of my own racing heart and the pounding of blood in my ears, I noticed the low yowl of a vacuum cleaner. There really was a cleaning crew on the floor. Then I swallowed bile.

After all my screaming and shouting, there hadn't been even a single "Are you all right?" inquiry. I could have been killed and no one would have known. And, I realized with a shiver, I still would be killed, or at least imprisoned, which to me was about the same thing, if I didn't get myself in hand and figure out what to do.

It took another two minutes of leaning against the cool surface of the wall to calm myself before I could search out the source of the sound.

It came from the offices in the far corner of the building, next to the elevator and stairwell. I was going to have to go past the cleaner to get out. I crept down the hall until I was next to the glass wall. Peering in, I saw the familiar rounded figure of Rosie, vacuuming furiously. At least something was going my way.

I tapped on the glass until she saw me and opened the door, a dust rag hanging from her belt. "I was looking for you earlier, Rosie."

She looked up and grinned. "Oh, it's you. Maybelle said someone was asking for me." Her brow furrowed. "They left without me and I ran out of gas two blocks away. It took forever to get here." She glanced up and down the hall then said, "You better come inside. I'm not supposed to have visitors. And, you can't tell who's listening around here."

I slipped in and followed her to the next room, where we were out of sight. "Would you know about—"

"I know a lot." She shook her finger in my face. "A lot more about what happens than anyone else, more even than that Lizzie who thinks she's so almighty smart." She sniffed. "You'd be surprised what I know."

"I don't doubt it."

She nodded slowly. "There's lots going on in that office that's nothing more than monkey business. It's a wonder God don't strike 'em dead in their chairs."

"Who are you talking about?"

She looked me straight in the eye, her chin stubborn. "What was it you wanted?"

"You knew about Helene's journals. Do you have them?"

Her lips thinned out into a look of trouble. "Wasn't going to leave them for that husband of hers. That Stewart was a pile of trouble, believe me. She never said a word, but I could tell."

"So you took her journals because he might read them and find out that he was a jerk?"

She snapped the dust cloth over the desk top, scattering dust motes. "I didn't say I took them, but if I did, it wouldn't be for that reason. He already knows he's a jerk."

"The current one she was writing in and the other most recent two, starting from January a year ago, were taken. That's the period when Julia Orbach died."

Rosie flicked her cloth over the chair, wiped off the telephone, and picked up a stack of papers from a box on the floor. Her voice was gruff as she said, "Look at this. Now here's another mess. Leave this recycling paper all over the place for me." She yanked the papers out of a wastebasket. "Too flaming lazy to put it in the bin. They leave them for me to haul down. Don't they know I've got a back injury? They think I'm some kind of pro weight-lifter?"

"A central recycling bin!"

"And you're 'bout the worst." She eyed me. "I pulled papers out of your basket, how many times? You think God puts those trees down here for you to grind up into paper endlessly? Don't you even think about the forest and His little creatures losing their homes to the cutters? Where they gonna live?"

"Where's the bin, Rosie? I'll take these down."

She sniffed. "You don't even know—"

"You're right. I don't. Where is it?"

"It's in the back, next to the trash bins."

"How often do they collect it?"

She jammed her fists onto her ample hips. "Well, now don't I have enough to do without keeping track of the trash and the recycling, too? Who do you think I am?"

141

"I think you're a blessed saint who's grumpy tonight." I gave her a quick hug. "Thank you, Rosie."

"Hey, wait!"

I stopped.

Her eyes had softened. "Helene didn't fire you to be mean. She was worried about you."

"Hey, Rosie, you sure you didn't know Julia Orbach? She used to work for Helene."

Rosie looked up and beyond me, her expression stony. "We got company," she said softly.

I turned. The woman I had spoken to earlier at the back door stood with her hands on her hips and a scowl on her brow. I shrugged and dug in my pocket, pulled out a twenty and handed it to Rosie.

"Thanks, Rosie," I said. "I wanted to get this back to you. Didn't mean to cause trouble."

I sidled past the angry woman and hustled to the elevator.

Outside, I found the trash bins and the recycled paper bin in the darkest corner. How could I have missed it? It looked as big as a boxcar and was probably half the size of one. Four black plastic door flaps lay open on the upper portion of each side, too high to see down inside.

I ran to the Rust, fired it up, and eased it over next to the recycle bin so that the trunk of the Rust was under one of the plastic doors. Then I cut the engine, climbed out, and crawled up on the trunk, lifting a door flap to peer inside. The opening under the plastic flap was discouragingly narrow and the bin itself was half full with thousands of sheets, some in shreds and bagged, some loose, and some newspapers. A mess.

I would have to go in head first and getting back out would be a real challenge. It was late and I had no flashlight. I heard a skittering sound. Oh, sweet Jesus, there were mice in there, too. Big ones. I decided I'd come back in daylight, with a flashlight, rope, and maybe some help.

I got home about midnight, walked my neighbor home to make sure she didn't trip, and thanked her for staying with Mac. She's a little frail at seventy-eight, with bilateral hip and knee replacements.

"Oh, honey, no trouble. I hope he's a fine man, not some two-timer wasting your precious years."

"What are you talking about?"

"About your young man." She looked worried. "He came as soon as you left, dear. Such a good-looking man. I told him you said you were working late."

"Dark hair?"

"Tight jeans, good legs. Nice smile and such good teeth. You notice teeth at my age. He caught up with you, didn't he?"

I smiled as though I was trying to be discreet instead of trying to keep my heart rate below 170 and said, "Thanks."

Back in my own house, I warmed a cup of milk, spent an hour going over the printout with Harris's money transfers, and then stowed the paper under the stove for safe keeping.

The next day I entered Level One with one thing in mind: work hard, leave after four hours, and search the recycle bin for my report. It was all I could do to place phone call after phone call to people who had zero desire to talk about funerals. After four fruitless hours, I hung up my headphones, sneaked past Ethel's office to avoid another "You're-failing" lecturette, and headed out.

Inside the Rust, I gnawed my way through my peanut butter sandwich, dry and partially mummified because I'd run out of plastic baggies. Then I poured in another half bottle of brake fluid, coaxed the Rust into action, and took off for Techlaw, leaving behind a great stinking blue cloud of exhaust. The car seemed to be dying a slow death.

On the far side of the recycle bins the Rust wasn't immediately obvious. I parked so that I could climb on the trunk of the Rust and easily reach the bin flaps, without being easily visible from the back of Techlaw.

In the light of day, it was clear the window was quite small. I'd have to go in head first and hope my fall would be cushioned by paper shreds. At least the distance from the window to the papers inside seemed to be about four feet, so it wasn't too far. And I could still get back out.

I scraped through, fell, managed to curl enough to land on my shoulder, and rolled to my back. But I had miscalculated the distance. It was a bitch. It hurt. The good news was that the papers were fluffed up and there weren't any mouse squeaks. The bad news was, the papers were so fluffed up, it was at least five feet from the bottom of the window and I hadn't done a pull-up since I was in fourth grade. Getting out was going to be real tough.

I decided to do a Scarlett O'Hara. Think about it later.

It had been nearly three weeks since I was fired, three and a half since I'd printed out the draft report and tossed the pages after proofing them. I checked the pages underfoot. They were dated the first of this week. I went to the far end of the bin, which was piled higher with papers. There the dates were last week. I started digging, looking for the right date.

An hour later I was on the right week, but I had a headache of gigantic proportions and the flashlight batteries were dimming. As I changed the batteries I wondered, if I didn't find the report, could I possibly recreate it? And if I did, would it tell me what I needed to know? Or was it something else that Helene knew that made it so significant to her? I started digging again.

About forty-five minutes later I found papers from our office, three sheets I recognized as mine, but not the right project. I scrabbled furiously, squinting, grabbing, reading, and tossing away. Finally, I found a page of my report, but then I heard a deep male voice. "We'll empty this bin into the compactor even if it isn't full."

I hollered, "Hold it!"

A motor roared. Something metallic bumped the end of the bin. Then the motor died again.

I yelled. "Hey! I'm in here."

The first voice, sounding a bit familiar now, called out louder. "Sure no one's in there? It'll kill 'em."

A second voice said, "I didn't hear anything."

The window on the opposite side of the bin swung open. Light poured in. Wolfe's head rose in a bin window. His voice was practically laughing. "Oh, look who's here. What could you be doing in there?"

Dammit, he must have followed me. And this little charade was no doubt to make a point. "Working," I said, pawing feverishly through papers, grabbing a handful of papers to let them slip slowly from my fingers as I scanned each sheet for a date.

He muttered something, which I ignored.

Where was the rest of the report? There should have been at least ten pages altogether. I jammed the one sheet inside my blouse and grabbed another handful. I found another sheet, and another. Stuffed those inside my blouse and reached for more.

Another head, another voice, deeper, rumbled out, "Who are you? What are you doing here?"

I ignored him as well and reached for another handful of paper. Not the right ones. Pawing desperately, I riffled through more sheets. "I'm looking for the proof pages of the report I gave to Helene. The report no one else seems to be able to find."

"And have you found it?"

I continued ruffling pages. If I said yes, he'd want them and I'd never get to go through them. If I said no and then produced them later, he'd assume I simply made it up. Would he let me copy them before taking the originals?

"A few pages. The rest must be here."

"Come out. I'll have an officer finish up here."

"He won't know what to look for."

"Come out of there, right now!"

"I can't. It's too deep."

"How did you think you'd get out?"

"I was going to think about it later. Would you move? You're in my light." I looked up. "Are you calling an officer to come and find the rest of the pages?"

"Not until I see what it is you've found."

"Then I'll stay until I've found it all. It has to be here."

I found three more of the sheets before he totally lost patience, and then another two after he started threatening me and I had to think seriously about getting out. That was eight out of ten. It would have to do, for now. I put them all together, folded them, and stuffed them inside my jeans so they wouldn't fall out.

Then I went to the other end of the bin and shoved the papers into a heap, under the window opposite the top of the Rust. I climbed up on it and tried to pull myself out. Of course I couldn't.

"Give me your hands," Wolfe said and reached in.

"You're standing on the roof of my car."

"You bet."

"You'll make dents."

"You'll never notice. Give me your arms."

"If we do double grips I can walk my feet up the side of the bin." I used to be pretty athletic and limber and, somehow, my body would remember how to do this.

"I don't think so. The opening is too small."

"Trust me." I heaped up the papers underfoot again, grabbed

his hands, and tried to walk my feet up the side of the bin. I was nearly there when his grip failed and I fell.

He stuck his head in. "Do it my way. Pile all the papers up and come out with your arms overhead. I'll grab you under the arms and pull you out the rest of the way."

I piled the papers up until I had my arms out and my head about even with the opening. If the papers hadn't slid so, I could have maybe managed, but there were so many plastic bags between them, they were like paper avalanches.

Wolfe pulled until my arms were out far enough to get some leverage. "Let go of me. I can do this."

"I doubt it," he said, but he let go and I eased a bit farther out. The bin opening was so narrow I couldn't maneuver myself the last bit. "I'm stuck."

"Thought so." Great satisfaction sounded in his voice.

"Do something! Please!"

He wrapped his arms around my chest in a bear hug and pulled me the rest of the way out. We ended up face-to-face, chest-to-chest, thigh-to-tingling-thigh, both panting. It had been a long, long time since I'd been held close like that. He even smelled nice, a kind of warm, sweaty smell. It took me by surprise. His wife was very lucky. Oh my God, it was humiliating and very hot. What a way to get a hug from a sexy guy.

He seemed as surprised as I was. He let go abruptly and jumped to the ground in one athletic move. My knees shook, my hands shook. I caught my balance and clambered down slowly to the bumper and then to the ground, trying to gather my wits and conceal the pain of my scraped shins. The net result was complete embarrassment and two new dents in the roof of the Rust, although, as Wolfe had pointed out, the dents didn't alter the overall appearance.

He stood before me, hand out. "The papers."

"After I copy them. The whole report isn't here and they

aren't going to make sense to anyone but me."

"There's a copy place a few blocks from here."

I started to get into the Rust.

"Oh, no. We'll go together in my car. Chain of evidence."

Oh, boy. He meant he had to see the papers the whole way. I hesitated. "I don't have much time. I have to pick up Mac—"

"You weren't worried about that when you were in the bin."

"I'm worried about it now."

He glared at me. "Then give me the papers and meet me at the copy shop."

I wasn't letting the papers out of my sight. I got in his car. He generously let me pay for the copying, took the originals, and dropped me back at the Rust.

As I was getting out of his car I said, "You followed me here last night. And you arranged for the guard to call you if I showed up again."

"Don't know a thing about it," he replied. "By the way, there was a break in at Foster's garage yesterday afternoon. Were you looking for those papers there?"

I shook my head and climbed into the Rust. "Don't know a thing about it."

"You going to need a very good lawyer, Ms. Starzel."

Was the look in his eyes worry? Or something else?

CHAPTER 16

That night about eight o'clock my phone rang.

"Have you looked at your report?" Detective Wolfe's voice, husky for some reason, came over the telephone line.

I checked my watch, trying not to disturb the skin on my back, still stinging from the scrape that afternoon. "Not really, not yet."

"If I came over, would you go over it with me?"

I peered out my kitchen window into the hostile eyes of Mrs. Folsom staring back at me. She turned off her lights so I could see only her black silhouette, backlit by the glow of light from her living room. What would she think of a man calling on me at night? Did it matter? Would it change her obvious opinion of Mac and me? "Is this an official visit?"

Pause. "No, it's education for me."

Would he stick to such a promise? I was tempted. A compromise came to mind. "Come ahead, but we'll sit on the porch. There's plenty of light there."

He was quiet for few minutes. "Okay. That'll do."

He arrived before I had time to do more than a quick brush of my hair. So fast I decided he had phoned from his car, probably only a block or so away. His eyes were reddened, as though he had been reading for hours, and when he walked, his shoulders seemed weighed down with fatigue. He settled heavily on the glider.

Mac hustled to the door, clearly curious. Wolfe asked polite questions about what he was doing this summer and what grade he would enter in the fall, but I had a sense that he was remote from us, as though he were emotionally somewhere else. Or maybe in pain.

In my family cops were "them," the enemy, the other side of the jailhouse door, anything but people to whom we could relate. I had never thought about cops as ordinary people who had emotions other than the love of a good chase or wielding power. It was bad enough I had to worry about Mac and how I'd straighten out all this mess—having a cop appear human was an unwanted complication. I didn't like it and felt disturbed. Even so, I heard myself asking, "Are you okay?"

He nodded. "Long day. That's why I thought if you could go through these with me, explain them, it might save some time."

A trap? Dad would say, "Give them nothing. They're paid to get you." But I was tired too, and needed to pick my battles. I couldn't fight everyone and everything all the time. Maybe going through these papers with him would help me to see what I must have missed before.

Mac went back to the living room to watch television while I walked into the kitchen, fished Harris's printout out from under the stove, and made a pot of Nepalese black tea in order to give myself time to calm my nerves. I wanted to be in full control of myself when dealing with Detective Wolfe. I was helped in this effort by Mrs. Folsom, whose head was visible as a silhouette peering out her window into my kitchen. Did the woman have nothing else to do in her life? No television to watch?

Wolfe took the tea and sipped it gingerly, as though he thought it might contain some disreputable substance. I settled next to him on the glider, a safe four inches away, but not quite out of range of his body heat.

I spread the pages out on the top of the old steamer trunk we used for a table. "This is Helene's calendar, the dates she was in the office, important meetings, the dates she was on the road, the companies she visited for either sales or support."

"Support?"

"Follow up on sales. She would do the product installation and a trial run, then in four to six months she'd go back and check to see that it was running as intended."

He picked up a page of graphs.

"That's a graph of inventory flow. And that one is sales volumes by date. I was trying to see what the correlation was to her on-site visits, if any."

"And?"

"A very high correlation. She was a superb salesperson. Even on the callbacks she got additional orders."

"No unsatisfied customers?"

"There's always at least one. That table compiles complaints and their origin. You can see there have been very few, which is pretty surprising for a software program, but both Harris and Sam are fantastic programmers. And the bugs are pretty well worked out before they're shipped."

"Each program is written new for each client?"

"Not quite. The basic program is set, then Harris and Sam only need to alter a few things to customize the programs for the companies. Because Techlaw targets law firms, quite a lot of the programs are boilerplate, with little or no need to individualize them."

"I don't see a sales graph here."

He reached across, his arm brushing mine. It felt so good I made myself ease another inch away. It's one thing to decide a cop might be human; it's another to sit there and get hot.

Words tumbled out of my mouth in an effort to cover up my discomfort. "That sheet is missing, but as I recall, sales were remarkably consistent. Most done by calling, demonstrations, and full presentations, all handled by Helene. Word of mouth accounted for some. My primary recommendation based on this was for increased advertising and an interactive demonstration booth at an American Bar Association conference coming up in the fall."

"What about revenues? I don't see that sheet anywhere."

"It's under that set."

"I don't see it." He moved closer, looking for it.

A cool breeze would have been real welcome. "It should be there. Look through them again while I get the fan."

He ruffled the sheets. "It's not."

"Then it's also missing. I only had revenue records for the first and second quarters." How could I have forgotten that? "Helene gave me raw deposit history for the third quarter. She said the computer had gone down and they were working with totals for some of this."

"Wasn't there backup?"

"Apparently a client sent an attachment containing a virus and Lizzie's machine went down. It managed to destroy the backup as well."

"But she would have had secondary backup."

Even with the living room fan blowing out the door to us, it was hot. "Should have, but evidently didn't. Helene said the data wasn't available. I had no reason to disbelieve her."

He looked at me, his gaze so direct and unblinking that I could see tiny gold flecks in the dark, dark brown of his eyes. "That was odd, wasn't it?"

"I thought it was, but I didn't say so." A bead of sweat trickled down between my breasts. I stood up and pulled the fan clear outside so it blew at me. If I ever got a decent job again, air conditioning was top on the must-have list, even though it wouldn't have helped in this situation.

"What were collections like?" Wolfe scratched his chin, his gold wedding band flashing in the light from the lamp at the end of the couch. Lucky, lucky wife.

I thought for a minute. He knew I'd gone to Techlaw last night. There was little to gain by holding back what I'd learned from Harris and his printouts. I retrieved Harris's printout, smoothed it out, and tried to compare it to the collections sheets. There was no match. Dang. I really needed to have the missing sheets of my report. Still, it was enough to know he was depositing amounts very similar to those removed from his savings, if my memory for figures was accurate. I took a deep breath and launched in.

"The collections were poor, but deposits always matched. I learned last night that someone, Harris I believe, because his withdrawals appear to match the company deposits, has been feeding in cash to keep the company afloat. My guess is my sheets made that clear to Helene."

"Wouldn't she have had the same information as Harris?"

I shook my head. "I don't think so. This printout I picked up last night indicates he has kept two sets of books, one for himself and one for everyone else. Possibly he believed Helene was siphoning cash out."

"How would she do that?"

Again, I shook my head. "I've been thinking about that, and I simply don't know. I suppose there are several ways . . ." I rubbed my cheek. "You see, I've been thinking that Helene's murder goes back to the business. It's the old money trail sort of thing. Someone has been leaching cash and I figured it was probably Harris, but after last night, I don't think so. However, I think he suspected Helene was embezzling and that she brought me on board to assist in her scheme. That would explain why he was so against me all along."

"You have proof?"

"No. But if each of them suspected the other, they wouldn't talk to each other. I'm sure Helene brought me on to help find the leak. And something in this report gave her the answer she sought."

"And the person who killed her?"

"Is the person taking out the cash." I was the puzzle expert, so why couldn't I figure out who? I finished my tea. "There are two sheets missing, but from my recollection, those were simply a couple graphs and my recommendations, which were simple. One, advertisement, through personal contact sales, and two, big picture, through hard copy ads in business journals and at conferences, like the American Bar Association conference in the fall. Probably the most important was to purchase a decent antivirus program for Lizzie's computer. It was always breaking down."

I put Harris's printout on top of the sheets. "Harris's savings withdrawals correlate with Techlaw's cash deposits. Either Techlaw was bleeding cash and Harris was shoring it up, which seems unlikely, or Harris was shifting funds to cover up an embezzlement. There were three people in a position to easily embezzle—Harris, Helene, and the company auditor, Laurence Gifford. I believe Helene discovered the embezzlement from the report, and fired me to protect me. But in doing so she must have alerted the embezzler, who killed her to keep her quiet."

Wolfe's mouth twisted in a cynical smile. "Odd way to protect you, isn't it? She caused you a good deal of hardship."

He was still trying to stack the cards against me and it pissed me off. "You're the detective here. While you're looking into things, look into a death a year ago. The person who last held my job, Julia Orbach, died suddenly in an auto accident about a year ago. A little too coincidental, wouldn't you say?"

I expected him to get defensive, but he merely said, "I'll do that, but before I go I'd like to ask Mac a few more questions about finding the gun at Fosters'."

"Only if you do it out here and I can be present."

"I'd rather do it privately."

I shook my head. "I'll be quiet, I won't interfere, but I want to be present." I had a bad feeling about that gun. Actually, "bad" wasn't the right word. "Bad" didn't come close to describing the gripping, nauseating feeling I had thinking about Mac with that gun. Could he have taken it from its hiding place? Or had someone stolen it from our house to frame me? Either way I felt sick.

I knew all too well the traps a kid could fall into during an interview with the cops. A wrong word or two uttered in an effort to please a frightening authority and suddenly the kid is seen as having "confessed." Oh yes, I knew those traps. I'd fallen into them as a youngster. I wasn't going to let it happen to Mac. "What is it that you need to know?"

He seemed to bite back information, then sighed. "Look, it doesn't ring true to me that he found the gun in the linen closet. My men went through that house with a fine-tooth comb and they'd have found it. I think he found it somewhere else."

He sounded truthful, and I'd wondered about Mac's explanation myself. I said, "Here's why I'm concerned. I know perfectly well that the way you ask your questions can affect what Mac says. Kids sometimes make up answers in an effort to please, especially a strong authority figure."

"Fair enough." Wolfe smiled. "I'll do my best and if you think the questions are leading you nudge me."

Nudge him? I'd almost rather hug him, but I shoved that thought away and called Mac to come out.

He came cheerfully, seeming pleased to be included, and eased into the chair. "Whassup?" Spike perched on his shoulder, all eight little furry feet clutching his T-shirt. "Grandma Lil says Spike's really an attack spider. She could kill a person."

It was all for effect, but I still had to repress a shudder. "I thought Dude said her bite was like a bee sting."

Wolfe grinned at Mac in an easy, slow way that seemed to connect with Mac. "I'll bet Spike could scare a person to death. It takes a lot of nerve to handle a tarantula."

"Yeah, you want to hold him?"

Ah, the test. Wolfe didn't flinch a bit, just held out his hand and waited while Mac set Spike in his palm. Spike marched straight up Wolfe's arm to his shoulder.

"He likes you." Mac took Spike back, obviously impressed. Score a big one for Wolfe. He'd pretty well won Mac's approval.

"I hear you're into wrestling," Wolfe said.

Mac nodded, carefully checking out Wolfe more closely.

"I wrestled in high school a bit," Wolfe said. "For East High."

"What weight?"

"Middle. I wasn't all that big until my junior year, and then mostly lanky."

"I'm doing heavyweight."

"And I'll bet you're pretty good."

"Coach says so." Mac looked at him slyly. "Are you trying to warm me up?"

I smothered a grin. Mac was nobody's fool.

Wolfe grinned, too. "Yeah. I asked your mom if I could talk to you. I need some help understanding how things were at the Fosters' house the other night."

Mac's expression grew wary, his face still. He busied himself putting Spike back in his cage.

Wolfe waited until the cage door was safely latched, then continued. "You see, the closet where you said you found the gun had been searched earlier by the officers and no gun was found. So, I wonder if you can help me out?"

Mac kicked at the floor, then looked at me, then back at Wolfe. "I really did look in the closet . . . for toilet paper."

Wolfe didn't say anything, but he moved to mimic Mac's body posture. Trying to put him at ease, I guessed. An old interviewing trick they probably taught at the police academy in Grilling 101. Finally Wolfe said, "I think someone brought it to Fosters' that night, trying to frame someone."

"She was never in that room." Mac stopped, his lip caught in his teeth as if to stop himself from saying any more. He looked at me.

Wolfe caught the look. "What room?"

"The dining room," he whispered.

Wolfe's expression was bleak. "You were worried I'd blame your mom, right?"

Mac nodded, his eyes filling.

"It takes courage to trust I won't hurt you or your mom."

Mac stared hard at the floor. "But I don't trust you."

"Mac, I'm only trying to find the truth. You believe that?"

He didn't answer.

Wolfe looked at me. I knew he wanted me to say "the truth won't hurt," but I knew better. Sometimes it did and I wasn't going to lie to Mac.

He turned back to Mac, a light frown on his brow. "Mac, I know this is scary, but you're in trouble and the only way out is to tell the truth."

I leaned forward. I couldn't tell Mac the truth wouldn't hurt us, but I could urge him to tell exactly what happened. Whatever it was, Mac needed to tell it. "Sweetie, think back to that night. We walked in, you and Sam went to the dining room, and I left you to talk to Mr. Foster. What did you do after that? It might help to start by telling us about the food."

Mac is like a bear, he never forgets a meal. I hoped that by focusing on food he might relax.

Wolfe looked dubious, but once Mac began with the shrimp, words poured from him as he listed a horrifying mountain of food, ending with a glass of ginger ale.

"Then I felt kind of full and really hot, so I went over to the window. I was looking out over this pot of vines, you know, Grandma Lil has those kinds, they grow all over her floor toward the light? Kinda heart-shaped leaves? And I thought maybe I'd throw up, so I got real close to the plant and was looking in it. And there was this little gun. I pulled it out and it looked like . . ." His eyes were round and frightened. "Kinda like, a toy, sort of. Anyway, I got kind of sicker, so I stuck it in my pocket and went upstairs to the bathroom."

"And then?"

He kicked at the floor awkwardly.

At that moment, I realized he must have thought he recognized the gun, thought it was mine, and that was why he'd pocketed it.

"Then in the bathroom I took it out and was playing like it was a real gun, only down at the floor, and it went off."

Wolfe nodded. "It must have scared you."

Mac's face relaxed. "Yeah. It jumped in my hand and I dropped it and it went off again. Bam, right through the door."

"How'd you decide to go to the upstairs bathroom? There's one right downstairs by the front door."

Mac was solemn again, his gaze stuck on the floor, as though he knew something he thought he shouldn't know. He rubbed his head. "I thought someone might, uh, need to use the toilet, so, uh, I went upstairs."

I started to rise up but Wolfe put a hand on my knee. How could one man make my skin burn that way? I glared at the gleaming gold band on his ring finger and cooled myself right out. He's taken, I told myself. Chill.

Wolfe said, "Why didn't you use the downstairs bathroom?"

"Someone was in there."

"Why did you go through the kitchen?"

"It was closer, and I figured there was a big sink in there and if I had to throw up . . ." He let it hang there.

"And then what?"

"One of the cooks in there asked what I was doing and pointed me up the back stairs when I told her I needed a bathroom."

Mac was looking at me funny. I tried to smile encouragement but I thought I saw a pleading little look in his eyes. I wasn't sure what it was about.

Wolfe asked, "Is there anything else?"

Mac shook his head, his gaze sliding to the floor again. "I'm sorry I lied about finding the gun in the closet."

"You've been a real help, Mac," Wolfe said and stood. "I know it was worrying you, but telling the truth is important. It's the only way we can really find out what happened."

Mac nodded, but his gaze stayed on the floor.

I gathered up the copies of the report and stuffed them into a folder, then walked Wolfe to his car.

"It hasn't clarified much for you, has it?"

He looked at the ground.

Irritated I said, "You and Mac both look at the ground when you don't know how to answer a question. It's beginning to seem a lot like a male gene thing."

A telltale flicker of humor showed in Wolfe's eyes. "Some questions are hard to answer."

The night was warm, the air still, and his eyes were dark in the faint light from the porch. An expression I didn't understand lurked there. Was it longing, or was that what I was feeling? As quick as it came, it left, and his expression was again carefully guarded. "Be careful, Francie," he said and climbed in his car and left.

When I came inside, Mac was sitting on the couch holding Spike, gazing into her beady black eyes. I had a feeling that there was more he hadn't told us. Much as I didn't care for the spider, I sat next to Mac and put an arm around him.

He didn't pull away.

"Is there something you're worried about? Anything you weren't sure you should tell Detective Wolfe?"

He shook his head, staring at the floor. "Grandma Lil wouldn't have let a cop in the house."

"I'm not Grandma Lil. Everybody has their own rules. I have mine and she has hers." I could feel tension tightening up my neck and shoulders. "Did you call Grandma Lil recently?"

He nodded. "You said it was all right."

"It is. I was just surprised. You know, Mac, sometimes Grandma Lil exaggerates a little. Like about Spike being an attack spider. It's okay to brag a little about her, but the truth is important, too. Really important, Mac."

"That's why we moved, isn't it? Grandma Lil doesn't always tell the truth."

It was so tempting to move into a lecture about the importance of not lying. After all, in my family lying was regarded as an art form and Mac was also getting very good at sliding away from the topic at hand—his truthfulness. "Mac, I think when *you* were talking to Detective Wolfe, maybe you left out something because you were a little worried."

He kicked at the floor, scuffing the toe of his tennie across the polished hardwood. I waited him out. There was only so long he could work on his toes. He dragged his gaze up from his foot to meet mine.

"I heard someone in the hall," he said, "and got scared."

My heart beat faster, but I tried to keep the excitement out of my voice. "Did you recognize the person?"

"Just a woman with fuzzy hair. I didn't look at her too good."

My breath caught in my throat. Rosie? I thought back to the wake. When I had asked her about the journals she looked surprised, as though she hadn't thought of them, but right after that she excused herself. Then last night she had nearly admitted having them. I'd practically handed them to her.

I looked at Mac. He still had a secretive glint in his eye. "Is there a bit more you haven't mentioned?" He didn't answer. "Maybe something about the way the gun looked."

He finally nodded, staring straight at the floor.

"Did you think that gun was mine?"

He whispered, "I didn't want to get you in trouble."

A nasty knot of worry burned in my gut. I rubbed his head. "I know, but you should tell the truth. I discovered the gun was missing that night before we went to the Fosters'. But you have to believe me, I didn't kill Helene."

He nodded. "I know."

"Detective Wolfe will find out who did."

"Are you sure?"

I couldn't have Mac worrying. "Of course." Sometimes lying is justified.

He leaned into me and I held him until the phone rang. When I answered it, Wolfe's voice came over the line. "Julia Orbach's car ran off the road on Berthoud Pass. An accident."

What if it wasn't? A chill crawled over my arms, raising goose bumps. Mac's gaze was glued to my face. I knew he was wondering if I would tell Wolfe about the gun. God, what a double bind these moral lessons turn out to be.

"Uh," I said into the phone. "The gun that Mac found, is it the murder weapon?"

"Why?"

"You should know, it might be mine. I don't know for sure, but mine is missing. I only discovered it the night of the wake."

Long silence, the silence of disbelief. Then, "That's quite an example you set for the boy. If you lie to me again, I'll set an example for him that he'll never forget."

My cheeks burned. I knew Mac had guessed what Wolfe said.

"Look," I said. "Put some time into rechecking Julia Orbach's death."

He hung up.

Mac's face was tense. "What's going to happen now?"

"Now we're going to talk about lying—yours and mine, and the trouble it causes."

CHAPTER 17

I wrapped Mac in my arms. "You don't need to worry. I'm real proud of you for telling the truth. I love you and everything is going to work out."

He was ramrod stiff with tension, but his arms went around me, and it was a sweet, sweet feeling.

Mac went to bed and after a while to sleep, his survival book under his cheek. For me, sleep was impossible.

In my whole roller-coaster life, never had I been so happy and so frightened at the same time. Happy that Mac and I were finally getting closer, but frightened because of the shadow of Helene's murder. I had no idea what lay ahead of us, only that I had to make good my promise to Mac that it would all work out.

The truth was out there somewhere and I had to find it. I pulled out a paper but before I could start a list, my cell phone rang.

Without preamble Lil said, "What's happening out there?"

"What do you want me to say, Mom? That I've got the hots for a sexy married cop, that I spent the afternoon in a recycling bin, and that I got pulled out by the same hot cop?"

"Stop right there. Not a single Starlinski, or Starzel as you call yourself now, has ever disgraced herself with a cop. Don't even joke about it. Now tell me the truth. I get more information from my grandson than from my own daughter. What are you doing about all this? Mac says you went to a wake and he shot a gun and ruined a ceiling in Helene's house."

Bless Mac's heart. I told her about finding most of the pages of the report but that there weren't any answers. "The only thing I can think of is that Helene would write any worries she had in her journals and I'm positive Rosie took them."

"I don't suppose she'll just tell you."

"I doubt it, but I'll give it a try."

Lil was quiet a moment, then spoke in a hushed voice. "Do you need a little *heat?*" Lil's code for a gun.

"Mom, no. Absolutely not. Don't even consider it."

"I can be there in a heartbeat, Francie."

"No, Mom, please. It's all under control."

After assurances that she'd do anything she could to help, she rang off. Her call and the two cups of Nepalese black tea I'd drunk while Wolfe was there made it hard to calm down.

Julia Orbach's slide off the mountain pass may have looked like an accident then, but with Helene's murder, it was too coincidental. If Julia had been killed because of something she knew about Techlaw and Helene had been killed because of something she figured out from my report, then I was a prime target. Helene's attempt to degrade my report and sever our connection would not be enough to protect me. Or Mac.

At least three times I checked on Mac and peered out the front window. I didn't see the white car or Wolfe's, nor did I spot anything odd outside. Still, I couldn't shake the feeling that someone was keeping an eye on my house.

I wondered if Lil had suffered similar feelings, her sleep eroded by gut-deep worry due to my father's so-called "career choice." I didn't remember her complaining about it, but she was never a complainer. Of course in her case she only had to worry about the law coming, whereas I had the law and a killer to consider.

Tidying up to wear myself out a bit, I thought about my list from the other night, with all the options, including running and where we could run.

I knew we would not run. Running would begin a lifetime of fear and I wasn't going to let that be my lot, or Mac's. Mac's dad, Dave, and I had talked about the life we would one day have together, the life we'd make for Mac. I had loved Dave for his idealism, his determination, and his belief in a good, stable, proud life.

It didn't matter that I later learned it wasn't what he was, or how he lived and died. Whatever mistakes Dave McGraw had made, I knew in my heart he loved both Mac and me, and he'd left Mac with me believing I'd give Mac that kind of life we'd talked about. And I would, if it killed me.

When the alarm rang at quarter to six in the morning I was already awake, thinking about Helene's journals. At the wake I'd seen two dust strips on the shelf, indicating two missing journals. I was betting Rosie had them. But there was still Helene's current journal. The police hadn't found it. And a current one probably wouldn't have been on the shelf, so it was still unaccounted for. That was the one that would have her thoughts about me and my report. That was the journal I had to find.

By six-thirty Mac was mostly awake and slouched into his chair at the kitchen table to consume no fewer than three bowls of corn flakes.

"Can I have my allowance early?" His wide gray eyes were clear, no signs of devious thoughts.

"Why?"

"I have to buy Spike some crickets. They cost ten cents each."

"Ten cents for insects? How many does she eat in a week?"

"The pet shop said three to four should be plenty, but she already ate up the ones they gave me. I think the move made her hungry."

I shuddered. "How about if I give you fifty cents, you get five, and we'll see how fast they go?"

"I suppose." He finished off the beige flakes that he loves. "Barry gets three dollars a week."

I put down my coffee cup. "I think we'll both have to live with what we have now. It's real tight, Mac."

"Are we poor?"

"No. We're only short of cash right now."

He thought, then said. "Do other people get short of cash?"

"Of course. Why?"

"When we get some money, can I get new shoes?"

I looked at his tennies. They were a bit worn, but still holding together and only four weeks old. They should last a bit longer, at least another couple weeks. "Do they hurt your feet?"

"They're not the same kind as the other kids."

"Do they tease you?"

He blinked rapidly. "Not too much."

"Do the other kids all have the same kind?"

His face wrinkled up. "No."

A desperate flutter beat in my chest; some things are never forgotten. "The kids teased me when I was a kid, too. I hated it."

"What did you do?"

Had my brother beat them within an inch. "Uh, I don't remember. I only remember how angry I would get. After a while they started teasing someone else. It took me a long time to figure out it wouldn't matter what I wore. Even if my things were exactly the same as theirs, they'd find something to tease me about. What do you do when they start in?"

He looked troubled. "Uncle Andy said to steal their lunch money or smash their faces."

"Sweetie, some of Uncle Andy's ideas aren't really a good way to handle things. You know that."

He kicked the floor. "I go away. I'm not a good enough fighter but I'd really like to smash them."

So would I, right then. Everything was conspiring against us. "You want a ride to day camp this morning?"

He looked at me, horrified. "No offense, I think I'll walk."

"Are you embarrassed by the Rust?"

"Aren't you?"

I sent Mac off to day camp with a whole dollar and an extra peanut butter sandwich. As soon as he left, I placed a call to his day camp leader. Fortunately she was in early.

She sighed. "It's a real problem this year. There's a child whose parents are having a lot of trouble and he's acting out by picking on the others. You know how it is with single parents. The kids are always in trouble, the kids always feel like they're cheated, and—"

Talk about pain! I felt like I'd been stabbed. "*I'm* a single parent. And Mac is *not* in trouble. Maybe it's an attitude that comes from higher up that motivates the kids."

"I'm so sorry. I didn't know. I try to keep an eye on the kids, but I know teasing goes on. Believe me, they aren't picking on Mac alone. I'll try."

Fat lot of good that would do if she thought it was all the fault of single parents. It was hard enough without that. And what was I going to do about it? Hire a dad? Pay someone to go to camp, and later to school, with me so we could present a united front? It shouldn't be necessary, dammit.

Practically throwing the dishes, I cleared the kitchen table, wiped it down, and then wiped down the counter. What was I going to do about any of this mess? I felt like I was going to explode.

I threw the dish cloth on the floor and stomped on it. Since no one was looking, I jumped up and down on it, until I felt exhausted and the rag was practically an organic part of the floor. When I looked up, Mrs. Folsom was staring out her kitchen window into mine, her mouth agape. She turned abruptly away and disappeared.

Oh, fine! I was definitely going to have to work on the control thing. Now added to everything else, she could tell the cops I was nuts and had temper tantrums. She probably heard me snore because our houses were set so close together. I wished I'd thought to ask her if she had a television. Or told her to get a life.

I got to work at ten that morning, a little shaky, with my hair wrapped in a knot right on top of my head. Just for the fun of it, I stuck two chopsticks in it for decoration. Who knows, if I got in a pinch I could always use them as weapons.

Ethel, my boss, was closeted in her office, but a note to me was pinned to the bulletin board. I opened it. "Your sell rate is quite low," it read. "Please use the following paragraph in your calls."

I slunk to an empty carrel, of which there were many again that day. I accepted the first call with a certain fury.

"My name is A-nice Euphemism. I'm calling you about a great opportunity that has just come on the market."

I unfolded the note, placed it before me, and read, "If you act quickly you may be one of the few people accepted into a new program in which the lucky participants may arrange to have their remains compressed into a lovely diamond, a fitting, eternal memorial of you and your wonderful life."

"I've had a bad life and it ain't getting better with this stupid call."

Oh, enough. "You know, mister. We all have bad days. I have more than most, because I have a job that takes me into the homes of people like you. People who can't wait to be rude and nasty to someone they can't see. Who do you think I am? Some computer with no feelings? I have bad times or I wouldn't be doing a job like this, so lighten up."

A pause, then, "You go, girl."

"Do you want to hear about funeral arrangement plans?" I heard a clock striking in the background and a tinny music box playing "Jesus Loves Me."

He answered. "Yeah, well, I'll think about it. If they can make me into a diamond, think they could make me into a statue?"

"I'll be glad to put you through to the people who can give much more information. What are you thinking of?"

"A third finger pointing up."

By the time I'd put in three hours, it was one o'clock and I was fried, but I made myself stick to it. All I had that morning were the I & I calls, the Irate and the Insane. And thinking of the irate, I thought of Stewart and the wake and the falling ceiling.

The memory of the ceiling crash brought an instant wave of guilt for having left Stewart without so much as even a half-hearted offer to pay for the damage Mac's shooting, however accidental, had caused. But how would I ever come up with that kind of cash? Georgia had been so enthused about Stewart and what a great guy he was to work for. Generous. Thoughtful. Would his generosity extend to a fallen ceiling?

From Stewart, my mind wandered to Helene and her missing journals.

Stewart would know about Helene's journals. And unless he was mentioned unfavorably or was the killer, he probably had the missing current one. Further, since the police hadn't found it, he'd probably hidden it. If he wanted to hide it, what better place to hide a book than among other books, and who had books in their office? Lawyers. Well, actually, who didn't have books in their offices, but lawyers were notorious book people and Helene's journal would presumably be safe from the police and any other prying people on Stewart's bookshelves.

I was itching to visit Stewart and Georgia in his office. By skipping lunch and working through to two-thirty, I kept at the calls and talked up those diamonds. Four people were actually interested in wearing their spouses as diamonds. My best sell record yet.

I put in four and a half hours for a total of twenty-one hours that week. Two hundred and ten dollars, minus FICA, minus withholding, minus who knew what else. I could maybe count on a total of one-seventy. I had to increase my hours and my sales, or the hole in my savings would be as deep as the Grand Canyon and we'd be eating macaroni and cheese until we turned orange.

I parked at a meter north of Eighteenth Street and hoofed it to Stewart's offices, located in a renovated office building in lower downtown, "Lodo" to the natives. Situated below street level with an iron railing that skirted large window wells which lit the rooms, the offices had a certain cachet.

Peering over the railing, I could see through the large paned windows into two offices. In a flash I understood Mrs. Folsom's fascination with watching in my window. It was much better than a movie;, it was live and real-time. Stewart was bent over his immense desk, law books stacked high, papers everywhere. No bookcases. The waiting room where Georgia sat at a smaller, far tidier desk, contained only a single set of bookshelves. How could Stewart practice law without more books?

Inside, an elevator from the ground-floor lobby deposited me directly in the little waiting room where Georgia looked up, surprise all over her face. "Francie!"

Oh, my God, I hadn't figured out what I was going to say. I stretched my face into a huge grin and said, "Georgia!"

She stared at me, waiting.

I sucked air. "Uh, Georgia . . ."

Journals, books, I'd come to look for Helene's journal. Now how to say I want to go through your books. "Georgia, uh, I have a little legal problem and I wondered if I could . . ."

She tilted her head in query.

"Uh, use Stewart's law library."

"You know the law?"

"No, but I don't have any money to pay a lawyer, so I thought maybe I could browse through Stewart's books a bit." *Oh, feeble, feeble.*

Fortunately, she held up an interrupting hand and said "Excuse me," then pressed a button on the telephone. "Foster and Gladry attorneys, may I help you?" she said, and I realized she wore a headset and was speaking into the microphone.

She listened, her eyelids lowering a fraction. "Please hold." She pressed a second button. "Mr. Foster? Lizzie, I mean Mrs. Bruckner, is on line one." Silence. "Yes, I'll do that. And you remember the workmen were coming to your house to fix the ceiling this afternoon? Someone needs to let them in. Do you want me to go?"

I couldn't make out the words, but his tone was emphatic. "Okay, but are you sure you want to—" She winced. "Yes, sir. I'll see to it."

So Stu wasn't as charming today as she had described him at the wake. Or maybe his nerves were working on him. Guilt?

Keeping an ear on the conversation I quickly scanned the one set of bookshelves, looking for Helene's journal. It wasn't there.

Georgia listened, her gaze drifting to the clock on the opposite wall. "Yes, sir." She returned to line one. "Mrs. Bruckner, he asked me to tell you he would be working on it 'til late tonight. Yes, I'm readying it for printout right now."

And I said I didn't believe in coincidence. What was 'it'?

Techlaw stuff? It couldn't be. Stewart wasn't the attorney for

Techlaw—Lawrence Gifford, possible embezzler, was. How could I get a look at whatever it was she was working on?

Georgia hung up and looked at me. "Actually, Stewart doesn't keep his books in his office, except for these state statutes and a couple of professional periodicals. He uses the law library in the building. It's upstairs, but I don't think you can use it. You can use the Colorado State Law Library, though. It's in the basement of the Colorado State Judicial Building on the corner of Broadway and Fourteenth. They're real helpful over there." She looked at me rather obliquely and said, "Know anyone who can be hired to open a house?"

Oh, my. I wanted into his house. It was worth a try. "I'm available. Not too expensive."

"I'm not sure . . ." She shrugged. "He said I could hire a bag lady if I had to, but . . ."

"I've got a bag." I held up my rather large black purse. "Seriously, I don't mind. After all, I feel a little responsible." Remembering his look of exasperation that night I added, "Of course you should check with Stewart first."

She rose. "Wait a minute. I'll be right back." She left and entered Stewart's office, closing the door behind her.

I immediately peered into her computer screen. She was entering information on a restraining order naming Harris Bruckner. I riffed through the papers on the desk. Lizzie was filing for divorce. And Stewart was doing the work. Oh, my.

Georgia returned before I could get back to the front of the desk.

I held up my hands and made an apologetic face.

"You're not supposed to do that," she scolded.

"I'm not surprised, though, Georgia. Harris is a difficult man."

"Promise me, you won't say anything to anyone about it. Harris doesn't know."

"That Lizzie is filing or that Stewart is doing the work?"

"Either. And it must stay that way. People frequently change their minds at the last minute. Please make sure you keep it to yourself."

"Promise."

She held out a set of house keys.

Remarkable. I couldn't believe Stewart agreed. "You are sure Stewart knows that I'm the one opening his house? I wouldn't want him not to know. He'd be pretty bent out of shape."

"He knows. Leave the keys under the little concrete frog at the side of the front steps."

My brother Andy would love that. Those habits cut his entry time by ninety percent. Stewart must be losing it. "I suppose Stewart has been really upset about Helene. It must make things so much more difficult for him. I suppose he's brought some books and things here from the house. Journals—"

"No. In fact, he took stuff home to cut down on the clutter here." Georgia sat down, the expression on her face a mix of feelings. "Frankly, I don't know what he feels, but I'm almost relieved. You have no idea what she could be like."

"You worked for her for a while."

"Not long, trust me. But Julia, poor thing, put up with her for two whole years."

So she did know Julia. "Julia didn't get along with Helene?"

"Oh, she did. Or said she did, but"—her voice dropped to near whisper level—"Helene was harsh, no appreciation, no support. And then the accusations she made about Julia's work were intolerable."

That sounded uncomfortably like my experience with Helene. "What accusations?"

Georgia's pretty face twisted. "Julia had worked so many hours on a report for Helene, and she trashed it. Said Julia made it up. I think that was what drove Julia to distraction.

That's why she missed that turn on Berthoud Pass . . ." Georgia stopped. "Oh, dear. I'm so sorry. I should never . . ." Her voice drifted off. "The real truth," she said. "is that I hated Helene. I blame her for Julia. I always will."

Georgia must have seen something in my expression because she hastily said, "But I didn't kill her."

Then she looked me straight in the eye, hard, as though she wanted me to understand that what she was going to say was of the greatest importance. "But I wouldn't turn in her killer. Never. Because I think whoever killed Helene did the world a huge favor."

I blinked. "I didn't kill her either."

Georgia smiled slowly, her chin raised. "Trust me. I'll never, ever, tell."

The fact that Stewart trusted me to open his house for the workmen pretty much said he was innocent and had nothing to hide—or he'd already cleared anything incriminating. So, I'd go on the theory he was innocent but Helene may have tucked her journal away herself. And if not the journal, maybe something else. She was an inveterate note-taker.

I arrived at Stewart and Helene's house slightly out of breath and very fearful that the scent of burning oil was a warning sign from the Rust of an imminent and ugly demise. I hoped it wouldn't be mine, as well.

The workmen were sitting on the porch and smoking cigarettes. They rose as I came up the walk.

"You better get that car looked at, miss. It's really smoking. Probably needs a valve job."

"I think a valve job would cost more than I paid for the car."

"You *paid* for it?" He laughed.

I let them in, got them started on the ceiling repair, and danced all the way upstairs. I figured with my background, I had a better chance than most people, even most cops, of finding some kind of clue. I was looking for something of Helene's that others would overlook, like a scrap of paper or note to herself.

I started with the library, her former home office, and her telephone pads, bits of paper in her desk, under the telephone, even behind pictures on the wall. For a moment I was caught by the very blue eyes of Helene and Stuart as they looked happily out of an enlarged snapshot after a marathon race, still wearing their paper ID race numbers, sweat dampening their hair and slicking their skin, triumph written over their faces. Happier days for both.

Having found nothing, I went next to her closet off the master bedroom, searching her clothes pockets because she habitually stuffed notes in them, then through everything on her shelves, her dresser, even her shoes. Carefully, quickly, and thoroughly. Nothing. No journal, no note.

The bathroom yielded only the information that she used sunscreen religiously and in large quantities, and one or the other of them worried about fungus. Stewart, I decided.

Then to the basement laundry room. After all, she wouldn't have stuffed things into clean clothes, only things she'd worn.

I was working my way through the dirty laundry when I heard footsteps on the stairs.

Stewart's voice rumbled into the room. "Stop right there."

I held a pair of Helene's jeans. My hand in the front pocket closed around a scrap of paper. I palmed it and dropped the jeans back on the heap of unwashed laundry and turned to him.

"Yes?" I said brightly.

"I'm going to have you arrested."

CHAPTER 18

Very smoothly, I shoved the scrap of paper from her jeans into my pocket and said, "I knew I shouldn't have agreed to this. You set me up, didn't you?"

Stewart stood in the harsh light of the bare overhead incandescent bulb, his lean runner's body coiled in anger, his cold blue eyes hidden in the shadow of his brow. Was he a man with a killer instinct? He was a trial lawyer, after all.

I shivered lightly and wondered: if Stewart attacked me, would anyone think to look for me down here? I tried to moisten my lips with my tongue and found I had no spit in my mouth, which had gone dust-dry from nerves. The acrid, floral scent of laundry detergent was sickening and, I hoped, strong enough to cover the smell of my fear.

Helene always said Stewart prided himself on his ability to be reasonable. I figured it was my main, best hope. "You have always been the most reasonable man I know, Stewart, and while it might look strange, I'm merely trying to find who killed Helene. That's what you want, isn't it? Let's go upstairs and look at what facts there actually are."

"I know who killed her. You did."

"No, I did not. Someone is framing me for it."

"What a laugh! You're doing everything you can to screw this case up and hide your tracks. And to destroy my home."

I noticed his fist flexing. He could snap me in half despite my karate training, which consisted of three lessons after which the instructor refunded my money and said I had a singular ineptitude for it.

Maybe going upstairs where he could no doubt still see the damage from the broken water pipe wasn't a great idea, but staying down in the cellar with the dirty linen was more than dangerous.

Easing toward the door, I smiled the best I could under the circumstances and said, "I thought you couldn't leave the office because of work tonight."

His lip curled. "That's right. I'm overloaded with work, I've got court dates looming and briefs to prepare, and I'm haunted, thinking you're probably prowling around my house." His voice rose to a sharp edge. "So instead of getting all that done, I have to come out here, only to find you sifting through my late wife's dirty laundry."

"I can explain. Let's go upstairs where I can be clear."

"Where you think you'll be safe because the workmen would witness my wringing your neck? Well, they're gone now. I sent them away."

"Then you have lead-footed mice up there."

He lifted his head to listen. I stiff-armed him and dashed up the stairs to the kitchen, hoping my panic would outrace his speed. At the last minute I caught sight of a large bucket of plaster at the top of the stairs. I leaped and miraculously cleared it.

Stewart didn't see it, or he couldn't clear it. One foot landed square in the bucket. Arms flailing, he went down like a core-rotted cottonwood tree, big, broad, and bad.

Plaster splattered everywhere in the kitchen, even onto the hanging copper pan collection. The place looked like a snowstorm had hit. At the swinging door I realized he was down for the count and halted.

I went back to where he lay, swearing, his fists doubled

dangerously. Staying out of range of his long arms I said, "I'll get the workmen organized to clean up some. The housekeeper can get the rest of the plaster up."

I raised my voice to be sure the young man already scraping up the plaster on the floor would hear. "I know you didn't mean it when you said you would wring my neck. You were angry, right?"

He glared at me, murder in his eyes. "Go away. Please go away and don't come back here."

It's hardly fair to take advantage of a wounded, whimpering man, but he was down and I could still run and I still needed some answers. "Where did Helene put her latest journal?"

His eyes were screwed into narrow slits. "The last I saw, it was in her briefcase. She took it to her office."

"Just one more little question. When did Helene find out about your affair with Lizzie?"

His eyes popped open and he raised his head. "I wasn't having an affair with Lizzie. I'm only doing her work as a favor."

"Helene thought you were having an affair, though, didn't she? And she—"

"I don't know what Helene thought." He raised himself to his elbows, kicking hard at the bucket and wedging his foot in even tighter than before. "Damn! Go away!"

By the time Stewart had sat up. he was in despair. He pointed at the astonished workman eyeing the two of us. "Come here and get this bucket off my foot. But get her out of here first, before I kill her."

Edging toward the door I said to the man now gingerly at Stewart's foot, trying to help him out of the bucket, "You heard it here first. If I die, you heard him threaten me. Note the time and the place, please."

He shook his head and grinned. *"No comprendo, señorita."*

My luck.

Once safely in the Rust, I pulled from my pocket the note I'd found in the pocket of Helene's jeans. It was a little Post-it note, folded in half, sticky strip in, with the words "mars stone" scrawled in Helene's hasty handwriting. Mars stone? What, or who, was "mars stone"? I stowed the little note carefully in my inner, zippered purse pocket, the one where I keep my chocolate mini-bars. I ate the chocolate.

If Helene took her journal to the office, it was now gone. In fact, her briefcase hadn't been there either.

Of course, Stewart was downplaying his involvement with Lizzie. I was sure of it. Well, pretty sure. I decided to find Lizzie and hear her version.

It occurred to me that I kept coming back to Lizzie; every time anything came up, there was Lizzie. Always in the middle of things. In the middle of the office, in the middle of Helene and Stewart, in the middle of all my questions, not unlike a spider in the middle of its web.

I reached Lizzie at Techlaw. She was reluctant to meet me until I said I'd just been at Stewart's house and had something she might want to hear. Suddenly, she was more than eager. Thinking it very unlikely she'd rip out a pistol and shoot me in front of the happy-hour patrons, I insisted we meet at the Avenue Grill on Seventeenth, where the crowd would leave us fairly anonymous, yet in full view.

Lizzie swept in, her normally tidy hair loose, noticeable fatigue smudges under her eyes, and her cuticles bitten. I ordered wine for us, hoping it might knit up her frayed edges. "I was at Stewart's this afternoon," I said, "to let in the workmen and—"

"When did you and Stewart get so friendly?"

179

Friendly? I barely kept a straight face and waved a casual hand. "Oh, I wouldn't call it friendly, merely . . ." I stopped and looked at her with my best naïve expression. A little jealousy might well loosen her tongue. "I didn't think you'd mind . . . given the situation you're in."

"What do you mean? *What* situation?"

"That you and Stewart were . . . shall I say comforting each other when Helene was killed?"

Lizzie's mouth drew up in a sour knot.

"Stewart says it was only . . ." Again I stopped short and waved a hand. "You know . . ." I waited.

Lizzie's face clouded over, her gaze tight on the table top. Her wine glass wobbled slightly in her hand and she put it flat on the table. She swirled it, her lips compressed as if she were only containing her words with effort. Her lips barely moved when she asked, "Meaning what?"

I took a leisurely sip of wine. "I think Stewart made light of something important to you."

"What?"

"It wasn't mere platonic support, was it?" I barely stopped myself from mentioning the divorce work.

She blinked rapidly and whispered, "Did he make a pass at you?"

Well, certainly not the kind she was thinking of. I bit my lip, still playing on her jealousy without strictly speaking, lying. "Not . . . really."

"Dammit." She glanced nervously around the room. "I don't know what to do."

"Look, Lizzie, Helene was murdered. That's a fact. You and Stewart were having an affair, that's a fact. Stewart's saying it was platonic and is avoiding you." I couldn't say that's a fact because it was sort of supposition. "Where do you stand on all this? It doesn't look good for you. I want to hear your side of things."

She didn't seem to think that was unreasonable, although I couldn't quite figure out why. I assumed it was because she felt Stewart was denying her and her feelings were hurt.

In any case, the words she had been holding back burst forth. "Well, he better not be denying me because he was in on it every bit as much as me, more in fact. Our affair started when I was still working in his office. One night he had a brief due and I stayed late to help him and it all just happened. He took advantage of me when Harris was totally distracted with Techlaw. Helene was always gone on one trip or another and Harris . . . well, Harris was Harris. Continually at the office and unbelievably uninterested in me or what I was thinking. And Stewart was different.

"Neither of us planned it, but we had things in common. Stewart was so sweet, so attentive, so wonderful. I felt like I was living in a kind of bubble of excitement and love. Stewart said it was the same for him and it would never end."

Her eyes were huge and brimming with tears of self-pity. She took a healthy sip of wine, emptying her glass. I signaled the waiter for another for her, nursing mine.

"Then everything changed. Harris and Helene insisted I move to Techlaw and Georgia was brought to Stewart's office. Harris said it was to save money and because Helene couldn't stand Georgia." Lizzie's lips twisted in a bitter little grimace. "I'm positive Helene began to suspect something, got jealous, and insisted on the switch. But it didn't stop Stewart and me. If anything it brought us closer."

"And where did you and Stewart meet after that?"

Her gaze drifted up and to the right. "Different places, but mostly at the Sands Motel on East Colfax. It didn't really matter then, we only wanted time to be with each other."

"What about Harris? Does he know?"

"Oh, no. He's oblivious. The only thing that matters for him is the company. I could be dead for all he cares." She accepted the fresh glass of wine and sipped, licking her lips.

"There's almost nothing left in the bank and he's borrowed against our IRAs. He got a second mortgage on the house. He even forged my signature on the loan. I only found out by accident. Then I pulled a summary of our assets. That's when I decided I had to get a divorce." She shook her head. "There's nothing there now."

"You discovered this recently?" I asked, thinking of the bank sheets I'd seen in her desk the night I scampered into Techlaw.

"About a month ago. Something told me to get a printout from the bank. Sure enough, it all matches deposits into the company."

"Maybe he's simply lending it to the company."

"There's a difference?" Her jaw jutted out. "He didn't talk to me about it. He went right ahead and did it. It's the same as gambling or pouring money down a rat hole. What's going to happen to me?" She bowed her head and looked at her hands, clasping and unclasping. "I didn't mean to say all that. I don't know what happened, it just erupted."

"But you're really worried about something else, aren't you?" An uncomfortable feeling, probably guilt for taking advantage of a heartbroken woman, was gnawing at me, but I didn't let it stop me. "Lizzie, something is really eating at you. It's like poison and you'll be better if you let it out." I expected to hear that she thought Stewart was hot in pursuit of the lovely Georgia.

In a soft, almost inaudible voice she said, "Helene once mentioned to me she'd take Stewart to the cleaners if he so much as thought about divorce."

Where was she going with this? "When was that?"

Lizzie pursed her lips. "Before I switched jobs with Georgia, while I was still working for Stewart." She looked at me. "Do you think she suspected something way back then?"

Duh. I nodded. "Helene was not slow on the uptake. She'd have sniffed out Stewart's little affair with you within seconds of its initiation."

Lizzie swirled the wine in her glass. "Stewart had ideas about getting a judgeship, maybe even running for political office. A divorce could have hindered that." She finished the wine. "You know what scares me?"

I raised my brows in question.

She stared at her hands, now curled loosely in fists on the table. Her gaze lifted to meet mine. "I . . . I'm afraid Stewart killed Helene. I wake up nights in a sweat thinking about it."

Surprise made my voice husky. "I thought he was in Albuquerque."

"No, you don't get it. What if he *arranged* the murder?"

I had one of those moments when time seemed to shift sideways, slipping away from me for seconds, then I emerged into normal time and the sound around me started up again. It wasn't that I hadn't thought of it. What was so chilling was hearing it from another person, one whose lips had tasted Stewart's and enjoyed him, who knew him far, far better than I ever would. "How—"

"I don't know how, but he could do it. You don't know him; he's vengeful. It doesn't show, but he does things, little things to get back at people who hurt him. Or who he imagines hurt him."

That was a truly ugly thought. Secretaries learn a lot about the people they work for. More than is realized much of the time. But I needed specifics from Lizzie. She too easily threw accusations. "Like what, for instance?"

She looked at me. "Like when he blew out a picture window

in his neighbor's house because the guy cut back Stu's apricot tree where it hung over the fence."

"You saw it?"

"Everyone saw the window."

"I mean, you saw Stewart do it?"

She shook her head. "Of course not, but I was still working for him when his neighbor called and threatened to sue. Stu laughed. I thought he was really strong at the time, you know, a big he-man; now I know he's only vengeful."

"But you don't know for sure he did it."

"As good as. I'm surprised you haven't had something happen, for instance. My God, you've about done everything a person can do and survive him."

And she didn't know the half of it. I quieted my beating heart. "What else has he done?"

"Oh, I don't know. Lots of things. Something always happens to those who cross him. You wait, it'll happen to you, too."

It was a sort of secondhand threat, but it worked. My chest tightened and a chill ran down my back. As calmly as possible I said, "Well, let's hope you are wrong about him."

"You'll see," she said and gathered up her purse.

I put the tab on my poor old credit card, because, as she reminded me, I had invited her. We walked out together. "Lizzie, have you ever heard of 'mars stone'?"

She shook her head. "Doesn't sound like much to me. Certainly not a gem stone. I know all those. Maybe it's a rock, like granite. For kitchen counters. You think?"

We were nearly at the Rust when she pointed and shrieked, "I told you!"

The back window was smashed in. Little squares of glass sparkled all across the back seat. A note was pinned under the windshield wiper. Rough printing in block letters said: THIS CAN HAPPEN TO YOU, TOO.

The neighborhood around the Avenue Grill isn't the best, but I'd never had any trouble before. No one loitered on the street, no one seemed to be watching in order to enjoy the excitement of their vandalism.

Lizzie was almost triumphant. "See? I told you. Something always happens."

The glint in her eyes made me wonder, briefly, if she had arranged it to prove her point. I watched as she marched down the block to her own car. All the time I thought, *What kind of person declares her love for a man, thinking he's a murderer?*

Maybe someone who wanted to scare me.

It worked.

I shuddered, thinking about the close call I'd had that afternoon at his house. What if the workmen had not been there? Would he have killed me then? No, of course not. He was no fool. He'd be aware that Georgia knew I'd gone there.

A breeze ruffled the hairs on my neck, chilling me. No, a vengeful Stewart would wait, lurking in the shadows, until he could sneak up on me. And he'd probably do a whole lot more damage than a broken window.

CHAPTER 19

I spent half an hour trying to find someone in the area who had seen my car window get broken. I had no success. In the end, I had a lurking feeling that Lizzie had done it merely to prove her point. All the same, I decided preparations were in order, in case it became necessary to flee the Denver area with Mac.

A simple list helped. *Important papers, extra clothing, fluids and tire for the Rust, money. Rent a locker.*

On the way home I bought a case each of brake and steering fluids and put them in the trunk of the Rust. Next, I went to the gas station to check the spare tire. The Rust actually had an extra real tire. It was the weekend, so I'd have to wait until Monday when the bank was open to get big money, the last of my savings, but I withdrew some walk-around cash from an ATM, just in case.

That night, after Mac was asleep, I got all our important papers together—our passports, bank cards, social security cards and birth certificates, house and insurance papers—along with a small bag with extra clothing for each of us. Figuring someone might be watching the house, I carried the bags to the car under a coat, and I sweated in spite of the cool night temperatures.

I also decided I desperately needed to nail down some facts. I'd had one person or another telling me things, but none of the information had been verified. It could all be nothing more than lies. I went through my photos from the past few months and pulled out snapshots of Lizzie, Harris, Stewart, Helene, and

Sam, and put them in my purse. Tomorrow I'd work on truth and who was telling it. And I would start with Rosie and "mars stone," whatever that was.

The next morning, Saturday, at breakfast, I underscored to Mac that he should be careful and not talk to strangers, but how do you tell a child not to trust friends? And yet, that is what I did.

He chugged a glass of milk and looked at me like I was nuts. "I never talk to strangers."

"And for now, Mac, I don't want you to get into anyone else's car but ours, with me."

"Not even Barry's mom?"

"She's not with Techlaw. Barry's mom is okay. No one else, though. Even if they know your name and all. I don't know who to trust, so I'm not trusting anyone for now. And I want to make sure you're careful, too."

He wiped his mouth. "I'm always careful."

"And this morning I'll give you a ride to wrestling."

"Aw, I want to walk."

"Ride, Mac. Besides, you'll be late."

He picked up his sack lunch and headed out the door. "They all make fun of the Rust." In less than five steps he noticed the broken car window. "What happened?"

"It was simply a kid playing. He didn't mean to do it."

Mac blinked solemnly, his face worried. "It doesn't look like a kid threw a rock."

"Well, he did. Now get in. You're going to be late."

"Do you think we should bug out?"

I grinned to put him at ease. "We definitely do not need to bug out," I said to keep him from worrying.

After I dropped him at wrestling, I took the bag with the papers and clothing to a twenty-four-hour locker at the bus station. I pinned the key to my bra. I don't go anywhere without a bra—had a strict upbringing in that area.

I turned the Rust into the street and melted into traffic, as much as I could with smoke belching from the exhaust pipe every time I accelerated.

The truth was out there, waiting for me to find it. Because it was too early to call on Rosie, who had to work the night shift, I decided to start by verifying stories.

Stewart said his affair with Lizzie was platonic. Lizzie maintained it was passionate. I was pretty sure Lizzie's was the more accurate account.

Careful to look to see if I was being tailed, I drove to the motel she'd mentioned. It was located past some of the seediest parts of East Colfax, but it wasn't luxurious. Stewart hadn't exactly blown a wad on their trysts. The parking lot was tarmac, the hedge trimmed, the walls stucco and recently painted, but the lobby was depressing. A matronly woman sat behind the desk going through accounts. I smiled and in a chatty way asked how long she'd been running the motel.

She looked puzzled, but said, "About two years now. The hubby and I took it on as our retirement. I thought it would keep the hubby busy. He's not much of a one to sit around."

"Lucky." I surveyed the area. "You all keep it really clean and neat."

"It's a lot of work, too. I hadn't realized how much when we started this."

"And I'll bet your insurance bill is a tough one to pay, as well."

She looked very directly at me. "Now you didn't come in here to learn about the motel business, I'm sure, so what is it you're working up to?"

I looked down at my hands. "I'm not good at lying, and I don't see a need to. I need to know if a certain couple stayed here during the last year. The woman says they did, the man denies it. The answer will be kept private, you won't be involved, but I need to know. I'll give you two names—"

"Our records are not for public information."

I didn't respond and I didn't move.

"I can't hand over our register." She looked nervous. "It isn't really important, is it?"

"Yes, it is. And if I don't get the truth, I'm going to call Detective Wolfe of the Denver police, homicide, and he'll come get it."

"Oh, dear." She looked anxiously at the front door, then caved. "What are the names?"

She entered them in her computer, pulled up a list of ten dates. "You understand they paid in cash, so I have no verification that these are the real people. They could all be false names."

I pulled out the snapshots from my purse. "Do you recognize any of these people?"

She took them, her fingers trembling lightly, adjusted her glasses, and peered at them. "This one," she said.

"Stay long?"

Her face hardened. "He pays in advance and I don't see him leave."

"But he doesn't stay the night?"

She flushed. "Now see here. I don't run a brothel if that's what you're implying."

"Not at all. I need to know how long he stayed. No insult intended."

She huffed. "He pays for the night."

"One last question. Do you have anyone registered under the name Mars Stone?"

"I've never heard of him," she said and typed in the name. "Nope, nothing here."

I thanked her and got back into the Rust. After sitting in the sun for even that few minutes, the car was hot enough to slow-cook a mountain goat, which was what was happening to me. I congratulated myself on having confirmed Lizzie's account of things, but instead of lifting my spirits, it lowered them. There was no triumph in learning that Helene had been betrayed by two people she knew, one of whom had once vowed to love, honor, and cherish her.

I tried a self-affirmation, but it didn't do much. Even with three more self-affirmations, including a desperate promise that I'd get my hair cut as soon as I had an extra few bucks, my dauber was really down.

Having discovered Stewart lied big-time and Lizzie's account of the affair was the most truthful, I decided to delve into the words "mars stone." Was it at all possible she was referring to tombstones or countertops? I was no geologist, and knew next to nothing about rocks, but I figured a cemetery would know a lot about rocks and I wasn't far from the one Helene was buried in.

I drove over there, found a shady place in the parking lot under a linden tree for the Rust, and walked to the office. A somber young man with a dreadful habit of wringing his hands shook his head and said there was no "mars stone" that he knew of. Granite and marble were the customary tombstones, although there were other varieties of markers available. He gave me a pamphlet.

The cemetery itself was quiet, almost park-like, the grass green and peaceful. I strolled to Helene's grave and sat on a nearby bench in the shade, a gentle breeze lifting my hair from my neck, the sun dappled and warm on my face. A temporary marker and a simple vase of lilies stood at her grave.

I was alone except for a man in the distance, lingering by a grave, probably communing with the person therein. A few minutes of peace for me and then I'd go forward in my quest for the truth.

I skimmed the pamphlet. Then sleepy, I closed my eyes, enjoying the faint, dry scent of pine and dust in the air, listening to the birds and the distant sounds of traffic, muted by the pines along the cemetery. Cicadas droned in the rising heat, a kind summer surf sound that left me nearly asleep until a shadow fell over my face. I raised one eyelid.

Detective Wolfe stood before me, his dark eyes narrowed to near oblivion in his face. He wasn't smiling. "Let's talk."

Before I could stop myself I said, "What, are you staking out her grave now?"

Wolfe sat heavily on the bench beside me, then pulled out a pencil and little notepad that nearly disappeared in his hand.

I swore to myself. I should have known the cops might be watching Helene's grave. Every third mystery story said so. Even I could begin to understand why they'd think I was guilty. Everything I did added to their suspicions.

He looked straight into my eyes, close enough that I could see that the amber lights I had noticed before were dark, his emotions masked. His gaze dropped to his notepad. "I've been doing a little checking. You come from a very distinguished family, which you carefully never mention."

"You never ask."

"Did you think I wouldn't find out?"

"Why would I tell you about my family? You don't tell me about yours."

"I'm not a suspect in a murder case."

"And my family has nothing at all to do with this."

I tried to tell myself it didn't matter, that it didn't prove a thing, but my cheeks turned hot and my temper rose. "I love my family and you're denigrating them. I had hoped you'd approach this case with an open mind and a dispassionate view and I rightly figured that my family's background would not tend to leave you objective. I was right, wasn't I? Now that you've read a little background, you're ready to wrap up the murder of Helene."

He crossed his legs. "You see, I don't understand why Helene Foster would bring you all the way out here for a job she could hire anyone for, unless she had a little pressure to hire you." He looked at me steadily. "You wanted to get out of Chicago, right? A little matter of your family's reputation made it hard to keep a job there, maybe. Starting over would sound very attractive, wouldn't it? Enough to pressure Helene for a job."

"Helene came to *me* in Chicago. Ask Lizzie. She heard Helene say she had someone in mind for the job."

"Lizzie has no memory of this and the telephone records for Techlaw show telephone calls from you to Helene a month before she came to Chicago."

"She sent an email saying she'd be in Chicago and suggested we get together."

"You have proof?"

Of course I didn't, unless the old message was still out there in the ether, available to techie whizzes. But that was the stuff of television shows. "Helene asked me to meet her in the bar that evening. Her invitation. She brought up the possibility of a job."

"You have a witness to that?"

I thought back. "There was a dark-haired suit sitting next to her at the bar when I came in. Could have been anyone. She picked up her drink and we sat in a booth. I don't even know when he left. If he left."

I stood.

He ignored me. "It plays this way. She fired you before you could pass probation, while she still could without having to give a reason. You went to see her Thursday night, lost your temper, and killed her. Then it was simply a matter of finding a place to dump her body."

"She owed me money, why would I kill her? I never saw her again after she fired me. Didn't even talk to her. You're hassling me when you should be looking long and hard at Stewart Foster. He was having an affair with Lizzie Bruckner and had plenty of reason to want to be rid of Helene."

"Stewart Foster was in Albuquerque that night."

"He could have purchased a hit."

Wolfe's mouth twitched. "You have more contacts with that sort of person than Stewart Foster does."

I nearly saw red. "I don't think you've even looked into anyone else. What about Harris Bruckner? Sam Lawson? Neither of them had any great love for Helene! Have you even begun to look into them?"

"Sam Lawson was out of town from Wednesday to Sunday that week. At a conference. Verified."

"And Harris? And Lawrence Gifford, or do you think that because Gifford's an attorney he has to be innocent? Seems to me you've been sitting on your assets, trying to figure out how to hang it on me because I'm not in a position to make trouble for you."

Wolfe straightened, the expression in his eyes hard and angry. "Look, I have been checking it all. You are the one with the problem."

I walked away, fast, angry, and a little frightened, clenching my teeth and fists. Wolfe's questioning left me shaken, almost ill. Did he really know something, or was he merely fishing?

Worse, he was doing his best to nail me for a murder I hadn't committed, yet simply sitting on the bench with him had set me vibrating. How could I be attracted to this man? And yet I was, and it only made everything worse.

Opposite the place I'd first seen the man I now knew was Wolfe, I slowed. A single white rose lay at the foot of a simple granite stone engraved "Elizabeth Wolfe, Beloved wife, June 4, 1970–November 19, 2002." Today was August nineteenth.

Oh dear, no wonder Wolfe had been so tired and bitter.

I had wished Helene dead and she was now dead. I had wished for a new car and got one new to me. I had wished for excitement and found a body in my car trunk. It was ridiculous, but out there in the bright sunshine and the ninety-eight-degree dry heat, I shivered.

As I was climbing into the Rust, Wolfe came across the parking lot toward me. He had waited for me. A thousand different feelings flooded through me, leaving me unable to think straight or say a word. I slammed the car door and started the car. A cloud of blue exhaust belched from it.

Wolfe knocked on the window. I lowered it.

"What happened to your rear window?"

"Someone wanted the valuables I keep in the car."

"And the note?" He pointed to the passenger seat where the note lay printed side up. "Looks to me like you've rattled someone's cage."

I shrugged. "Seems to be my life's story."

"You should take it very seriously, Francie. And get yourself a lawyer. A good one."

CHAPTER 20

Easy for Wolfe to say "Get a lawyer." Not so easy when you don't have the cash to pay for one. They don't come free.

I left the parking lot in a small cloud of exhaust—in search of more truth, although so far, it hadn't brought me joy or even relief. But it would. It had to.

Next I'd talk to Rosie, about Helene's journals and maybe a little truth about Julia Orbach.

It was nearly ten in the morning; I still had plenty of time before I needed to pick up Mac. The Rust had a sort of smoky smell, so I chugged down the street toward Rosie's house at a stately pace, trying to ease the strain on its obviously suffering motor.

Her address lay north on the dismal end of Denver's downtown diagonal streets, an area of mildewed homes in a bewildering meltdown of old age. Some were small gingerbread Victorians of two and three stories, others tiny brick hovels shrouded in decay and sumac trees. Nearly all of the oldest homes were in a state of disrepair and wore a minimum of five mailboxes, indicating slumlord subdivisions.

The windows of the houses were curtained against the street life, except for Rosie's. Her house had wide silvery strips of duct tape covering cracks in the front window pane. The cracks were in a stellar pattern, as though the window had been shattered one dark night by a thrown rock. Or a bullet.

Rosie's house was a tiny one-story brick, with porch-fatigue and peeling paint. It had only one mailbox and cowered in the shadows of a two-story brick Victorian whose latest coat of paint probably dated from World War Two and contained enough lead to poison a small Chinese city of a million or so.

Rusty iron grills covered Rosie's windows, all on ground level. The house was so small it seemed to shrink behind a birch tree that someone had hacked off halfway up and which had since sprouted several defiant shoots trying to maintain life. Underneath the tree a scrawny rose bush pushed toward the sun. Sort of the way I thought of Rosie, struggling against all odds.

The little yard was denuded, hard-packed clay, the grass worn away years ago. Even before I reached the porch, I smelled house halitosis as years of musty, moldy odor oozed from it.

I stepped onto the porch. The boards groaned under my weight. Generations of dirt coated the worn porch boards and the sandstone ledge of the single round-topped front window. Lace curtains sagged in the window. Depression leaked out of this house.

I told myself I shouldn't have come; Rosie was probably sleeping; I would only add to her troubles. I started to leave.

And then I noticed the front door was ajar.

Jesus, Mary, and Joseph, give me strength. Good burglars don't leave the door ajar; it's too much of a clue to the rest of the world that they've been there.

A small voice that sounded a lot like Dad's voice, in the back of my head, said, "Run. Put one foot in front of the other and leave."

I couldn't do it. A front door ajar in this neighborhood, even in this heat, was a very ugly omen. Rosie might need help. God, I hoped she needed help. Needing help implied life and hope.

I raised my fist and banged on the screen door. No answer.

The possibility that I could help her impelled me to open

first the screen door, then push open the front door, using a knuckle so I wouldn't leave a print, another lesson from Dad.

I called out, "Yoohoo!" but my voice was barely audible, even to me. No answer.

Despite the grime outside, inside Rosie was a meticulous housekeeper. The thin carpet was swept, the cushions straight on the sagging couch and chair in sixties-style Spanish gothic with scratchy, worn orange-plaid upholstery. No dust on the old floor-model television. Framed pictures hung on the walls, sat on the end tables, crowded the top of the television. Family, friends, mementos of happy days. And no dust anywhere. She would have to clean daily to keep it under control in this grass-less neighborhood.

The air was heavy and seemed to drag on my legs and feet as I moved toward the back of the house. My heart pounded with fright. I wanted to run away, scamper out to the safety of old Rust, yet even hesitating brought the thought of Rosie suffering, praying for help. I couldn't walk out on her if there was any hope of life.

"Rosie?" I squeaked. Ashamed of the fear in my voice, I repeated myself, louder. "Rosie."

The floor creaked under my feet. The carpeting was ancient, faded until the pattern was no longer visible except as a brown-ish under-footing. I crept down the hallway to the first door. Her bedroom.

A crucifix hung on the wall over the head of a double bed that nearly filled the tiny room. A chipped mirror, held together with wide, clear package-sealing tape topped the only other piece of furniture, a dresser on which lay a hairbrush and comb, neatly aligned. The window shade was pulled tight to the sill. I flicked on the light switch.

Her purse, upended, spilled contents across the bed. No wal-let or coin purse. Carefully, I poked it open. No credit cards

197

that I could see, though maybe she didn't own any.

Dreading what I would find, I continued down the hall to the kitchen where sunlight fingered through a vine-covered window in shafts that gave a subdued golden glow to the small square room. For a moment the light held my gaze, then I looked down to the cracked linoleum flooring.

Feet.

I eased forward, aware of an odd silence. Not even the hum of the refrigerator or the buzz of a fly against the window pane broke quiet.

Her toes pointed up and outward; her thickened ankles were mottled. She wore a lightweight, short-sleeved housecoat of well-washed pink-and-white-striped seersucker. Her head was turned to the side, her eyes open, glazed and sightless, her mouth open in a mute cry. Her hair was a tangle of dark curls, made darker by clotted blood.

Rosie was dead. I knew it. I could feel it in my bones. All the same, I knelt over her and felt for a pulse. In hopes.

The skin on her neck was still warm, but not warm enough for life and her wrist was too cool. There was no pulse, not even a flutter. Like Helene, she had a neat, deadly little hole above her ear—small, but deadly. Probably shot by someone she knew and trusted. Someone for whom she may have been going to make a cup of tea.

Blood pooled under her head in a dark, dead stain. A teakettle lay on the floor, surrounded by a similar pool, only that pool was water. She must have dropped the kettle when she was shot. It had rolled to the wall and leaked, just as she fell and bled. And from the amount of blood, I guessed she had lived for only a few minutes.

Tears would have helped, but I had none. I felt cold and a terrible helplessness pressed down on my shoulders and made my breath come in ragged gulps. One day I would weep for both Helene and Rosie, two very different women, both of whom I owed something to. It would be a hard debt to discharge.

"Gott im Himmel," I said, slowly and softly like Granny used to say. *"God in heaven above, take this woman to your breast. Care for this loving soul and give her rest."* Granny outlived most of her friends and family. There were a lot of funerals and I went to most of them. I'm as good at funerals as I am at picking locks.

I stood. *Forgive me, Dad, but I've got to call the police,* I thought. Feeling ill, I rummaged in my purse for my cell phone. I found it, pressed 9-1-1 and gave the address and the information, then pressed in the numbers for Detective Wolfe.

He answered, listened, and then said, "Go outside and wait. Don't go anywhere and make sure no one goes in. You think she's dead?"

"I couldn't find a pulse or a breath." I couldn't describe her head, the words stuck in my throat. "Please hurry!" I rang off and put my phone back in my purse. And then, my teeth chattering with a chill that had nothing to do with the temperature of the air, I started to shake. First Helene, now Rosie. Who would be next? Too frightening; I couldn't think about it. As if on autopilot I forced myself to concentrate on things at hand, burying messy emotions. This would be the last time I had a chance to look around.

Washed dishes air-dried in the drainer. The back door had three locks, one a chain lock, engaged. Whoever killed her had walked in and walked out the front door.

Why? Why kill Rosie? Was it the journals? Had someone thought she might have taken them? Or was it something she knew? Something she said to the killer that let him or her know she had tumbled to them? What would Rosie know?

On the counter a basket held mail—bills straightened out, ready to be paid, probably waiting for her next paycheck. I took a pencil and used the eraser end to do a quick riff through, but all I found were the usual heat, light, and water bills. A bank statement revealed a pitifully small checking account. Her telephone bill showed regular calls to several out-of-state numbers, all to area code 505. Probably family. I jotted down the two most frequently called numbers and let the bill fall back into the basket.

I tiptoed into Rosie's bedroom and looked quickly under the bed and under her mattress. No journals, not even dustballs. I checked her dresser, careful not to leave prints, and then went to the living room.

A stack of magazines sat on the floor next to the end of the couch, where it was evident she sat to watch television. I sifted through the stack. No diaries. Not there, not under the cushion of the couch.

Stymied, I started looking through the pictures that covered the top of the television and the walls. One card showed a picture of a young, rather plain young woman with cynical eyes, smiling broadly, sitting in the midst of a petting zoo with a goat looking over her shoulder and chickens at her feet. Printing at the bottom said simply: "Me, at the Orbach family reunion. Love Julia."

I hadn't found the journals, but I had found this small proof of a relationship with Rosie, and I figured it was Julia and her relationship with Rosie that was the key to Helene's murder.

Without even thinking, I slipped the picture into my purse. I was halfway across the living room when I realized my family genes had kicked in. Do those automatic impulses ever go away?

I pulled the picture back out, wiped it down with the edge of my T-shirt, and replaced it on the TV. Dad would have been so disgusted.

CHAPTER 21

I sat on Rosie's porch, still dry-eyed but shaking. My watch said it had been five minutes, but it seemed hours later when the fire rescue truck wheeled up, followed by a squad car.

Pointing to the door, I squeezed a word out of my dry throat, "Kitchen." In what seemed like five seconds but was actually five minutes, a paramedic came back out, shaking his head. More police arrived; the paramedics piled back into the fire rescue truck and left.

Within twenty minutes Wolfe came, face grim, fatigue written all over it. His jacket was rumpled, his navy polo shirt open at the collar, his trousers loose as though he'd lost weight recently. He looked at me with an expression I couldn't read. His voice was gruff. "Wait here, I've got questions for you."

He looked too tired to remember it was Saturday, which meant Mac had to be picked up early. "I have to pick up Mac from wrestling at one."

"He'll be all right there. Don't leave."

I called the YMCA, explained I was unavoidably delayed, and asked them to hold him there inside until I could pick him up personally. The straggling rose bush in the little corner of Rosie's yard had only one last blossom. As I gazed at it, a light breeze scattered its petals in a flurry of blood red across the hard-packed dirt. Was that how rose bushes wept?

Wolfe returned forty minutes later and stood close. I could feel his body heat and see the tiny creases at the corners of his eyes. "Let's go to my car."

I felt my cheeks go cold. Was he going to arrest me? Please God, no.

He looked at me for a long minute, then his expression softened and he drew in a breath. "All right, your car."

I turned away, blinking so he wouldn't see the quick, hot sting of relief in my eyes, and walked quickly to the Rust. Then I remembered. The Rust stank of exhaust and the front passenger door didn't open from the inside. "I don't think it's such a good idea. Maybe we—"

"Do you have to argue with everything I say?"

"But the door—"

"Get in! I don't have time to argue."

His dignity was going to regret it. I would give him maybe fifteen minutes before sweat would gather on his forehead. It was already trickling down my sides in miserable little trails.

He yanked open the door and slid into the passenger side.

I called out, "Don't shut your—"

He slammed the door drowning out my last word, which would have been "door."

Oh, well. I took a couple of deep breaths to jump start the oxygen in my arteries and slid in behind the steering wheel.

He pulled out his little writing pad and flipped to a new page. "Okay, talk. Everything. Not some edited version you think will play for me. I'm sick of you carefully feeding me an edited version because you think I'm some moron who can't be trusted with information."

I waited until I thought he'd cooled off a bit, then told him about finding Rosie, putting in every detail I could think of to make the story long and seemingly complete. I omitted the examination of her bills. And the look under the bed and through her magazines and through her family pictures. And the little episode where Julia's picture jumped into my hand.

I did my best to look innocent and vulnerable.

He muttered something to himself. He was an unhappy man. He turned directly to me, eyes steady. "I want everything."

"Everything? Okay, here it is. Lizzie and Stewart were having a torrid affair. Helene discovered it. I don't know what she did about it, or intended to do about it, but knowing her, she'd do something. Sam said he thought she was asking for a divorce. He also implied that Helene wasn't entirely without fault, but I don't know what he meant. Perhaps you can look into that. And finally, Julia Orbach continues to surface, and I believe your investigation into her death was superficial."

Wolfe rubbed his temple where a sizable drop of perspiration had started to run down his cheek. "But why did you come here in the first place?"

I didn't want to tell him about Mac's additional confession Thursday night. It would be setting Mac up for trouble with the law and God knows I knew how devastating that could be to a kid, innocent or not. The trouble was, omitting things to Wolfe was hard, but outright lying was *real* hard. I wasn't good at it anyway. "I just figured Rosie would know about Helene keeping journals."

His face stilled, his gaze tight on me. "Francie . . ."

I swallowed. I tried not to, but I felt my breath coming a little quicker.

"Talk, dammit." His eyes were dark, thunderous. "I mean it."

Even my scalp burned. I flapped my hand, fanning my face, and wondered if this was what a hot flash would feel like.

He caught my wrist, his fingers easily wrapping my forearm, and leaned in close, crowding me until I could feel his anger hot on my cheeks. "The whole truth, Francie. Every bit of it, or—"

"Or what?"

"Or we go downtown right now."

He was so close I could smell his shampoo. A flicker of something showed in his eyes and he let go of my arm, so I capitulated and told him about Mac's second confession Thursday night, the one he hadn't heard. "I'm sure the woman he saw was Rosie. I hoped she would let me see Helene's journals and tell me about Julia Orbach."

He looked at me sourly. "And you saw no reason to let me look into it? I've got half a mind to jail you for obstruction of justice. Maybe that would make it clear to you that lying to me is not going to work. I don't know any other way to get you to listen to me."

"I meant to tell you, but the next morning Mac told me about being teased and that drove everything else out of my mind. Then work was the pits. And then, after I went to Stewart's house and he chased me out of the basement and stepped in the bucket and fell over, I forgot."

"What else has Mac confessed to?"

"Don't pick on him. He's been through a lot in his short life." I checked my watch. "I need to pick up Mac. I can go through this story without varying details for the next six hours, or we can simply agree that once is enough, for now."

I looked straight into his eyes. What was he thinking? Why so irritable? Had Rosie's death gotten under his skin? A cop with feelings? There was a novel concept.

His jaw set. "And if I said you were under arrest?"

"I'm not trying to be defiant or obnoxious. I really need to pick up Mac. If I'm late after all he's been through lately, he'll be terribly worried. I just can't do that to him."

The front door of Rosie's house opened and the coroner's men rolled out the gurney with the body bag on it and bounced along the uneven front walk. The small crowd that had gathered melted back into their homes.

Everything crashed in on me. I could barely draw a breath.

My eyes stung. I was riding some kind of emotional roller coaster, one moment angry, the next tearful, the next curious about a cop's feelings. At once distant from, then entwined in, emotions I'd buried for years.

With Wolfe, I had no idea. Half the time he seemed fair, aboveboard and dealing straight. The other half of the time there was a certain reserve and, I swear, an absolutely hot attraction. Him for me. And me for him. Like opposite poles of magnets.

Given my family background, an attraction to a cop was impossible, a capitulation to the enemy. I would never be able to take him home to meet the relatives, for fear they'd all be on wanted posters. Besides, although his wife was dead, Wolfe wore a wedding band, so if he hadn't remarried, he still felt wedded. To her. The deck was stacked against any relationship other than antagonistic. And yet, it was almost moth-to-flame time.

I swallowed and said as clearly as I could, "Out of my car, please. I have to go." I wished my voice had been a little stronger, but at least I said it.

He looked at me and glanced at his watch. "Don't leave town, don't go nosing into anything, and—"

Before I could stop myself I interrupted with, "And don't take candy from strangers?"

His chin raised. "Don't push me." He worked the door handle.

I had forgotten about the door.

He yanked. The handle came off in his hand. "What?" Scowling, he tried to roll down the window. The window crank turned without moving the glass. He turned to me. "What in blazes?"

"It has a few flaws," I said and got out of the car to open the passenger-side door. He stepped out, his expression fierce, his cheeks flushed.

I shoved the door shut. "I tried to tell you."

He caught my forearm, his fingers firm but not bruising. "Look at me. Are you snooping around in this just to try to earn Foster's ten-thousand-dollar reward?"

"What reward?"

"The one he announced on TV last night and in the papers this morning. That reward."

"I didn't know about it. Great idea, though."

Wolfe's cheeks turned dusky. "Have you thought about the danger? That woman in there was doing the same thing you're doing, snooping. She wasn't a fool, and yet she's dead. Do you want that for yourself? Who will pick up Mac if you're six feet under?"

The warmth drained from my cheeks. "I get your point."

"I hope so. I really hope so. One of your small circle of friends is killing all the others. You could be next. You'd make a lovely corpse, but I'd hate to see it. And it would devastate that kid of yours." His dark eyes were intense. "By the way, I did some checking. You've never had a baby and there's no record of a marriage or an adoption."

That was true. I had guardianship; the adoption wasn't final. I could control my facial expressions, but not my autonomic nervous system. In spite of the sweltering heat, I went cold and rigid. "What are you saying?"

"Where are his birth parents, and why isn't he with them?"

"Because they're dead. He's mine and he's a very bright kid with a ton of potential if he just gets a break. And I'm here to see that he gets it. That's my mission, and nothing will stop me." I was a little surprised to hear my voice quake as I finished.

Wolfe wasn't impressed. "You have papers?"

"Of course." My hands were shaking, my heart thumping. This hit too close to home. Why did Wolfe bring it up?

One more time he moved in close, his head bent close to mine. In a voice so low I barely heard him, he said, "Francie, this could go farther than you imagine, way beyond you."

He turned on his heel and walked to his car, then before he climbed in, he looked back at me, a play of emotions crossing his face, as though he was at war with himself. Was he going to say more? He shook his head and got behind the wheel.

What did it mean? Was he truly worried about me? Yes, I thought, but it's bigger than that. I sensed he knew something worse, something far, far more important.

There was only one thing worse, a threat to Mac.

The face of the adoptions judge in Chicago flashed before my eyes. "To love and protect . . ." And that meant . . . I couldn't bear to finish that thought.

CHAPTER 22

Suddenly very frightened, I drove a couple blocks, then pulled to the curb to add the essential fluids to the Rust, pull myself together, and assess my situation, which was bleak.

I had to do something. I was down to flight or fight. Would I run? Hide out? Get a gun? And do what? Kill the rest of the world? The only thing I knew for sure was that there was no way I'd risk anyone taking Mac from me.

I drove through downtown to the bus station and retrieved my bundle of essentials from the locker. Then I made for home, threw some clothes into a brown paper bag, added the cell phone charger, a few snacks and swimsuits, shook the remaining crickets into Spike's cage, locked up, and got back in the car. I also decided that I wouldn't talk much in the car, just in case it was bugged.

My actions didn't seem so much paranoid as just plain sensible, given Rosie's murder. If Julia also were murdered, and I believed she had been, then this killer had done in three women. No reason to think he wouldn't do another. And if the killer didn't come after us, the cops would, or perhaps social services.

By the time I picked up Mac I had myself under control, had a plan, and had left a message on Wolfe's office phone that I was staying in the metro area, but I was vacationing. I emphasized vacationing.

I made a quick call to Sam, to let him know about Rosie and

to tell him we were taking some time off.

"I'm glad you're doing that," he said. "You've got to keep Mac safe. He was looking a little stressed at practice today."

"You stopped by the gym?"

"Yeah. I like to see the kids. Mac's got real promise, you know."

"What made you think Mac was stressed?"

"He looked kind of down. Maybe I'll go to the mountains for a bit, too. Might be safer."

"So far, just being male seems to be safer."

Avoiding the front because of the door, Mac climbed into the back seat. He seemed unusually subdued. I asked, "How was wrestling today?"

"I'm quitting."

Uh, oh. "Why? You love it. And you're doing really well."

"Just am." The two parallel lines between his brows were practically an inch deep in frown and his brow formed a little shelf, hiding his eyes.

"You're a natural wrestler, Mac."

"I'm not going back."

My stomach clenched at the very thought that some of the kids were teasing him and he didn't want to admit it. What a terrible day. Everything had gone to pieces and the day wasn't over.

Then another, more horrendous, thought hit. "Did someone do something to you?"

"I'm not talking."

Teeth clenched, mind churning with all the vicious possibilities, I drove until I reached the Holiday Inn at the Tech Center, south of the city, and parked. Mac and I would be close enough to Denver without being exactly there and, I thought, it was definitely not the first place anyone would look for us.

I'd kill whoever hurt him, but I kept my voice neutral. "Did anyone touch you in a bad way?"

He looked at me, surprised. "No. Not *that*."

Oh, relief. "Then what?"

He shook his head. "Nothing!"

"Drugs?"

"No. Stop it!" Mac's jaw was set, his mouth compressed. "I'm not talking."

I grabbed the bag from the back seat. "Okay. Come with me."

"Why are we here?"

"We're taking the weekend off. It's a vacation."

"Oh."

I expected to hear "Wow!" It's Mac universal word for anything he likes. Something truly terrible must have happened to him.

Feeling ill from anxiety, I signed in for the room, using the name Bagylady, paid cash, and we settled in.

"Anything to eat?" Mac asked.

I handed him the sack with snacks. He ripped open a bag of chips. Compulsive eating—the sign of trying to fill the void of a loss, I thought, and reached for a handful myself.

We went out for lunch. Mac shoveled the food in, I picked at mine, and we both suffered the elephant-in-the- living-room effect. If we wouldn't talk about the big thing, then we couldn't talk about anything else. Mac struggled silently with whatever demons were bedeviling him. I mulled over what I could do next.

After a brief rest, we went to the dome and I watched Mac swim. I had two huge problems: Mac and the murderer. Mac took precedence.

When we were back in our room, showered, dried, and dressed, I broached the subject again. "Mac, either you tell me what happened or I'll call your coach. Which would you prefer?"

"It's not your business."

"Yes, it is. I'm your mother, I love you, and that makes it my business. We have to hang together."

"So?"

"That means we are honest with each other. We share the things that matter. Believe me, it makes it easier in the long run."

His face wrinkled. "*You* don't tell me everything. You didn't tell me about finding that woman this morning. I saw the news at the Y. The television crew panned the whole street and I saw the Rust and then I saw you, so I know you were there."

"I was afraid it would bother you."

"It does."

"Is that why you're quitting wrestling?"

He curled up in a stubborn ball on the bed. "No."

"Mac, I'm going to call your coach." My cell phone rang just as I reached for it.

It was Mac's coach. "Miz Starzell, I don't know what happened. He's doing great. He's in the heavyweight class for his age, he's a natural at wrestling, and I thought everything was going great, and then after he got dressed he said he was quitting."

"Was that before he watched television?"

"Yeah, had to be. We were still in the locker room and I was doing my team talk. We've got a big match coming up next Saturday, a week from tomorrow. I was counting on Mac."

"Don't take him off the roster. I'll see what I can do. By the way, what was your team talk about?"

"Honesty and responsibility. I like to give the kids a shove in the right direction. This time I was talking about being responsible, taking care of business, and the importance of being honest. Next practice is Tuesday. He *must* be there to be in the match."

I promised the coach I'd try to find out what was bothering Mac and rang off. Mulling it over, I thought that responsibility was something Mac took to easily. Taking care of business was also easy for him, so *honesty* had to be the problem. I wondered if this was tied to Mac's story about the gun.

Mac caught me looking at him. "What?"

"I'm thinking about everything that's happened and all the things you've told me."

The sneaky look I'd seen on Mac's face when Detective Wolfe asked him about the gun again crossed his face. There *was* more that he hadn't told me. "Come over here."

He slowly moved to where I sat on the bed and dropped beside me, slightly uncomfortable. "Yeah?"

Of course he wasn't just going to spill his guts, nothing so easy as that. "I know you think about things a lot. Especially at night when you're going to sleep."

I waited.

He sucked on his lower lip. In all it took about fifteen minutes of saying a few little words, but mostly just waiting him out. Finally, he said, "I think everybody is lying."

That wasn't quite the answer I'd expected. "Like what?"

"Like, Mrs. Foster lied to you about the job."

"And . . . ?"

"Then she lied about you being lousy at your job, and they lied about paying you. Maybe Mrs. Foster lied about something more, and they found out and got mad—"

"You think the lying led to her getting killed?"

He swallowed. "Coach said lying causes bad problems. Liars can't be on the team. And that lady that got killed today . . . she might've told lies too and caused trouble."

Lying was the million-dollar theme here. "Has that ever happened to you? Maybe you said something not quite right, not meaning to cause trouble? Maybe a while ago?"

Silence.

"Maybe some time when the words just fell out of your mouth?"

"I don't lie."

"But maybe accidentally?"

He hung his head. "Maybe."

"Like about the gun at the Fosters'?"

He nodded.

"The gun wasn't really in the plant, was it?"

He shook his head, his gaze on the floor.

"It was my gun, wasn't it?"

"Yes," he whispered.

There was only one way he could know for sure it was my gun. "You had the gun before that night, didn't you?"

"Yes," he whispered.

"I think I need to know the whole story, honey. When did you get the gun?"

He squirmed. In halting words he said, "The day before the Fourth of July. I wanted to show it to Barry. He didn't believe that I . . . I mean, we had one."

"Did you show Barry?"

"Just a little bit." Mac raised his chin. "It's a cool little gun. No hammer—it fit right in my pocket."

My God! I hadn't had the gun lock on it, either. How could I have forgotten? If Social Services learned of this, they'd have an even stronger case against me. There were so many things I forgot. How did people learn all the parenting things necessary to keep a kid alive until twenty-one? Feeling sick, I pushed on. I needed to have the whole truth, bad as it might be. "And then you took it to Mrs. Foster's house?"

"I stuck it in my pocket before we left. It's not very big. I thought if anyone bothered us, I could just . . . shoot 'em. I

213

know how to shoot. Dad used to take me to the shooting range."

I felt a chill go right down my arms and spine. This child had carried that unreliable, dangerous weapon around ready to kill. "How did it go off?"

Mac wiped his eyes with the back of his hand. "When that woman came back out of the room, she was covering up some books with a coat."

So Mac had seen a bit more than he'd told me before. And Rosie had indeed taken Helene's journals.

Mac continued. "She looked right at me. I got real scared and I got the gun out. I backed up and bumped into the toilet and started to fall and the gun went off. And then I dropped it and it went off again."

He swallowed, eyes brimming. "I was real scared again. And then water started coming up from the floor . . ." Tears spilled out of his eyes and streamed down his cheeks.

"Do you know who the woman was?"

He nodded, wiping his face with the back of his hand. "They showed her face on the TV. It was the one who was killed this morning."

My God, how close he had come to killing himself and Rosie. I couldn't say a word, my mouth was so dry just thinking about it. "Now tell me why you were frightened."

"She looked so fierce at me. I thought she was going to get me."

"Did she come toward you?"

"I thought she was—that's why I backed up and fell over the toilet."

More tears, flooding his face.

"Come here. Sit on my lap."

"It isn't big enough."

"Try it." I patted my thighs. He sat. I put my arms around him. He really was getting big. "Mac, whatever happened to

Rosie isn't going to happen to us."

He was silent for a long moment, then shifted painfully on my legs and said in a hushed voice, "How do you know?"

"I think she was killed because of those books you saw, the journals Mrs. Foster wrote. Rosie took them and the person who killed her wanted them."

"Now that they have them, they'll be satisfied?"

"Something like that," I said and hugged him. "Did you quit wrestling because you knew you had lied?"

"Yeah," he said. "Do you think something bad will happen? Is that why we're here? Hiding out?"

"I thought it would be sensible to be somewhere else for a while."

"Maybe we should go to Alaska."

"We're as safe here as we would be anywhere. If we leave town now, Detective Wolfe will think we're running because I'm guilty. Mac, I need to know, do you have any more secrets?"

He shook his head and wiped his nose with his sleeve.

"Any more weapons?"

"No. I wish I did." His jaw jutted out in stubbornness and worry. "All I've got are those old handcuffs that are sort of broken. Even a baby could get them off. We should call Uncle Andy. He'd get us another gun."

"No. We don't call Uncle Andy or Grandma Lil. Guns don't solve a thing. I wish I'd known earlier that you had my gun."

He dropped his chin to his chest. "I'm sorry. I was afraid if Detective Wolfe knew you had a gun he'd blame you." He looked at me, his eyes filling again. "I don't want him to take you away."

"Sweetie, he's not going to take me away. I'm yours now. Always. I don't go away. We just have to be careful for a little while." I squeezed him. "And now that the person has the books, we're safe. And I think it's almost all over. Detective Wolfe has almost got it all figured out." May God forgive me for that lie, but I wanted him to stop worrying, at least a little bit.

He put his arms around me, strong and tight. "I'm glad," he said.

Tears stung my eyes. I had no idea how strong he was; he didn't either. I could barely breathe in his grip, but those words, "I don't want him to take you away," were so wonderful, I just hung on and enjoyed it and hoped I wouldn't black out from lack of oxygen.

CHAPTER 23

Sunday morning dawned bright and cool for a change. Sometime in the night the air had cooled and freshened and a little breeze blew from the southeast. It was welcome. And so was the call from Mom. Her crisp no-nonsense voice on my cell phone filled me with a sense of security, way beyond reality. I wished I could do the same for Mac.

Handing the phone to Mac, I cautioned him not to mention anything about Rosie, the gun, or any other trouble. "Keep it light. We don't want to worry Lil."

He nodded and took the phone. "Hi Grandma, guess what? We're on a vacation at a motel with a swimming pool."

I cringed, but he talked on about day camp and Spike and when I rang off, Lil was her usual cheerful self, no piercing questions, and I breathed a sigh of relief. The last thing I needed was Lil out here to "help." As Dad always said, "She means well but creates Hell."

I finished the Sunday *LA Times* crossword, cut out the *New York Times* puzzle, and took Mac to the dome to swim. It was late enough to call the numbers I'd jotted down from Rosie's telephone bill. I was hoping whoever was at the other end could shed light on what Rosie had been involved in before she was killed.

While Mac splashed and played, I rang the first number, the one Rosie called most often. A flat female voice answered on the second ring. I said, "I'm calling about Rosie Donaugh . . ." I let my voice trail off.

"Sheriff said she was murdered."

"I'm so sorry for your loss. She was a wonderful woman. I wonder if I could talk to you about her? I'm trying to find out what I can do to help out up here and I found your number among her things. Are you a relative?"

"I'm her sister, Ruth."

"I talked to Rosie a week ago and I knew she was worried about something. Did she talk to you about it?"

Long silence. "I guess it can't hurt. She said she got some books from that other woman that was killed, the one she used to work for. She thought they'd tell her how Julia died."

"Was Julia your daughter?"

"Niece. But don't call Julia's folks. They're mighty upset and Julia's mother has been a little off ever since Julia passed over. Know what I mean?"

"It's hard to ever accept someone we love is gone."

"Well, Julia was no angel. She was a sassy little girl, too smart for her own good, but she didn't deserve to die like that. Rosie thought she could prove it was murder if she found those books. I guess she must'a told the wrong person about them."

"Rosie was convinced Julia was murdered."

"We all are. Julia did a lot of things well and one of them was driving. She used to hang out with the boys at the little stock car racetrack we got here. She could drive those cars better than most of them. So hearing she didn't make a curve on some mountain just doesn't hold true. But your fancy-pantsy cops up there wouldn't listen to us."

"So Rosie decided to look into it?"

"Well, she felt a little responsible. See, she invited Julia to go work there. Julia always wanted to go to the big city. Said she'd just grow old and ugly buried out here. So she got to die young out there, instead. Just about killed her folks."

"So Julia was Rosie's niece?"

"Yeah, but they was always close. I think on account of Julia's mom being a little spooky, even back then. I think it was the hot wind took her wits."

"Did Rosie tell you who she thought had killed Julia?"

"To tell the truth, I think she was scared."

"Did she ever mention 'mars stone'?"

"No."

"Did Julia ever mention friends of hers here?"

Long silence. Then, "Well, not really, just her roommate. Julia shared a house with a Georgie somebody."

I'd bet two to one, Georgie was Georgia Jenson, Stewart's lovely secretary.

"We was hoping we'd get to meet her," Ruth continued, "but it never happened." She sighed. "So many things never happened."

There were little sniffling sounds, then her voice somewhat choked said, "You know, Rosie left a message on the phone day before yesterday when I wasn't home. She was going to call yesterday morning 'round eleven our time. That's how come I knew something awful had happened even before the sheriff came to the door. We always talked on Saturday morning. Sometimes more, but always on Saturday morning."

"Do you know Georgie's last name?"

"Nope. Might'a known it once, but I sure don't remember it now."

"Do you remember Julia's address?"

"Oh, yeah, it's here somewhere. Hold on."

I could hear the sounds of rustling in the background. Also, a television evangelist. Then Ruth said, "Here 'tis. As I thought, it's 4244 Hayward Place."

Upstairs in the hotel room, I looked up Georgia Jenson's address: 4244 Hayward Place.

After yesterday's tongue-lashing, I carefully left a message for Wolfe with the information I'd just learned from Rosie's sister in Kansas. Just as carefully, I did not mention I was taking Mac for a ride to see Georgia Jenson. She and Julia had shared a house. Georgia had to know more about Julia's death than she'd admitted. With Rosie dead, Georgia was the only one who'd really known Julia before her so-called accident.

I changed into a navy slacks and simple white cotton blouse, in order to look a little official and still be reasonably comfortable.

We got in the Rust, Mac in the back. "I always have to ride in the back," he grumbled.

"You can ride in front."

"Yeah, sure. I can get in but I can't get out because it doesn't open from the inside. And the way the engine smokes it'll burn up."

He was right. At the rate it was deteriorating, I figured it would barely last another week. I released the hood. "Yeah, but this way you get to add oil and brake fluid."

Mac happily poured in oil and brake fluid, spilling only a little.

I drove north on I-25 to the viaduct over Platte Valley and the train yard and continued west, timing stop lights to avoid unnecessary stops. Georgia lived in a northwest Denver neighborhood with mature trees, shaded lawns, and small, tidy homes of varying ages and styles on single lots.

I passed her tiny blond-brick ranch house and parked in front of a modest house with an overgrown spruce tree.

"What now?" Mac asked.

"Here's what I need you to do. Watch to see who drives by." I handed him a pad of paper and a pencil. "Write down the license plate numbers of each car that comes by, especially if they're going slowly or if they park. Stay low. Don't let anybody see you."

"Gotcha."

I didn't really need Mac to do that, but if he didn't have an assignment, he'd be out of that car in plain view in no time. "Wait for me, stay low, and keep the car locked."

I crossed the street to a house where I'd seen the curtain move, and knocked with a firm hand.

A small woman, thin and wiry with springy graying hair pulled back from her lined face, answered so quickly I knew she'd been standing by the door. "If you're selling magazines I don't want any. The last time I ordered, it took more than six weeks before they came." She glared to make her point.

Trying to be ingratiating I said, "I'm not selling anything. I can't tell you what agency I'm from, but I'm doing a background check. It's routine when anyone applies for a government job."

"Sunday's a kind of odd day to work, isn't it?"

"Can you tell me who all lives with Georgia Jenson?"

"Nobody, except that awful basset hound that humps everything and everybody on the block."

"Basset hound?"

"That thing molests tree stumps and small children. He digs out of her yard all the time. Just tunnels under the fence." Her head jerked up and she pointed to Georgia's house. "See? That beast is out again."

Across the street a huge basset hound tore down the block, ears flopping, thick little legs churning, tongue out at the side, a string of drool whipping beside him.

"There *she* goes now."

Georgia burst through the gate in her back yard and raced down the block after her dog.

"The only thing that'll solve that dog problem is the

graveyard."

"Thank you for your help," I said and left to cross the street, tempted to enter Georgia's house.

I knew the neighbor was watching me, though, so I waited until Georgia returned, panting and dragging the basset at the end of a leash, his tongue nearly on the ground. I swear he was grinning.

Georgia saw me and alarm spread over her face.

I grinned, trying to disarm her. "You're a very good runner."

She shortened the leash on the basset and said through gritted teeth, "Careful, he's been known to bite."

Yeah, like I'm known to trust people. I smiled. "What's his name?"

"Seymour. He's a trained watch dog."

"Nice. Georgia, I need to talk to you, either here, in your yard, or in the house."

The expression on her face told me she would rather gnaw on a raw rat. "What about?"

"Julia Orbach. Your roommate. Why didn't you tell me she was Rosie's niece and lived with you?"

She shrugged, still trying to catch her breath. "Oh, come on in. I guess if you're going to kill me, you'll do it wherever we are."

"If I were going to kill you, you'd already be dead."

Her expression said she believed me. She led the way through the gate into her tidy but barren back yard, the grass scratched off by Seymour's fat little toe nails. Bricks and stones lay along the bottom of the fence in an attempt to keep Seymour from tunneling, but he obviously dug past them whenever the spirit moved him. It appeared to move him fairly often.

Georgia pulled a plastic lawn chair under the shade of a walnut tree, and sat. Seymour rolled onto his back at her feet and stretched his hind legs out long, begging for a good rub.

Georgia absently stroked his belly with the toe of her tennis shoe. All of which merely reinforced his behavior. The neighbor was right. Death would be the ultimate trainer for this creature. As I set a chair in the shade, I noticed the smell of dry, baked earth, hot bricks, and a faint scent of doggy urine. "Why didn't you tell me about Julia?"

Georgia's pretty face, flushed from her run, wrinkled. "What difference would it have made?"

"Rosie's dead now, too. Maybe it would have stopped that."

She glanced away. "Maybe nothing would."

She looked back at me, her cheeks pale. Little beads of perspiration lined her brow. "Maybe you didn't notice, but Rosie was more than a little passionate about what happened to Julia. She was convinced Julia was murdered."

"But you accepted it as an accident."

"Sure I did. The police investigated, and they said it was accidental. You should have seen how Julia drove. She put the pedal to the metal, especially when she was upset. And she was very upset then."

Georgia dropped her head onto her chest and looked at Seymour as she petted him with her toe. "You had to know Julia. She said her mother was a little unbalanced and had a history of hospitalizations for it. Rosie overreacted to everything too, but when she heard Julia was dead, she really lost it."

A little breeze fresh with the scent of green leaves cooled my forehead. "Rosie's sister said Rosie thought she knew who killed Helene and Julia."

Georgia raised her head, her gaze moving slowly around the yard. "I don't believe her. Julia maintained that an odd strain ran in the women of the family."

I remembered the card in Rosie's house with the picture of Julia, but I wanted to move her off the family eccentricities. "You and Julia lived together, right?"

She nodded. "We kept it quiet. Julia felt that if we told anyone at the office, it would look peculiar . . . too close, I guess. I never worried about it. I loved Julia like a sister. Not sexual, just soul mates maybe. I didn't think it would make a bit of difference, but she did."

Georgia's blue eyes were vague and troubled. She blinked rapidly as though she were clearing away memories as well as gathering tears. "There were so many things Julia thought I didn't pay much attention to. I didn't think they were important. I guess I should have listened."

"Like what?"

"Like when she wondered if Gifford had his hand in the till. 'Tentacles everywhere' were her words."

"Did she say anything to Helene?"

"When she first hinted at it, Helene exploded, so Julia decided to put data together to show Helene. According to Julia, Helene yelled at her." Georgia shook her head. "You always had to take a bit of the emotion out of what Julia said. That's why I only sort of listened."

"And then?"

"Julia stayed angry for a couple of days, and then she was found in the mountains. Dead. She missed a curve."

"And the report?"

"I never saw it."

"Did she leave any papers or anything?"

Georgia bit her lip, then dodged the question. "Julia lived with Rosie when she first came to Denver and Rosie didn't want Julia to move here."

"Julia's family knew her address was here."

"Yeah." Georgia smiled sadly. "Julia wrote home a lot and she finally just used my address. I don't know if she ever told them I lived here, too."

"You didn't go to her funeral?"

"I wish I had." She shook her head. "But it was in Kansas and I couldn't afford to take the time and I didn't know how to handle her family."

"What did you do with her things?"

Again Georgia scanned the yard, as though looking for an escape. Finally she said, "I gave all her clothes and stuff to Rosie. I just kept one box." She looked my way. "Do you think Rosie was killed because I told people she had Julia's stuff?"

"When did you tell them?"

"Last year."

"More likely Rosie was killed because she said she knew who killed Helene."

Georgia sighed. "We all do such stupid things."

There wasn't much to say to that. She was right. We all do stupid things. I'd done a number in my lifetime.

I walked to the car and told Mac he could play in Georgia's back yard with Seymour, the drooler dog. Then I descended into Georgia's unbelievably tidy basement and started through the box of papers.

Julia had indeed been pulling things together, but her data was different than mine. She had printouts showing a downward trend in revenues and a rise in client cancellations. The data I had pulled was nothing like Julia's, yet the tables seemed the same. How had they changed? And something else I hadn't gotten was a list of clients who inquired but didn't follow through. I scanned Julia's list.

Halfway down was a lightly penciled notation on the side of the page. "Mars Stone." Both words were capitalized, as in a name. Below that was the name "Lawrence Gifford."

Upstairs, Georgia was standing at the kitchen window, watching Mac playing with the basset. She turned when she heard my footsteps on the stairs. "Find anything helpful?"

"Possibly. It would be real smart not to tell anyone, though.

Did Julia ever mention Mars Stone?"

Georgia's eyes widened. "You know, the night before her accident she had the phone book on her lap and rang a whole series of people asking for Mars or Mark Stone, but she never found him."

Well, dang. Mars Stone probably wasn't a variety of granite. He was probably a killer. "Did she say why she was trying to find him?"

"No. She wouldn't talk about it."

CHAPTER 24

I was nervous about being seen, but Mac insisted that a food reward was in order, and because we had to eat sometime, I stopped at the Dairy Queen for cuisine rustique. I argued with myself about eating healthfully and lost, settling for a hot fudge sundae and iced tea. Tea is healthful. Mac washed the drooler dog's slime off in the restroom, downed a large fries, burger, and Coke, and finished it all with a Snickers Blizzard. He scraped the last of it and said, "Francie?" He looked troubled. "We've got to feed Spike."

"She'll be okay till tomorrow."

"But—"

My cell phone rang. Even with a quick call, my ice cream would turn to mush. I let it go to message. It was Sam. After I scraped up the last of the hot fudge, I rang him back.

"Would you consider a movie and a pizza?" he asked.

I tossed the empty ice cream cup into the trash. "Thanks, but no, not this time. We're sort of bonding here."

"Bonding?"

"That's where you spend time together with someone you like so you know them better."

"Well, the three of us could bond."

"I need to get a good start with Mac first, Sam."

There was a prolonged silence. I imagined Sam trying to get his glasses to stay up on his nose. Finally I said, "I've got a question for you, Sam. What does Mars Stone mean to you?"

I heard him breathing on the other end of the line. "For God's sake, Julia Orbach asked me the same thing, not long before her accident. If you're snooping, it could be real dangerous."

"What does it mean to you?"

"It doesn't mean a thing, except that you could end up getting hurt. Maybe you don't care, but I do. You and Mac matter to me."

"Look, Sam." I used his name to make sure he listened. "I'm a big girl and I can take care of myself."

The silence again. "This means we're not going to the movie?"

"Yes, I guess so."

I don't think it ever occurred to him that tonight was the one-week anniversary of my finding Helene in the trunk of my car. Not an event to celebrate under any circumstances. It had seemed much longer than a week to me.

That night at the motel I looked through the phone book for Mars Stone. Marissa, Mark, Marshall, Marvin, Mary, but no Mars. Thinking Mars might be a nickname, I called all the initial "M" Stones and the Marshall Stone, and got nowhere. I even called Wolfe's office number and left him a message about Mars Stone on his tape recorder.

The next morning, Monday, I took Mac to day camp. I circled the block and let him out at the back door so he could scoot inside unseen and the other kids wouldn't see the Rust belching exhaust, which was clearly worse today. I reminded him not to tell anyone where we were staying and not to leave day camp with anyone but me.

When I got to Level One, I parked the Rust in the lot next door, on the sheltered side of a large van. Then I stole down the alley and entered the building by the back door. By the time I reached the office it was a bit after nine o'clock and a quiet buzz of sales pitches filled the room. I checked my mail slot, found my third paycheck, for Friday only, since I hadn't worked Saturday morning, and opened it. Good thing Spike didn't eat more, because forty-five dollars minus withholding, minus FICA, was barely enough to buy crickets. I had to start putting in more hours. I tossed my purse in the drawer and pulled on a headset.

By eleven o'clock I was feeling ill from tension. If I didn't work more soon, we'd go hungry, but if I didn't clear myself, it wasn't going to matter because I'd be fed my three squares in the pen. I decided I'd give telemarketing another half hour. Then I'd put my energy into action, stir up trouble, and see what, or rather who, surfaced.

If I reached Techlaw's attorney's office before noon, most likely I could catch Lawrence Gifford going to lunch and ask about Mars Stone. No doubt the interview would be brief and tense. I just hoped it wouldn't be deadly.

Thinking about it made crawly tension sensations in my chest, growls in my stomach, and I almost hoped Wolfe would come by so I could get into a huge fight and relieve some of my nerves.

Finally, at eleven thirty, after three unsuccessful sales pitches and two hang-ups, I took a call from an elderly man with a gentle voice. He hesitated as he spoke, as though he was a bit unsure of himself. "I might be . . . interested . . . in talking about . . . a funeral."

"There are a large number of options from which you can choose to personalize the service you select."

"Like what?"

"For instance, you can choose what kind of coach your loved ones ride in to the cemetery, the kind and quality of resting case—"

"You mean casket?"

"Er, yes. You also can select music, either live or recorded."

"Could I record something to be read at the service?" He seemed to have perked up considerably.

"You can talk to the Everlasting Life Funeral Home representative about it. I'm sure you can arrange it all just as you like."

He was quiet for a beat, but when he spoke, his voice was significantly stronger. "See, what I also need is someone to provide the body."

Uh-oh. "Provide the body?"

"As in, I give the name, they go get them."

Oh, great, a nut case. And he had sounded like such a nice man. Nice and gentle. Harmless. Would I ever learn? "If you'll write down this number I give you and call right away, you will receive a great deal of attention, no charge to you. The man who answers may help in ways you haven't thought of."

"Great."

I gave him Wolfe's number, the one that goes directly to his desk phone, which I assumed would be recorded and caller ID'd. Now let Wolfe say I never called him.

"If you'll hold, I'll have my supervisor verify everything." I marked him for material and a referral to the funeral home and switched him over to Ethel. Give her something to do. Yeah!

I continued to think about the soft-voiced, gentleman-killer who wanted to record his own service. It troubled me that I'd so totally misjudged him, simply because he had a soft, almost musical voice that I associated with kindliness. How many times had I done that? And then I wondered if I had made a mistake not to take him even more seriously. At least I still had his name. I dialed Wolfe and left a message for him, including the name of the man I'd spoken to.

I was still thinking about it twenty minutes later, wondering what other situations I was blinded by discounting the danger, when the pencils on my desk chattered with an approaching storm. Ethel. Her scowl was so deep her eyes were nearly invisible when she hauled up at my desk. Maybe I'd discounted her danger index as well.

"I'm changing your assignment. Starting next week you'll be selling lawn fertilizer."

From funerals to happy horse shit, all in one week. "Is this a promotion?"

"I do not find that humorous. Your hours are low, your sales rate dismal, and if you don't do better in this new assignment, you may have to work elsewhere."

The few others near me in the room hid in their carrels as they listened. No one wanted to be associated with a funeral failure.

I worked steadily with somewhat better results, in that I referred three calls to Ethel. Between calls I thought about the fact that I had gone so far on hunches and assumptions, based on my personal reactions to people, without getting solid facts to back everything up. More importantly, without giving credence to their potential for danger. I especially thought about Laurence Gifford.

By eleven-twenty I couldn't wait any longer. I packed up and left for Gifford's office. Since his secretary doubtless wouldn't let me in the door, I planned to catch him in the little parking area behind his office. Once there, I lurked near the gray Mercedes SUV I figured belonged to him, versus the six-year-old Honda Civic that had secretary written all over it.

I was wrong, of course.

Laurence Gifford came flying out the door and went straight to the Honda. I caught him as he was climbing into the driver's seat. He had put his briefcase on the passenger's seat, so unless he packed a pistol under his fitted suit, which I doubted, I was safe approaching him. I stepped to his window. "Hey!"

"What do you want?" He snarled at me. His head jerked to the right and back. The tic movement again. Where else had I seen him? I was sure it was important, maybe key.

"What does the name Mars Stone, mean to you?"

He was slow to answer. "It means nothing to me, except . . ." He stopped, then said softly, "Julia asked the same question."

Did his lowered voice indicate menace, or was he thinking? In my case, was there a difference? I plowed on. "She thought you were guilty of dipping in the company till, didn't she?"

He jammed the key into the ignition. "I don't know what you're talking about."

"I'm talking about the constant drain of money from Techlaw, the Chinese drip of company destruction. Explain Julia's notation of the name Mars Stone and your name right under it."

"You're making connections that aren't there." He made that odd, jerking motion to the right again.

Then I placed the motion. "Chicago!"

That's where I'd seen the odd move before. "You were at the bar, sitting next to Helene when I got there, the night she offered me the job. Helene and I moved to a booth. You remained at the bar. I thought you were just some stranger."

"Impossible."

"My daddy used to say, 'If he lied, he had something to hide.' So what are you hiding?" Of course Daddy was referring to squeezing one of his partners, but it still held. I waited. No response.

I lowered my voice, hoping it would sound more ominous and *noir* and said, "Helene and Stewart were having marital problems. Helene was a *very* attractive woman."

His chin raised defensively and he did that odd little jerk to the right again. "I think it's time for you to leave."

I planted one hand firmly on the car window and leaned toward him with my best evil eye. It had always worked on my brother Andy. "Helene wanted a divorce, correct?"

"I was the company lawyer. I don't know anything about Helene's personal troubles."

"You flew to Boston, registered at your conference, flew right back here, and drove to her house that Thursday night because you knew Stewart was out of town. You argued with her. And when she threatened to tell your wife and blow this all open, you killed her. She was a small woman and you're a very muscular, fit man. All you had to do was put her in your car, drive to my place, leave her in the trunk of my car, and take the red-eye back to Boston. And a simple check of the parking stub from DIA will disprove it. I'll bet you can't produce it."

He was probably a good poker player—he kept his expression almost still—but I'm better, and I read the tiny lines around his eyes. They relaxed slightly. He probably had a parking stub.

His lips stretched into a menacing grimace. "Helene was attractive, someone I admired, but we were never lovers."

I'd missed the mark. If he didn't react to accusations about Helene, then he was sensitive to the audits. "But your audits weren't quite correct, were they? Were you just lazy, or did you fiddle around with them on purpose?"

His fist clenched. "Can you really afford a lawsuit? Believe me, threatening people results in short, ugly endings."

I gave him my best, inscrutable, snake smile. "Think about it, Mr. Gifford. An investigation of your audits wouldn't be pleasant, or discreet."

He gunned the engine, his confidence clearly rising. "I was in Boston from Thursday afternoon until Monday morning at the bar conference. And I have witnesses. Now take your hand off my car and stand back, or get run over."

I had to jump out of the way as he wheeled out of the parking space.

Back in the hot, sweaty safety of the Rust, I put together

what I'd pried out of him with what I suspected. He had either fiddled the audit figures, or dipped into the cash flow, or he'd rubber-stamped Techlaw's figures without checking. I suspected the latter and that he went to Chicago to plead with Helene not to hire me and to let him off the hook for his lousy audit. Others had killed for less.

I tried very hard to shrug off Lawrence Gifford's threat, but in the end I pressed in the numbers for Legal Aid, thinking that I could at least get them started on my various legal problems, not the least of which would probably be a suit by Gifford. They, however, referred me to the public defender.

At the public defender's office a tired, tinny voice said, "Lots of times the DA never files charges. We have too many cases to start working on ones that might not come up. We only take cases where the charges are clearly filed. Otherwise it could be a waste of our time."

A waste of time. So now I was not only suspect number one, threatened with a lawsuit by a nasty-piece-of-work lawyer, and the victim of a car-window smasher, I was a waste of time. Some days it was just plain hard to be upbeat.

I was still whining to myself when my cell phone rang.

Harris's voice boomed out. "Lizzie's missing."

CHAPTER 25

My first reaction was oh, no. Not another murder. Surely not Lizzie. "Did you and Lizzie have an argument?"

"What does that have to do with it? She's gone. Kidnapped!"

"Did you call the police?"

"Of course. They said they'd look into it, but I don't think they're gonna do a thing."

"When did you see her last?"

"Yesterday afternoon, about four."

Sunday afternoon? Why did he wait? "Why are you calling me now?"

"Because the police won't bother with it for three days and I don't know who else to call. And you helped before, at Helene's wake."

Like that made me some kind of rescuer? Still, Harris was clearly frantic. I pictured myself if Mac were missing. I'd be insane. He probably was, too. Then I thought about Lizzie. "Look, Harris, I'll try to see if I can find her. I'm pretty sure she just decided to go somewhere and cool down for a bit. I'll give you a call as soon as I know anything."

It was one o'clock. I was pretty sure I knew where to find Lizzie. Dealing with her, though, meant I'd need all the energy and control I could muster, so I swung through a fast food stand and snagged a sandwich to munch while I cruised east on Colfax.

Sure enough, I spotted her car at the Sands Motel where she

and Stewart had spent time together. Just to be on the safe side, I looked for Stewart's car, but it was nowhere to be seen. I parked and brushed crumbs from my clothes.

The woman at the desk recognized me and raised her chin defiantly. "I'm not talking to you."

I slapped the counter. "Have you seen her *alive* lately?"

The color in the woman's cheeks paled.

"We can go together, or you can give me the room number and I'll just quietly knock on the door."

She glared. "Sixteen."

Number sixteen was on the end of the row at the back. I knocked firmly. "Room service, Missie," I squeaked.

"I didn't order anything." Lizzie yanked open the door, saw me, and said, "Oh, crap! What are you doing here? I don't want to see you or talk to you. Go away."

My relief at seeing her alive withered. I stiff-armed my way inside, noting the sickening sour smell of old wine. "Are you all right?" I should have asked if she were sober.

"No," she answered and back-stepped until her knees hit the edge of the bed. She sat abruptly. "I feel like killing myself."

"Are you going to?"

She raised her chin in a show of attempted toughness. "If I did, Harris would get the Waterford."

I wasn't sure her weird humor was healthy, but at least she was trying.

The expression in her eyes was strained. "If you've found me, everyone else will. I've got to get out of here."

"Going home?"

"I can't. Harris is in a rage. He found out about Stu—"

"Hold it," I cut her off. "Where was Harris the night Helene was killed?"

"Working late. As always."

"Who saw him?"

"Rosie. He said she was his alibi." Lizzie looked at me, her eyes wide and blurry. "He doesn't have an alibi now, does he?"

No, he didn't. And if he was counting on Rosie for an alibi, it would make no sense for him to kill her. Unless she really wasn't his alibi, but a witness who had begun to blackmail him.

I made a mental note to check with the cleaning company to verify she worked the night Helene was killed, but I was sure Detective Wolfe would already have done that. "Tell me about Helene's message again. When did it come in and how?"

Lizzie's forehead wrinkled with the effort. "I got to work at quarter to eight. Harris came with me. At my desk I found a message on the phone that said, 'I won't be in today, please reschedule any appointments.' "

"Did it sound like Helene?"

"Of course it sounded like her. She said she wouldn't be coming in. She always said that."

"She called in often?"

"She usually worked from home on Friday."

"Did the police check your phone?"

"They took my message machine." A peculiar expression spread across her face. "It wasn't on the message machine. It was on my phone." She turned a little pale. "I had just signed up for a message service on the phone line. For personal stuff."

"Did Helene know about it?"

Lizzie shook her head. "No one did," she whispered. She pointed at the door. "Harris."

"Would he know?"

She shook her head. "No, he's here."

The door of the motel burst open. Harris stood in the doorway, his barrel chest practically filling it, his hair spiking in disarray. "Don't move! I have a gun."

A wild man waving a gun. It might have been funny but the gun was very real. My heart did a double loop and thump.

Guns have a nasty way of going off, when held by hysterical people.

Harris said, "What have you done to Lizzie?"

I kept my voice low, but couldn't keep the bitterness out of it. "Nothing. Nobody has done anything to Lizzie. She's right here, trying to think things through rationally. But, obviously, she called you before she started thinking!" What a mess.

Harris stepped inside. Still pointing his gun in my direction, he craned around the door until he saw Lizzie sitting on the bed. "Lizzie, get in the car."

Ashen-faced, she tried to pull herself together. She rose, walked stiff-legged to the dresser where she'd laid out her considerable cosmetics, and turned dramatically to face Harris. "I'm not going with you," she said and swept her collection of creams, lotions, and lipsticks to the floor. "I'm sick and tired of you bossing me around like a child."

He glowered at her. "You need it. You are a child."

Her chin jutted out farther. "I'm not, either. I'm a grown woman. I can think for myself, can't I, Francie?"

She had done pretty well for two sentences. I glanced at Harris. He flicked the gun dangerously toward me. "You, get into this chair."

I didn't move. I couldn't. My feet were rooted to the floor in sheer fright. Where were the cops? Where was Wolfe's great detective ability when I needed it?

Harris waved the gun again. I had visions of the back half of my head splattered across the room. "Careful! That thing could go off."

"And what a loss that would be."

"The manager knows I'm here. She'll get the police."

"I'll be out of here by the time they get here. Now move."

Of course I didn't move. Lizzie sat down again on the

unmade bed. Her voice softened as she said, "Harris, you don't
..."

She was losing her determination. A few more minutes and
she'd cave. So I spoke up, hoping to stiffen her resolve. "Lizzie
is furious with you for bankrolling the company. She thinks
you've jeopardized your future and she'll end up in the
poorhouse."

Lizzie crossed her arms across her chest in an attempt to look
forceful. "Like she says, I can too think!"

Harris ignored Lizzie and raised his gun until the barrel
pointed right between my eyes. His eyes narrowed down to
mean slits that started a shiver at my neck and moved down my
spine. He was desperate and furious. A deadly combination.
"I've had enough of you," he said.

My heart thudded, my ears rang with fright. Would I ever see
Mac again? "If you harm me, you'll take the fall for Helene's
murder and Rosie's murder. People will blame you."

His face seemed to expand and turn purple. "I've worked all
my life for that company. My only crime is that I couldn't find
the cause of the money loss."

"And you filed papers with false information in them to get a
loan for Techlaw."

His face turned even redder. "And some little worm has
ruined it for me." He turned to Lizzie. "Is that you, Lizzie?" he
asked, his voice low and cold. "Are you the little worm?"

She cringed into a corner of the bed. "I didn't do it, Harris.
Stop it. You're scaring me."

"But you betrayed me." His brows knit together in a long
dark line across his face. "You threw our marriage away."

The odds that the manager had spotted Harris with a gun
and would call the cops were not good. I eased toward the
bathroom. Maybe I could barricade myself in the bathtub.

He continued, "You think you can slime out of our vows

because I work late?"

"It just happened. All I really wanted was your attention. I didn't betray you, I just expanded our agreement a little."

Oh, Lizzie. Not a good thing to say.

He bellowed and swung around, the back of his hand and the butt of the gun clipping the side of my head. I went down, trying to catch myself, expecting to hear a gunshot and feel a bullet any minute. Instead I heard the beautiful warble of a siren.

Harris swore, stuffed his gun in his jacket pocket, grabbed Lizzie's arms, and pulled her toward the door. "Well, you've got my attention now."

"Oh, Harris," she breathed, "you're so strong."

"Lizzie!" I said through my pain. "What's your message password?"

"Dammit!" she squeaked and grabbed for his arm. She was a good-sized woman, but she snuggled in and put her head on his shoulder as he propelled her out the door and marched her to his car. He shoved her into the front seat.

Would he hurt her? I doubted it. Somehow, Lizzie would emerge unharmed. She was one of those people who walked through life without a scratch, while the world around crumpled. I had seriously underestimated Lizzie and Harris, but there was another person I had underestimated.

I reached for the telephone. The cord dangled in my hand. I ran from the motel unit as Harris pulled out of the driveway into traffic. An ambulance raced down the street, siren wailing. So there weren't any cops after all.

From the manager's office I called Wolfe, who was finally in, and told him about Lizzie starting the telephone messaging service and Harris taking Lizzie. He said he'd put out a pickup order for Harris, and asked me to meet him at Techlaw. He'd bring a search warrant. We could check Lizzie's messages. I prayed we weren't too late.

Wolfe drove into Techlaw's parking lot at ten past two, the same time as I did, so he must have already had that warrant. Interesting. He stepped from the car, pulled on a rumpled navy jacket, and met me on the front steps. His hair fell over his forehead in a dark thatch, but nothing hid the fatigue on his face.

As soon as he drew near, my heart started to pound. I was banking heavily on Lizzie's message still being on her phone. If it wasn't, I would be adding to my considerable trouble. We walked through the lobby and took the elevator up. Techlaw was closed. Where was Sam?

Wolfe looked at me, waiting. "You have keys?"

"Yes. Don't you? Didn't you find Helene's office keys?"

"We never found them. We believe the killer kept them."

I thought of Lawrence Gifford. He claimed to have witnesses to establish his alibi and he had sounded truly sincere, as well as angry, but he made such a good suspect. He was cold, arrogant, and a nasty piece of work. I wanted to blame him. "If the killer took the keys, maybe it was because he didn't have any, meaning he didn't work here."

"Or she had just been fired and didn't have any."

My throat constricted, making it hard to talk. "Well, Helene never asked me for mine, and I kept them. These are not hers."

"You can prove that?"

"Inside I can," I said and unlocked the door. Did Wolfe believe me? His thoughts hid in the shadows of his eyes.

Inside Techlaw everything looked as usual. Lizzie's desk was tidy, the wastebaskets were empty, the carpeting vacuumed. The air was still, stuffy, with no obvious scent, no lemony furniture polish. I stepped next to Lizzie's desk, scanning it. "Wait," I said. "Something's different."

"We don't have all day."

I laid down my keys and purse and sat in Lizzie's chair to try to figure things out.

Wolfe reached for the receiver, using a shield and two fingers. I told him to use "dammit" as the password. He pressed in the keys, then the speaker button. Then he pressed "one" for saved messages. Eerily, Helene's voice sounded in the stillness, barely distinguishable over the background noise of traffic. She sounded rushed, as though she were speaking as she walked.

"Lizzie, I won't be coming in today. I'll work from home and be in touch by cell phone. Thanks."

Wolfe said, "Was that Helene's voice?"

I nodded. "There should be a call-back number, 88. Press it. If it's Helene's cell phone or her house phone, you'll get her message."

Wolfe's dark eyes looked straight into mine. "Wouldn't your desk phone be disconnected?"

"Don't be funny, just try it. Please."

He redialed and replayed the message, then listened for the cue to call the caller and pressed 88. I moved in close to Wolfe in order to hear and became aware of the heat from his body. I forced myself to concentrate on the ringing in the phone receiver.

It rang several times, then an automated message came on to say the caller was unavailable.

Wolfe looked at me, his expression blank, shuttered.

I had another desperate idea. "Try ringing her cell phone. Her number will be here on Lizzie's roster."

But the roster was gone.

"Here," I said and pulled out my personal organizer. "Try this number. It's her cell phone."

He pressed in the numbers. His expression was dubious. After the third ring a woman answered. "Foster residence."

Wolfe spoke quickly, establishing that she was the Foster's housekeeper and she had answered Helen's cell phone.

"You see?" I said.

"That only proves she left the message from another phone." The expression in his eyes turned cold and hostile, as though he was getting ready to read me my rights and my cheeks grew cold. There had to be an answer. "Play her message to Lizzie again, please."

He pressed in the keys and Helene's voice came through. I listened through to the end and had him repeat it yet again. "There! Do you hear it? The little click? It's a recording."

"That doesn't make any difference."

"Yes, it does." My cell phone rang. Of all times! I snatched the phone from my purse and put it to my ear.

"Francie!"

"Mac!"

CHAPTER 26

Why was Mac calling? Was something wrong at day camp? There were odd sounds of adults talking in the background and maybe a crowd, but Mac wasn't on a field trip so far as I knew.

A low, muffled voice cut in. "Don't talk, just listen. Tell no one, or you'll never see Mac again. No one. Go to your car. Go west, out Sixth Avenue."

My face stiffened, cold.

Wolfe came toward me, his gaze questioning.

The soft, muffled voice continued to talk into my ear. "If you're followed, I'll know and you won't see Mac again. You have two minutes to get to your car." This time traffic noise filled the telephone receiver.

My throat constricted, my voice pitched high and hoarse. "Where is Mac?"

Was it Gifford's voice? Had he made good a threat to make me sorry? But how would he get to Mac? Mac would never go with him.

The phone went dead. "Wait!"

The room grew suddenly dark and cold.

Wolfe, stiff and intense, asked, "Did someone take Mac?"

I wasn't to tell anyone. The place could be bugged, and he, whoever he was, could be watching. The hair on the back of my neck prickled and a fine cold perspiration burst out on the sides of my forehead. I said loudly, "I have to go."

Wolfe gripped my forearm, his fingers digging into my skin.

"You have to let me help."

I had delivered Mac to day camp this morning and they had promised not to send him home with anyone but me. Surely he was with them and safe.

I twisted out of Wolfe's grip and speed-dialed Mac's day camp.

The office answered. I gave my name and said, "I left Mac off for day camp today. Is he still there with you? Please check for me. It's important."

I looked at my watch. One minute to go. I couldn't risk further delay. I had to go to my car. Phone to ear, I walked straight out Techlaw's front door to the elevator.

Wolfe burst out after me. "Where are you going? Is it Mac?"

I nodded. "I'm checking on him at the day camp. I forgot something."

The elevator was taking forever. I walked to the stairs, my feet almost tripping, and started down at a run.

The secretary from the day camp came back on the phone. "He's not here. His teacher said he left about an hour ago. The sign-out sheet says he's going home and it's signed by his father."

"He doesn't have a father. I said he wasn't to be signed out to anyone but me."

"I'm sorry, but it's right here. Although it looks kind of like a child's handwriting. If I see Mac, I'll hold him here in the office."

Still running, I thanked her and rang off. At the bottom of the stairs I yanked open the door, ran through the lobby, and out the front door to the Rust.

Wolfe came pounding after me. "You can't do this alone. You don't have a chance. Three people thought they could deal with a killer and they're all dead."

Maybe if I'd never laid eyes on Mac, never held him, never

grieved with him for his father, never seen him as *my* boy, I would be able to calmly approach this problem. But Mac was in my heart. And I had to do everything I possibly could to save him.

I shoved Wolfe out of the way, slid into my car, and turned the key. Miraculously, the engine caught.

Wolfe pounded on the door. "I'll go with you."

"No," I shouted. "If I'm followed I'll never see him alive."

I floored it and left Wolfe shouting at me, eating dust. His mouth still moved even after I'd spun out of the parking lot. He ran to his car, jumped in, and followed. I had to get away. If he were seen following me, Mac would be hurt. Or worse. I slowed, timed my crossing, and when Wolfe was close enough, I pulled out into traffic. I barely skinned the front of a semi and cramped the steering wheel hard left. Wolfe was stalled behind the semi. I was miraculously away.

As I reached the Sixth Avenue viaduct, my cell phone rang again. Still heavily overlaid with traffic noises, probably to muffle the voice, which said, "You're doing well."

How would he know? I watched to see if I was being followed, but didn't spot anyone. There must have been some kind of homing device or bug attached to the car. The Rust was barely moving these days. I'd neglected to put in oil and brake fluid yesterday. It was practically empty. I shouted into the phone, "You know how bad my car is. It may not make it much longer."

Silence. Then, "Listen carefully. Exit at Lowell, crossover and come back on Sixth Avenue to Washington. I'll be watching."

"I want to speak to Mac."

"No can do."

No can do. I recognized that tired old turn-down. Outrage poured forth. "You put him on, or I'll stop right now and call the police. You don't want to add killing a kid to your crimes, do you? You know what they'd do to you in the pen for that?"

Hesitation. Then Mac's voice, bright and tinny. "I'm sitting here—"

Did I hear a click? A recording? I thought so, but I couldn't risk it.

On Washington, going south, the phone rang again. The low muffled voice said, "Phone home."

The bastard had to be at my house. *In* my house, violating my safety, creating nightmare material for the rest of my life. And Mac's life. I tried to calm myself, to reason it out. There had to be a flaw or a way, and I had to find it.

Mac's voice, the little click I'd heard, had to be a recording. But if Mac wasn't there, where was he?

Sick with fright I turned south, then east onto a side street and dialed my home number.

He answered on the second ring. "Good. Now home, and use the front door."

Wait a minute, I thought. He couldn't see me in the car, at best he could only know approximately where I was. My throat tight from fear I said, "I've been caught behind an accident. It will take another few minutes." I held the phone away, made static noises, and then shouted, "The battery's going!" I muffled my voice with my fingers, and spoke in breaks as though the phone were breaking up. ". . . hel . . . no . . . keys . . ." and switched it off.

I pulled into the alley behind Mrs. Folsom's garage, grabbed my purse, and searched for my house keys. My God! I'd left them at Techlaw! How unbelievably stupid!

I jumped out of the car, left the door barely latched in case I needed it in a hurry, scooted along to the back gate of my house, eased it open, and crept in and up the stone walk. I pulled out my Sears credit card to try to slip open the back door. How ironic, I thought. Of all the times I'd cursed my family trade, I was going to have to use it and pray I could do it. The card bent, snagged, and failed. I tried again and again. Nothing.

Automatically, I glanced at Mrs. Folsom's house. She was nowhere to be seen. Dammit! She spied on me continuously, made note of everyone coming and going, and now she was nowhere to be seen. Where was she?

The little lock pick that Andy had given me several years ago was still in the lining of my purse. I worked it out and started to work. I was so out of practice.

It took me almost five minutes to pick my own back door lock and it wasn't even a good lock. My hands were shaking but finally I slipped the lock.

I took my cell phone from my purse, switched it on, pressed in Wolfe's number. When the call was answered, I gave my name and, leaving the phone on, slipped it in my pocket. This way there would at least be some kind of recording of what happened to me on Wolfe's office phone.

Now I needed a weapon. Inching across the kitchen floor, stepping over the squeaky board, I reached for the butcher knife on the magnetic strip at the side of the cupboards. But knives and stab wounds don't stop someone unless you're very lucky in the wound placement. I hadn't stabbed anything other than a carrot cake in a long time.

Something I could hide and use for surprise might be more useful. I took the smaller, pointed vegetable blade instead, and slid it into my waistband.

I listened for voices, telltale sounds of people. Nothing.

Almost out of the kitchen I stopped. One more weapon, something hefty to whack him. My old cast-iron skillet, holding a bit of bacon grease, sat on the stove to my right. I grabbed it and peered around the doorjamb into the living room.

It was empty. Overly careful, I made myself examine each piece of furniture. No one hid there. And no Mac. What if he wasn't here? Maybe he'd played hooky with Barry. I wished I'd thought to ask the day camp if Barry were still there.

I made one last glance out the kitchen window, hoping to see the familiar silhouette of Mrs. Folsom's long, long nose, but she wasn't at her usual post. I listened for a siren, hoping to hear Wolfe in the distance. Dammit! Where was everyone?

I listened until my ears rang, then crept around the corner into the living room and sneaked along the wall next to the doorway into the hall leading to the bedrooms. I raised the skillet chest-high.

Mac's bedsprings creaked. The floor squeaked. He was moving. Pray God it was not Mac.

Pan held high and somewhat level so the grease wouldn't drip out on my head, I waited.

The house phone rang. My heart nearly stopped. It came from Mac's bedroom. Oh, my God, why hadn't I thought before I entered to peer in his window so I'd have an idea of what I was walking into?

A muffled voice said, "Hello? She's not here, please call back later."

A slight pause, then irritably the same voice said, "No, I will not take a message."

The phone slammed down.

It was Sam's voice in the bedroom. Even though he'd tried to disguise it, I knew for sure it was him. How could he do this to Mac after all the times he'd been so helpful and supportive? How could he do it to me?

And then I remembered all the times I'd turned him down, all the rejections. A mature man would have accepted it and understood, but Sam was more child-like in nature, petulant and resentful when he felt rejected.

Was Mac in there? I hadn't heard his voice. Not a murmur. What if he'd been harmed? What if he was unconscious? Maybe,

I thought hopefully, he'd only been gagged?

If Mac was there, I needed to lure Sam away from him.

The floor creaked again. Coming closer.

A foot appeared. The nose of a gun. I swung. He jerked back. The skillet caught the tip of the gun. It fired. Grease flew, splattering him, me, and the floor.

Sam leapt out, faced me. His glasses tilted across his face. Automatically he raised a hand to straighten them.

I swung the skillet again, this time with all the strength I could muster.

The rim grazed his wrist. He screamed. The gun went off again, dropped, and spun away on the wooden floor under the couch.

He shook his wrist and screamed in a spray of outraged saliva, "You dumb, stupid bitch!"

I stiff-armed him out of the doorway, but my foot slipped in the grease. I stumbled, caught myself with a hand on the wall, and scrambled into Mac's room.

No Mac. I grabbed the door and tried to slam it.

Sam jammed his foot in the doorway. Then he threw himself against the door. I couldn't hold it. It burst open and he stepped into the room, his face red and furious, his eyes wild. "It's all your fault! You stupid, meddling witch!" His eyes were crazed.

Panting, I backed up and grabbed the vegetable knife from my waistband. Dammit, how could I have thought it would help?

Sam laughed, a brittle-sounding bark, snatched up a book and swept it across my hands, knocking the little knife away.

I was backed against the toy shelves, looking for anything to keep him at bay. Maybe he could be distracted. "Where's Mac? I thought you were concerned about our safety."

"Before you screwed it all up."

Was he nuts? Did the strange look in his eyes mean he'd lost his sanity? Could I bring him back?

Spike's cage sat on the edge of the shelf. I grabbed it and tried to hold Sam's gaze with mine. "What happened to the Sam who loves kids? Who took Mac to ball games?"

I shifted weight so that my knees were slightly bent and I was forward on the balls of my feet.

Sam didn't answer. His face was twisted in pain as he cradled his wrist. "You hurt me."

I held Spike's cage out in front of me like a shield. "Spike will be upset. She's sensitive to angry sounds and their vibrations. Come any closer and I'll let her loose on you."

My hand was shaking the cage. Spike would be in a real arachnid snit. "She's poisonous, you know," I said, barely able to speak. I lifted the cage so he would see it. "Deadly poisonous," I added.

His gaze flicked to the cage and back to me. He smiled, slow and lopsided. His eyes stayed cold and flat. "Spike's not home. What are you going to do with an empty plastic cage?"

I glanced in the cage. No Spike. Damn! Where was she? I had to do something to give myself regrouping time. "Where is Mac? How did you get him to leave day camp?"

Sam shoved his glasses up on his nose, puzzled, then his lips curled.

An awful, sickening feeling spread through my gut. Mac had truly checked himself out of day camp. He'd come home to visit Spike. That's why the cage was empty. So he was here at home, and I had just given it away.

CHAPTER 27

"Not so smart, are you?" Sam smiled in a kind of sick imitation of humor. "So Mac played hooky today. And the cage is empty. I'll bet he's here."

Sam scanned the room. "I wasn't going to involve Mac. When I called you on the phone and used Mac's voice to get your attention, I used a recording. I made it Sunday at the ball game. I told him it was a surprise for you."

"And the message from Helene for Lizzie was a recording, too."

"She always called in on Friday. I just got there early one Friday and recorded it."

He looked at the closet. "Come out, Mac. We're going to take a little ride."

No movement. No sound.

"Mac, come out or I'll hurt your mom."

"He's not here. He's at Barry's. And he wouldn't come out if he were here."

Sam made a face at me, started to turn away, then spun back, his arm out long and straight. His hand caught the side of my face with a crack that caused lights to flash in the back of my eyes. I hadn't anticipated that.

I barely managed not to scream. A scream would have brought Mac out of hiding. I prayed he was in the basement and hadn't heard anything. Blood dripped from my nose.

Ignoring the steady stream of blood and the pounding in my

ears, I threw myself at him, trying to get in close enough to avoid the worst of his blows.

He grasped my wrist and twisted my arm until it was bent up behind my back. "Mac, that sound was me slapping your Mom's face. Come on out or I'll have to beat her to a pulp."

A pulp? He was so trite! What, did he only read out-of-date comic books? It would have been funny, except my arm was nearly broken and I was practically helpless. "Don't move Mac! It's all a bluff!"

"I'm a black belt in karate, Mac. Get out here before I break your mom's arm." He twisted it harder. That time I yelped.

The closet door swung open and Mac came out, face red and distressed. "Don't hurt my mom!"

My eyes stung. He'd finally called me "mom."

Sam held him aside by the shoulder. "If you give me any trouble, Mac, any at all, I'll hurt her again. Now, we're going to take a lride." He marched me forward and snagged Mac's little metal handcuffs from the shelf. "We'll take your car, Francie."

"It's barely running."

"I know. Leaves a trail of smoke. All the better. Lead the way."

In the living room he stopped and ordered Mac to retrieve his gun from under the couch. Mac hesitated until Sam twisted my arm again. Then Mac retrieved the gun and brought it to Sam. "You give me any trouble, either of you," Sam said, "and I'll shoot the other one. I won't miss."

Mac nodded solemnly.

Sam released my arm.

From the back door I led the way as slowly as possible to where I'd parked the Rust. Where was nosy Mrs. Folsom? She had witnessed most of my embarrassing moments so far; how could she miss this one?

At the Rust, Sam slipped the toy handcuffs on Mac, put him

in the back seat, and said, "I know you can get those cuffs off but I've got the gun on your mom, so don't do it. Francie, get behind the wheel, real quiet."

He kept the gun pointed straight at me, walked around the car and slipped into the passenger seat, slammed the door, then held the gun in his lap, pointing it at me. "Drive. Go west, out Eighth."

I drove, hands gripping the steering wheel so tightly my knuckles were white and my fingers ached, but they didn't ache as badly as my heart did. I glimpsed Sam in the seat next to me, chewing his lower lip just like Mac did when he worked his arithmetic problems. That expression, so endearing in Mac, was what had blinded me to Sam as a killer.

And now, not only would I pay for it, so would Mac.

Sick, I glanced in the rearview mirror. Poor Mac's face was all eyes and fright. The pocket of his T-shirt bulged. And moved. Spike! What if she got frightened and bit him?

One way and another I steered the Rust through town and west to I-70 into the foothills, and then into the mountains. Julia had died in the mountains, too. An accident, supposedly. Had Sam done this same thing with her? Why hadn't Wolfe appeared? Surely he had followed me. Hadn't he?

For twenty minutes we drove, the Rust's exhaust growing steadily thicker and darker with each press on the gas pedal. Why couldn't the car fail here where traffic might help out?

"Take the Berthoud pass exit," Sam said.

"The car won't make it up the pass."

"Drive, dammit!"

Again I stole a glance in the rearview mirror. Mac was out of his handcuffs, looking back at me. I winked my left eye, hoping he'd be comforted. Four of Spike's furry legs poked out of Mac's pocket. Then her head appeared.

I needed to distract Sam so he wouldn't look back at Mac. If

I could get him to remember we were people he once cared about, maybe he'd let Mac go. "Sam, remember all the time you spent with Mac? Don't you care about that? You even asked me out and said you would be proud to be seen with us at the ball game."

"You'd rather stay home and clean your car than go with me."

Out of the corner of my eye I saw him turn slowly to me.

"You treat me like a kid," he said.

Oh, so true. Sam and Mac. I had thought them as equals, child-like and innocent and, therefore, not passionate, not furious, not ambitious and sensitive, even though I knew Mac was sensitive and got angry and hurt.

"I'm sorry Sam. I guess I was so worried about everything, I didn't think about you. I should have."

Oh, my yes, I should have. This was shaping up as the biggest mistake of my life. And that was saying a lot.

"I didn't want to hurt you," he said. "Or Mac. I had it all planned. If you had left it alone, you'd have beat the rap. I had it set to point to Harris. But no, you kept asking questions."

"After Harris was convicted, you would have the company."

"I would have solved the case for the cops and you would finally see me. You don't really see me when you look at me, you know?"

"You're right, but I do now. Sam, what happened with Helene?"

"The day she fired you, her little act made me suspicious that she'd figured it out. That night I found her journal in her desk and sure enough."

"Did she mention my report?"

"No. She just wrote that I was stealing from the company and crashing Lizzie's computer whenever she came back, to cover my tracks. Helene was wrong about that. I didn't need to crash Lizzie's computer. I had a program all worked out to cover my withdrawals and my stolen customers."

"But why kill her? If she didn't have proof, you could have gotten away."

He kicked the floor. "I lost my temper. She called me stupid. She wrote it right there in her journal." He turned to me, his face contorted. "I'm *not* stupid."

"No, Sam, you're not. And Rosie?"

He snorted. "She called and said she had Helene's old journals and that Helene had written that I killed Julia, so I went over to see. Rosie lied. There wasn't anything there, but it was too late. She knew."

I risked another glance in the mirror.

Slowly Mac put his hand up and let Spike crawl onto it. He had a furtive look on his face.

My mind was racing. "And Mars Stone?" The answer to that suddenly appeared like sunshine through the clouds in a B-movie. "You're Mars Stone. You're the competition sucking business out of Techlaw."

"Shut up. Keep driving."

"What does Mars Stone mean, Sam? Is it an anagram?"

He sneered at me. "It's my name. The name I use. The name that reflects the real me. Mars the Roman god of war. Stone because it's invincible."

"What do you use it for?"

"For my business, the customers I siphoned off of Techlaw. It's a name people don't forget. No one remembers Sam Lawson, but Mars Stone sticks right up front."

Mac piped up from the back seat. "It's the name of his comic book hero. I told you. He writes comic book stories."

Of course, he'd mentioned it right after he returned from the ball park that day. I drove on wondering how many things Mac had told me that I didn't remember? Then I shook myself.

Regret doesn't save lives. "You killed Julia this same way, forcing her to drive into the mountains. The cops won't believe it's an accident a second time."

"Won't matter. I'll be long gone."

I turned off at the Berthoud exit, drove up the ramp, making a long, slow curve around to the right, then began the ascent toward the crest of the pass. My hands were slick on the steering wheel. We breezed through Empire, more a crossroad than a town. No handy police cars, no one to alert.

The twists of the road grew sharper, the drop-offs steeper; my breath came hard and tight. Smoke was pouring out of the back of the Rust.

We were into hairpin turns leading to the upper stretch of the pass; beautiful but dangerous, because the road was rock cliff on one side and sheer drop-off on the other. *Don't pay attention to the drop-off,* I told myself. *Watch Sam. He'll pull something nasty any minute.*

Wheeling around a particularly narrow, tight curve, we came upon a white sedan with antenna and extra spotlights, parked against the rock wall, facing us. Police! Thank God.

I glanced into the rearview at Mac. I winked at him. It was going to be all right.

Sam caught it and laughed. "It's not the police. That's the car *I'm* leaving in."

I raised my foot from the gas pedal. No point in racing to our demise. The Rust slowed, coughed. The engine gauge was in the red band, seriously overheated.

In the rearview mirror I saw Mac lean forward and move his hand with Spike balanced on the back of it toward Sam's neck.

To keep Sam distracted I said, "Sam, you can't get away with this." Stress didn't make me very original. "You'll be lucky to get to the border."

"Pull up over on the edge."

We were twenty yards from his car. Mac held Spike next to Sam's neck.

Spike jumped. All eight fuzzy little feet landed on the back of Sam's shoulder.

I said, "You've got a tarantula on your back."

He smiled, but was he just a hair nervous?

"It's Spike," I said. "One bite and you'll be paralyzed."

He snarled, "Shut up," but turned to look at his shoulder. He jerked and yelled, "What the hell!"

Spike sprang to his neck and bit.

Sam yelped, "AAAAH!" His gun dropped to the floor as he slapped his neck.

It was Mac and my chance. I mashed the gas pedal to the floor and turned the car straight at the back end of his parked car. The Rust coughed, shuddered, then lunged forward.

"Duck, Mac!"

He dropped to the seat.

Sam grabbed the steering wheel. I whacked his Adam's apple with my forearm. He let go, choking and gasping. I stood on the gas pedal. The Rust roared toward the rear-end corner of his car.

Still choking, Sam unfastened his seat belt and yanked in vain on the door handle. The door on the passenger's side. The door that wouldn't open from the inside.

We reached twenty miles an hour. Not a deadly speed, but fast enough to do damage. We hit. The steering wheel jumped and twisted in my hands. It was all I could do to hold onto it.

We T-boned the side of Sam's car at the gas tank opening. Metal scraped against metal. Sparks flew. The Rust's fenders screamed. The Rust's hood buckled. We came to an abrupt stop.

Sam catapulted into the windshield.

I crashed into the steering wheel. For a moment I thought

my chest was crushed. I couldn't draw air.

The Rust's engine was buried in Sam's car, just over the rear wheel. No one would be going anywhere in either car. Smoke and exhaust, black and nasty, billowed up around us. Our engine glowed.

I gasped, "Get out, Mac," and released my seat belt.

"I gotta get Spike!"

"No, go now!" There was just enough of an angle for me to escape. I yanked on the door handle. Mac got out and pulled open my door. I rolled out onto the pavement.

Mac stepped over me and reached into the car. The sickly sweet smell of gasoline filled the air. Cars don't blow up that easily, I thought, until I saw low flames licking the Rust's buckled hood. I yanked Mac out of the car.

"Run, Mac, it's going to blow!"

"But Spike!"

Spike was crumpled on Sam's neck. Sam was cursing, beating on his door.

"Too late, honey," I said and grabbed Mac's hand. Together we stumbled to the edge, on the far side of the road. It was a steep drop for maybe twelve feet to a thick, fallen pine, just right to break a leg or head on.

Mac, frightened now, tugged on my arm and yelled, "Jump!"

I couldn't move.

"Slide!" Mac shoved my feet out from underneath me.

I landed heavily on my butt, pain shooting up my spine. I slid. Mac was right behind, his feet banging into my back. We rolled to a stop, crushed against the fallen tree.

"We've got to climb over," I said. "Sam may come after us."

I flung a leg over. Mac dove. We squeezed into the lee of the tree trunk. My chest pounded, pain spreading throughout, but my breath was coming easier.

We crouched there, peering up at the edge of the road. A car, then another, came up the pass. Wheels sliding. Brakes. Male voices shouting.

I wrapped my arms around Mac, pulled him close, and felt him hug me in return. Then the roar of an explosion rolled over us in a rush of sound, smoke, and heat.

Only a moment passed before I head Mac's voice. "Mom?"

It had a dreamlike quality, as though coming from far away. My ears were ringing, buzzing from the roar of the explosion.

"Mom? Don't die! Mom!"

The word "Mom" rolled around in my head, sweet and healing.

"Mom!" Mac shook my shoulder. I opened my eyes. He was peering into my face.

I looked around. Mac had pulled some broken pine branches up to hide us. "What, sweetie?"

"I was afraid you died."

Oh, sweet Jesus, so many people in his little life had died. No wonder he had been afraid to love me. "I told you, we're together in this. I don't go away."

And I held him until he wiggled free again.

"Someone's calling," he said. "I think it's Mr. Lawson."

"I can't hear anything."

"Listen."

"Francie!"

"I can't hear very well."

I shook my head. My ears cleared at last and I heard a strong baritone voice call, "Francie!"

I looked into Mac's worried eyes and said, "It's Detective Wolfe." My lips were stiff and my eyes burned.

Mac yelled, "Here!"

I pushed myself to a sitting position and turned to see Wolfe sliding butt-down toward us. I stood. Then he was next to me, his arms folding me into his chest. "God, I'm glad you're all right! I thought you were . . ." His voice choked off and he squeezed me tight.

Mac shoved against us and piped up, "Hey! That's my mom you've got."

Wolfe loosened his hold, but didn't release me. "Come here, Mac. I want to give you a hug, too."

Ambivalence wavered across Mac's face. He moved closer, but toward me. "How did you get here?" he asked.

"I was following your mom, but a semi pulled in front of me and by the time it moved I'd lost her. Then a call was routed to me from the station. I figured it was your mom. She called me and left her cell phone on. On top of that, your neighbor, Mrs. Folsom reported you broke into your own house and then she saw you leaving, to quote her, 'looking funny.' She thought you might be in trouble. I was pulling up as you left, so I followed you. How're you doing now?"

Mac frowned, his chin set. "Okay, I guess. What about Sam? Did you find him?"

Wolfe nodded. "Yeah. He got out of the car moments before the explosion and was thrown to the ground. Two officers have him. They'll take him to the emergency room at Denver Health Medical Center. He's alive, but not very coherent. He's talking about a spider killing him."

Mac nodded. "Did you see Spike up there? She was on his neck. She bit him. That's how Mom could ram his car."

Wolfe looked briefly at me, his dark eyes pained. He put a gentle hand on Mac's shoulder. "I think Spike is a hero today."

Mac's chin trembled. "Kinda like my Dad. Died for us."

I swallowed. Mac's dad hadn't exactly died for us, more like he'd died for drugs, but I wasn't going to go into that now, or ever, for that matter. "Mac saved the day, too. He helped Spike jump onto Sam's neck and he got me down off the road."

"Sam was so scared, he didn't see Mom ram his car till too

late." Mac's lower lip trembled. "Sam was really nice to me. Why'd he do that?"

"Money, sweetie," I said. "Sam wanted money and revenge because Harris didn't give him credit for all he did and how smart he was. Sam decided to steal from Techlaw by outwitting them, but Julia figured it out. I think he engineered her accident. That kind of anger can change you, and it ruined Sam."

"He said you asked too many questions. He was going to kill us." Mac gently shoved Wolfe away and put his arms around me. "Spike was really great."

I hugged him, feeling tears sting my eyes. I never thought I'd feel emotional about a spider. "Honey, I think Spike was proud to help us out. And I think Sam just went a little nuts. He really liked you."

Wolfe moved away, cell phone to his ear.

Mac's chin trembled. "I really liked Sam. He was like a kid, you know?"

A kid who played the game for keeps.

Mac noticed Wolfe standing off. "Hey," he called. "You don't have to leave, you just have to make room for me."

Wolfe closed up the phone and walked back. "Two things, Francie. They found your report. There was a CD in Helene's car. Your report was on that. You can—"

"I don't want to know," I said, shaking my head. "It will only stir up more emotional turmoil for me. What's the other thing?"

"You wouldn't know a small, red-haired woman with a large hat and a purple suitcase, would you? According to Mrs. Folsom, your neighbor, she just broke into your house."

I looked at Mac.

We said together, "Lil!"

Now how was I going to introduce Wolfe to Lil?

ABOUT THE AUTHOR

Christine T. Jorgensen is the author of the successful, humorous Stella the Stargazer series. A member of Rocky Mountain Fiction Writers and Mystery Writers of America, Jorgensen is an MSW, LCSW social worker. For over twenty-seven years she worked first at the Denver Department of Social Services and then the Denver Children's Hospital as the coordinator and co-director of the Child Advocacy Team and the assistant director of the Clinical Social Work Department. Before she left Children's, Jorgensen spearheaded the development of the Children's Hospital Rehabilitation Independence Scale.

She lives in Denver with her husband; her dog, Tyrannus Rex; her anole, Lips; and an African fat-tailed gecko, Spotty.